Taken to Heart

Taken to Heart

JANE JACKSON

ROBERT HALE · LONDON

To Mike, with love.

Typeset in 11½/14 Garamond
Printed in Great Britain by the MPG Books Group,
Bodmin and King's Lynn

Chapter One

Riding a sturdy brown gelding borrowed from the landlord of The Standard, Jenefer Trevanion rode along the track leading out of the village and up onto the moor. Over her gown of peach muslin she wore a long plain coat of yellow-brown linen fastened with a single button. A simple straw bonnet shaded her eyes from the sun.

She glanced towards the headland and the fire-blackened ruins of her old home. At the time she had believed her feelings of loss and dislocation would remain with her always. Instead, three years on, she felt part of the village in a way she never had while living at Pednbrose.

As the gelding plodded on she gazed down onto Porthinnis, so pretty in the late September sunshine. Whitewashed cottages and small houses built of local stone clustered around the small harbour. Larger more elegant properties were dotted over the hillside. Some stood alone, others in rows of two or three, comfortably removed from the noise and smells of the fishing fleet.

The occupants of those houses, the village's polite society, never missed an opportunity to shake their heads at how low she had sunk. Why, when she could easily afford to move, did she choose to live in a poky cottage behind the village pump? They were unable, or unwilling, to accept the simple truth. She was happy there.

But behind the picturesque façade the village was struggling for survival. Following two seasons of huge shoals, this year's pilchard catches had been disastrous. Were it not for the brandy, tea, tobacco and salt – goods the wealthy took for granted – smuggled in then sold on at a small profit, many families would be facing destitution.

Before the war with France, salt to preserve a winter's supply of pilchards cost three shillings and sixpence: a man's weekly wage.

Now the price was twenty-one shillings and still rising. How, Jenefer wondered, could the government justify a tax that forced a man either to break the law or starve?

She shook her head, deliberately setting aside both her angry frustration and all thoughts of invoices, account ledgers and the inevitable battle she would have with Will Prowse when she demanded the money he owed Mr Lukis, the Guernsey merchant who supplied the goods.

This afternoon she was free of it all. She shortened the reins and pressed her half boot against the gelding's side. His ears pricked as he surged forward in a canter.

Reaching the top of the moor she reined in, her blood racing and her quickened heartbeat making her feel gloriously alive. She vowed to do this more often. She was her own mistress and answerable to no one. For now.

Ahead of her lay a wide shallow valley. Weeks of dry sunny weather had ripened the crops and harvest was underway. In fields bordered by granite hedges, and swathes of land reclaimed from the moor, men moved in ragged lines, cutting oats, barley and wheat. Women followed, binding the cut grain into sheaves. Children ran across the stubble carrying the sheaves to be stacked in round arrish mows: cut ends out, so that should it rain the ears would be protected.

Taking the fork that led through purple heather and gorse bushes laden with fragrant butter-yellow blossom to Trescowe, she caught sight of a donkey cart ahead of her. Recognizing the familiar figure of Mrs Gillis perched on the seat she fought disappointment.

Instead of a delightful hour spent catching up with Tamara's news and playing with her toddler son, courtesy would demand she sit and listen while Mrs Gillis gushed about her daughter's marital bliss and made pointed remarks about the misfortune of being five-and-twenty and still unmarried.

Jenefer didn't blame Tamara, who hated her mother's crowing but was powerless to stop it. She even understood Mrs Gillis's relief that Tamara's wildness had been tamed. But today she was in no mood to be patronized or pitied. She would call on Roz instead.

Trotting along the drive she guided her hack into the stable yard. As a lad hurried out, she unhooked her leg from the U-shaped horn on the side-saddle and slid to the ground. Politely raising a finger to his cap, he caught the bridle.

'Is Mrs Casvellan at home?' Jenefer asked, ruefully aware of the thick layer of dust dulling her tan boots and wafting from the hem of her coat as she shook out her skirts.

'In 'er 'erb garden, miss.' The lad pointed. 'Loosen 'is girth and give 'n some water shall I?'

'Thank you.' Jenefer smiled at him. 'He would enjoy an apple or a carrot if you have one to spare.'

With a blush that turned the back of his neck scarlet, the boy led the horse away.

Walking through a stone archway, Jenefer paused at the gravelled path surrounding the house. Beyond a low box hedge Roz, wearing rose pink, a white lawn kerchief about her shoulders and a frilled cap on her dark hair, walked slowly between neat beds of herbs, bending every now and then to pick a few sprigs and drop them in the shallow basket she carried.

Observing the once painfully thin figure ripened now by mother-hood and happiness, Jenefer experienced a sharp pang of envy. She smothered it quickly. For her, domestic bliss demanded too high a price.

As she started forward, her boots crunching the gravel, Roz glanced round and a smile of welcome lit her face.

'Jenefer, what a lovely surprise!'

'I hope it is not inconvenient. It was my intention to call first on Tamara, then come here. But I saw Mrs Gillis ahead of me.'

'Ah.' They exchanged a glance of shared understanding. 'I saw Tamara this morning and she was saying she hoped you would visit soon. She misses you.'

'And I miss her. But—'

'You don't need to explain.' Roz laid a gentle hand on Jenefer's arm. 'We both understand how busy you are. She would happily ride or drive to the village, but with her confinement just weeks away I cannot blame Devlin for asking her not to.'

Jenefer's brows arched. 'Devlin asked?'

Roz nodded, amusement dancing in her eyes. 'He understands her so well. Had he forbidden, she would have defied him. But because he made a request she is perfectly content to agree.'

'Where's Enor?' Jenefer glanced round.

'She went up for her nap just ten minutes ago, protesting loudly. But Mary has the measure of her.' Roz listened, her head on one side. 'I hear no screams so she is probably asleep.' She looped her arm through Jenefer's. 'Come, we will go inside and have a glass of lemonade.'

'That sounds wonderful. My throat is parched from the dust. But it is excellent weather for the harvest.'

They crossed the gravel, walked up two shallow steps and entered a pretty sitting room through open French windows. A carpet patterned in pink, cream and jade covered much of the gleaming wood floor. Small rosewood tables with scalloped edges flanked two sofas upholstered in jade damask. An open bureau stood against one wall. Sunshine streamed through long windows framed by curtains of cream linen held back by braided silk ropes.

'I do like this room,' Jenefer said, as Roz set her basket on the carpet and tugged the bell-pull by the mantelpiece. 'It feels so tranquil.'

Roz laughed. 'You would not think so if my daughter were here.'

The door opened and a maid appeared.

'A jug of lemonade if you please, Amy. And some strawberry short-cake.' As the maid bobbed a curtsy and withdrew, closing the door, Roz sat on the sofa, patting the seat beside her. 'The shortcake is a bribe. I want all your news. Has Mr Ince proposed yet?'

Loosening the ribbons, Jenefer took off her bonnet and tucked it behind her. 'No, but he is becoming very attentive so I fear he may do so soon.'

'Fear?' Roz's brows lifted.

Jenefer nodded. 'I am still no clearer in my mind what I should do. I have spent long enough in his company to be certain he is a decent, honest man. Not at all like— ' She broke off.

'Oh my dear,' Roz sympathized.

'If I allow Martin's deceit to colour my outlook with bitterness or mistrust the only person to suffer will be me. I know that,' Jenefer blew a sigh. 'For goodness' sake, it was three years ago, and best forgotten.'

'So easy to say, but so hard to do,' Roz said softly.

'You always understand,' Jenefer said.

'From what I know of him, Mr Ince is a man of excellent principles.' Taking Jenefer's hand Roz held it between hers. 'The school is a perfect example. Faced with so many objections and setbacks a lesser man would have given up.'

Jenefer looked down at their clasped hands. 'He lost weight from the stress of it all. But he refused to concede defeat. And not once did he lose his temper.' She shook her head. 'I don't have that kind of faith, Roz.'

'Surely he would not expect it of you? The church is his calling, not yours.'

'Yes, but so much is required of a clergyman's wife.'

'All of it well within your capability,' Roz said gently. 'Think of the advantages.'

'Of being married to William? Or simply being married?'

'Are they not one and the same?'

'Believe me I have thought, considered, weighed. My mind is a battleground.' Aware of the strain in her voice, she forced a smile and spoke lightly. 'Being an object of pity is very irritating.'

'Yes, well, we need not concern ourselves with the opinions of Mrs Gillis and her cronies.' Roz's tone was uncharacteristically crisp.

The door opened and the maid came in. She set the tray on the table in front of Roz. 'Anything else, ma'am?'

'No thank you, Amy. Is all quiet?'

The maid grinned. 'Not a sound, ma'am.'

'The problem is,' Jenefer continued, as the door closed, 'I have grown used to my way of life. I enjoy my independence. If I accept William's proposal I must forfeit that. He would take control of all my money. And before you say anything, I have no fear of his gambling or drinking it away. Nor would I mind so much if it had come to me as a dowry or an inheritance. But this is money I worked hard for, Roz. William is already pressing me to sever my connections with the Guernsey merchants.'

'But he still wants you to continue working at the school?'

'Oh yes. Because that's *his* creation, and an acceptable occupation for a lady.' Jenefer shook her head. 'I'm sorry. You must be bored to sobs.'

'Don't be silly.' Roz handed her a glass of lemonade. 'You are my

9

very dear friend and this is the most important decision of your life.'

'Perhaps so. But I shall not resolve this afternoon. And we should remember that this is all speculation, for he has not asked me yet.' She shrugged. 'He may never do so. Though I will say this, if William loved me the way your husband loves you, and Devlin loves Tamara, I would have no dilemma.'

Roz cradled her glass between her palms, her cheeks pink, her eyes shining. 'I am so very, very lucky.'

'Then perhaps there is hope for me yet,' Jenefer said lightly, raising the glass to her lips. As the tart liquid slid down her dry throat, she tried to imagine William Ince looking at her the way she had seen Casvellan look at Roz. When the picture would not form she knew it was time to talk of other things.

She lowered the glass to her lap. 'You asked for news? I only wish I had some. My neighbour Lizzie Clemmow did rush back from the shop this morning to tell me two strangers have been seen down at the harbour.'

'Surely with trading brigs calling once a week— '

'Ah, but these were not sailors. According to Lizzie, who had it from Hannah Tresidder, they were gentlemen. And were observed taking measurements which one of them noted in a book. Lizzie was most put out that I could offer no explanation. When I reminded her I have not set foot over my doorstep for days—'

'Oh Jenefer, think of your health.'

'Why? It is excellent, truly. Yes, sometimes I am very busy. But at other times I am free to come and burden my friends.'

'Have some shortbread,' Roz said drily, offering the plate.

Taking a piece Jenefer bit into it, enjoying the contrast between buttery crumb and sweet-sharp fruit. 'This is delicious.'

'Taking measurements,' Roz mused. 'For what purpose I wonder? My husband might know. He is engaged at the moment with Mr Polgray. But when—'

'Polgray?' Jenefer interrupted, stiffening.

'Yes, why? Do you know him?'

Jenefer shook her head. 'No. But if his name is Charles Polgray he is the new owner of Pednbrose. The property was entailed to him on my father's death.'

'Then how is it you have never met? Surely he came to pay his respects?'

'Not to me. Nor to Betsy and Jared, for my sister would have been sure to tell me. To the best of my knowledge he has never set foot in the village.'

'Perhaps he intends calling on you later.'

'But why come here first?' Jenefer puzzled. 'What business could he possibly have with—? Of course: the famous Casvellan stud. They will be discussing horses.'

*

Standing shoulder to shoulder with his host, Charles Polgray pointed to a section of the drawing spread over the large oak desk.

'The extension to the western quay will offer additional protection to the harbour entrance and permit two vessels at a time to be unloaded.' He indicated the row of buildings along the back quay. 'With more cargo coming through the harbour in both directions obviously there will be a need for additional storage.'

'And this?' Casvellan tapped his finger on an area west of the quay extension.

Charles took a steadying breath, mentally bracing himself. This was an idea that had come to him during yet another sleepless night.

'Porthinnis has much to recommend it as a port, but the harbour is currently vulnerable to south-westerly gales. I propose to construct a freestanding mole fifty yards to the seaward side of the new quay extension. You will see that in cross section the mole resembles a triangle with the top cut off. The shallow sloping sides will absorb the power of the storm waves thus protecting the quay from damage.'

Casvellan was studying the drawing intently. 'My compliments, Mr Polgray. It is an ingenious idea. However, all this work will require a considerable labour force. Where do you propose to find the men?'

'From the village and surrounding area.' Charles met Casvellan's penetrating blue eyes. 'The pilchard catch has been disastrous this year. Every time fishermen put to sea they are at risk from press gang boats. And mine closures have thrown scores of men out of work. I'd hazard a guess that, even as we speak, many of them are helping with the harvest to earn enough to feed their families. But when harvest ends so does their money. By that time I should be ready to begin construction and will employ any man willing to work.'

'I am impressed, Mr Polgray.'

Charles nodded, accepting the compliment as his due. Since seeing the harbour and recognizing its potential he had been working eighteen hours a day. Branoc Casvellan was renowned throughout the county. Now in his mid-thirties he had been the local justice before retiring to concentrate on developing new farming methods and expanding his stud. His backing would carry weight with other investors.

Indicating a chair on the far side of his desk, Casvellan sat down. 'This development will greatly increase the amount of traffic to and from the harbour. How do you propose to deal with it?'

'By building a new road.' Charles leaned forward to indicate another area on the drawing. 'Commencing at the rear of back quay, between the lime kiln and the boatyard belonging to Mr John Gillis, it will cross this area of waste ground to form a new junction with the main road outside the village. By restricting all heavy wagons and pack animals to this road, the village centre will be kept free of traffic to and from the harbour.'

While Casvellan studied the drawing, Charles crossed one booted leg over the other, brushing a streak of dust from his fawn pantaloons. He wanted this development. Needed it. Not just for the financial rewards, though they would be considerable. Nor even for the acclaim that would accompany achievement. He wanted a project that would totally absorb him, leave him no time to brood. By moving into the village he would be available to deal immediately with any problems. *Only his father and his attorney knew where he was.*

As Casvellan's dark head was still bent over the drawing, Charles allowed his gaze to wander. The panelled walls, glass-fronted book-cases and large desk gave the room a decidedly masculine ambience, unexpectedly softened by a life-sized portrait of a dark-haired young woman.

A soft smile played at the corners of her mouth. *But at whom was she gazing with those luminous eyes? What secrets lurked in their depths? How many lies had spilled from that smiling mouth?*

He averted his gaze, appalled by this crack in his armour.

'My wife.' Casvellan's voice held pride and deep affection.

Charles's shirt clung damply to his back beneath the striped waist-coat and long-tailed frock coat of blue cloth. Perspiration prickled on his upper lip as shame surged through him. He cleared his throat. Clearly some comment was called for. Should he compliment the artist, or praise the beauty of the sitter?

'It is very lovely.'

'It does not do her justice.' Casvellan gazed at the picture oblivious to his guest's disquiet. 'She was reluctant to sit at all; her agreement conditional upon my remaining with her.'

She had been looking at her husband. Pierced to his soul, Charles focused his gaze on the ornate gilt frame. The portrait was too painful a reminder of vows shattered and trust betrayed. He struggled for words but they stuck in his throat.

Casvellan turned. 'But to the matter in hand.' He was brisk, busi-nesslike. 'How will you fund the project?'

Charles felt himself relax, back on firm ground. 'Kerrow & Polgray, our family company, will provide some of the investment. To keep the money safe, and secure from outside influence, I am setting up a separate company for the harbour development.'

'Let me know when you have completed the legalities.' Casvellan rose to his feet and Charles followed. 'I am interested in becoming a shareholder.'

As he shook Casvellan's proffered hand, Charles's relief and triumph strengthened his determination to succeed with this, his first solo project.

'I am very much obliged to you, sir.' Folding the drawings he stowed them in a leather pouch.

'Not at all. Expanding the harbour and increasing the number of cargoes will bring new prosperity to the village. God knows it's desper-ately needed. How much disruption do you anticipate?'

'I hope for very little. The fishing boats must be free to come and go, and cargoes loaded and landed as usual.'

Casvellan's quick smile softened the austere cast of his features, making him appear much younger. 'I wish you luck, Mr Polgray.' He tugged on the bell pull by the fireplace. 'Will you take some refreshment?'

'Thank you, no. I have another call to make in the village. On my previous visit to inspect the harbour there wasn't time. May I ask, were you acquainted with Colonel John Trevanion.'

Casvellan nodded. 'I knew of him.'

'When he died his estate was entailed to me. I had hoped to come before, but business commitments prevented it. Now that I am here, courtesy demands that I call on Miss Trevanion. However, as we are strangers, I am concerned that my arriving unannounced might cause her alarm.'

'Your consideration does you great credit, Mr Polgray.' Casvellan's mouth quirked. 'But you need not be concerned. Miss Trevanion is a lady of remarkable fortitude. She will bear your visit very well.'

While Charles was puzzling over the gleam of amusement in his host's eye, the door opened and a maid entered.

'Have Mr Polgray's horse brought round to the front, Amy.'

'Right away, sir.' With a swift look at the visitor she hurried out.

Casvellan accompanied Charles through a spacious entrance hall of rich dark wood and twin pedestals supporting huge curved urns filled with roses, lilies and trailing greenery. 'Where are you staying?'

'At The Standard.'

'I think you will soon be looking for a house,' Casvellan said, adding drily, 'If only for space to accommodate all the paperwork.'

Charles laughed. 'I swear it breeds.'

'I still have two rooms full from when I was a justice.'

They walked side by side down wide shallow steps. A groom appeared leading Charles's horse.

'A handsome animal,' Casvellan observed.

Charles inclined his head. 'From you, sir, that is praise indeed. He has excellent paces, but shies at his own shadow. I hope to train him out of it.' He put on his hat, replaced the pouch in his saddle-bag, then turned and extended his hand to Casvellan. 'I am much obliged to you.'

'Perhaps on your next visit you might care to see my thoroughbreds.'

Charles felt unfamiliar warmth in his chest. *How long was it since he had known happiness?* 'I should like it above all things.'

As Charles turned to his horse, the stable lad appeared leading the brown gelding and two young women came round the side of the house, their arms linked. He recognized the shorter one from her portrait.

'What remarkable timing,' Casvellan murmured. He turned to the women and extended his hand. 'My dear, this is indeed fortuitous.' He drew his smiling wife to his side. Ruthlessly suppressing bitter memories, Charles bowed as Casvellan introduced him.

Making a graceful curtsy, Roz smiled up at him. 'I'm delighted to make your acquaintance, Mr Polgray.'

'And I yours, ma'am.' His host had spoken the truth: the portrait did not do justice to her quiet radiance. His gaze flicked to the other young woman. Tall and slim, she stood motionless; her gloved hands linked in front of her, her features half-concealed by the brim of her plain straw bonnet. She emanated a dignity that seemed at odds with her unflattering coat. Was she an indigent relative perhaps? Taken into the household as a companion for Mrs Casvellan?

To Charles's surprise Casvellan beckoned her forward. 'Jenefer, my dear, permit me to present Mr Charles Polgray.'

She curtsied and Charles bowed stiffly, surprised by Casvellan's mode of introduction that intimated hers was the higher status.

As he straightened she raised her head and he looked into a heart-shaped face framed by feathery wheat-gold curls. Her fine straight nose was dusted with freckles and her mouth – her soft, full-lipped mouth— Wrenching his gaze away he met violet eyes whose cool direct gaze startled him.

'Mr Polgray,' Casvellan said gravely, 'regarding the call you mentioned? You are spared all anxiety. This is Miss Trevanion.'

Chapter Two

Turning away as Jenefer Trevanion and Casvellan's wife said their goodbyes, Charles frowned in puzzlement as the lad led a raw-boned hack to the mounting block. Why was she riding such an animal?

'She borrows it from the butcher,' Casvellan murmured, causing Charles a moment's unease that his thoughts, normally so well concealed, had been so easy to read. But perhaps he had not betrayed himself. The contrast between horse and rider was all too obvious.

'Jenefer,' Casvellan demanded, with equal amounts of amusement and frustration, 'when will you come to your senses and choose a mount from my stable?'

'When I have time to enjoy riding for pleasure.' She smiled at him. 'You know how much I appreciate your offer. But living where I do I have no suitable stabling. And if I kept it here I should have to walk over from the village, which entirely defeats the purpose. Mr Rollason's cob cannot be called handsome, but he serves me very well.'

'If ever you change your mind—'

'You will be the first to know,' Jenefer promised, then turned again to her friend.

'Will you permit me to offer a word of advice, Mr Polgray?' Casvellan's murmur recaptured Charles's attention. 'Miss Trevanion's standing among the villagers, and her business experience, could be of great benefit to you.'

'Indeed? In what respect?'

'The harbour development, what else?'

Charles felt a tingle down his spine as he registered what his host had said. 'Her *business* experience?'

Casvellan nodded, his voice pitched low. 'Do not allow the fact that she is a woman prejudice you. You would regret it. She has a shrewder grasp of finance than many men of my acquaintance.'

Seated on her horse's back, Jenefer adjusted her skirts, then gathered the reins.

While he would not dismiss Casvellan's advice, Charles preferred to learn more about this decidedly unusual young woman before making any decision. 'Miss Trevanion?' Her violet gaze met his. 'Are you returning to Porthinnis?'

'Yes.'

'Then as we are both heading in the same direction will you permit me to escort you?'

After a fractional hesitation she inclined her head. 'You are welcome to ride with me, Mr Polgray.'

'I am obliged to you,' he said drily. Politely and with some subtlety, she had made clear her independence. Common sense demanded he steered clear of this enigmatic young woman. But he had done the sensible thing earlier in the year. Now four months on, his attorney was still trying to extricate him from the mess. Besides, the longer the company continued using Hayle harbour, the more money they were losing.

Catching the gleam of amusement in Casvellan's gaze, he swung himself into the saddle and raised his hat in farewell. It took a moment to control his thoroughbred's prancing before he joined the young woman who sat poised and calm on her butcher's horse.

They rode side by side down the drive. Today had proved remarkably fortuitous. Casvellan's suggestion that he consult Jenefer Trevanion had taken him aback. But as he thought about it he saw how her connections in the village might prove very useful.

'Mr Polgray? Forgive me for interrupting,' – her smile softened the irony in her voice – 'but if you prefer to ride in silence, why did you apply to accompany me?'

Anger rushed through him. He controlled it at once, recognizing it as unfair and irrational. A deep breath steadied him. 'I beg your pardon, I—'

'Was deep in thought. So, now you are back with me, may I enquire why it has taken you so long to come and view your inheritance?' Her tone was courteous. Yet he sensed guardedness and realized that, like him, she was reserving judgement.

'I would have come sooner but for the demands of business.'

'And what is your business, Mr Polgray?'

'We have interests in copper and silver mines, shipping and cargo brokerage.'

'We?'

'Kerrow & Polgray. The company was founded thirty years ago by my father and his cousin.'

'What is your role?' Though her questions were surprisingly blunt there was no doubting her interest. He found himself responding with equal candour.

'Samson Kerrow, my father's cousin, runs the Cornish end of the company's business: the copper and silver mines. My father is based in Swansea. He ships coal from South Wales to Cornwall for the mine engines. The ships carry copper ore back to Swansea to be smelted. We also have a silver mine in Mexico. I was there for much of last year.'

'May I ask why?'

'Mining is a dangerous occupation at the best of times. But injuries and fatalities at our mine in Guanajuato had reached a level that was totally unacceptable.'

'And you were supposed to change all that?'

He nodded. 'That's my job: well, part of it.'

'So what did you do to put matters right?' The intensity of her interest surprised him.

'I employed a new manager, set new safety rules and altered various working practices.'

'Did it have the desired effect?'

'I believe so. By the time I left, the number of injuries had dropped to single figures, morale was higher and production had increased.'

'Congratulations. That was well done.' She sounded sincere. *But so had Eve, with her warm welcome, her delight to see him safely home. Had he only stayed in Mexico another month—* Too late for regrets. But anger still simmered.

'Mr Polgray, about Pednbrose—'

'I have not yet had an opportunity to view the property. Having lived there, you know it well.' He hesitated. If he allowed Eve's treachery to influence his decisions, he could all too easily forfeit valuable assistance. But he was wary of trusting a stranger, particularly a woman. *Casvellan was not a man to give his recommendation lightly.* 'I wonder, would you care to accompany me to Pednbrose?' When she didn't immediately respond he cursed himself for his clumsiness. 'Forgive me. It may be too painful—'

'Not at all,' she was quick to reassure. 'I visit regularly.' She laughed. 'It is a ruin, Mr Polgray, not a shrine. When I lived there we had a large and very productive walled garden. Since the fire it has become very overgrown. But rather than leave the fruit to rot, I have been picking it and making jam.'

His brows rose. 'Jam?'

She shrugged. 'If I am honest, my neighbour, Mrs Clemmow, does most of it. She's the expert. But my efforts don't burn or bubble over as often as they used to, so I think I am improving. We keep a dozen jars each. The rest we give away on Feast Day or at Harvest Festival and Christmas. I hope you don't mind?'

'Your generosity?'

'With your fruit.'

Charles shook his head. 'To object would be . . . pointless.'

'Then on behalf of all those who have benefited, I thank you.'

Was she mocking him in particular or men in general? He realized he didn't care. His next words surprised both of them. 'I need to find a house to rent. I should be most grateful for your assistance.'

She glanced at him. 'Surely you would do better to make enquiries from an agent.'

'I should much prefer to view the properties unofficially and at my own convenience first.'

'Which presupposes I have the time and inclination to abandon my business in order to help you.'

'What is your business, Miss Trevanion? And before you scold me for asking, may I remind you that your questions concerning my business were somewhat forthright.'

'A fair point, Mr Polgray. I am a bookkeeper.'

'Indeed? For whom?'

'Now you go too far,' she chided. 'Your assumption that I would reveal such information to a man I met barely an hour ago insults us both.'

He was actually considering an apology when he glimpsed laughter in her violet eyes. She was a most unusual and intriguing young woman. 'I most humbly beg your pardon, Miss Trevanion.'

Her laughter touched something deep within him and he felt himself respond as she shook her head. 'Humble? Oh no, Mr Polgray. I think not.'

'Well, at the risk of insulting you further, were I to offer a contribution to a worthy cause of your choice – I'm sure the village has several – might you perhaps find the time, and the inclination?'

Her gaze met his. As he held it he saw the pink in her cheeks deepen to rose. 'A generous contribution?'

'Naturally.'

'Then I might. On condition you are willing to wait until I have completed my current tasks?'

'Of course. I too have business requiring my attention.'

'Then shall we say Wednesday afternoon? Two o'clock?' Jenefer suggested. 'At Pednbrose?'

He nodded. 'I look forward to it. Meanwhile, tell me about the village.'

Her brows arched and her smile faded. 'Mr Polgray, your manner of address tells me you are more used to dealing with men. My father had a similar habit. Because I recognize this, I am not disposed to take offence at your abruptness. However, others might feel differently.'

His anger dissolved as swiftly as it had erupted. As much as he disliked being corrected, he disliked even more the fact that she was right. 'I beg your pardon.'

'Granted.' She smiled sweetly. 'To answer your question, the village is suffering greatly. Prices keep rising and pilchard catches have been disastrous. At least this year's harvest promises to be plentiful. But there is a desperate need for more work.' Turning her head she held his gaze. 'What has brought you to Porthinnis, Mr Polgray?' She raised a hand to forestall him. 'Yes, you wish to view your inheritance. But from what you have told me, I think it very unlikely a man as busy as yourself would come solely for that purpose.'

He was silent, once more weighing Casvellan's advice against his preference for working alone. 'If I tell you, it must be in confidence.'

Her brows arched. 'On such short acquaintance you would accept my word?'

'With Mr Casvellan's recommendation.'

'Ah.' The corners of her mouth lifted. 'You have my promise, Mr Polgray. Whatever you tell me stays between us.'

'I intend expanding the harbour and its facilities.' As he described the proposed changes and additions he saw her eyes lose focus. Assuming she had grown bored, and surprised by the disappointment lurking beneath his irritation, he fell silent.

'I can see it,' she said softly, and turned to him. 'Did Mr Casvellan tell you the harbour and surrounding land is owned by the Berkeley family?'

Unaccountably relieved he nodded.

'Should you need the name of their attorney—'

'I already have it. But I thank you for the offer. I have taken a twenty-year lease on the harbour and surrounding land. As soon as the legal and financial details are settled I intend to call a public meeting, tell the village of my plans, and offer work to all who want it.'

Relief and delight widened her smile. 'Really?'

Charles nodded. 'Obviously, once construction is complete the nature of the work will change. But men willing to adapt may be sure of continuing employment.'

Her eyes were bright and she seemed to glow. He couldn't tear his gaze away.

'Mr Polgray?' One gloved hand strayed uncertainly to her cheek. 'Is something amiss?'

'No,' he said hastily. 'No, not at all. Clearly the subject of employment matters a great deal to you. I just don't understand why.'

'No,' she said softly. 'You wouldn't. I intend no disrespect, but to you the villagers are simply a means to an end. You see them as a workforce. I, on the other hand, know what it is to be without money or a home. I worked in a fish cellar, Mr Polgray. Not for long: I was too slow and too clumsy. I would not have coped with even those few days but for the kindness of those working alongside me. So I know from experience how hard life is for most of the villagers.'

He stared at her, a frown tightening his forehead. 'You? A fish cellar?'

She nodded. 'I hated every dreadful moment.'

'But – *why?*'

'The fire,' she said simply. 'We – my sister and I – lost everything. But thanks to my education and the fact that after my mother's death I had taken over the household accounts and then my father's free trade transactions, I was able to offer my services as a bookkeeper. Village women don't have the luxury of choice.' They had reached the junction. She reined in her horse. 'And here we are. I'll bid you good afternoon, Mr Polgray. I must return my mount to his owner.'

Charles tipped his hat. 'Thank you for your company, Miss Trevanion.' Never had a journey passed so quickly. 'Until Wednesday.'

Chapter Three

Turning to the long glass Jenefer cast a critical eye over her reflection. The pale blue dotted muslin gown was fashionably cut with a high waist, low neckline and three-quarter sleeves. But conscious of village sensibility she had added a softly gathered kerchief of white gauze. Crossed in front and tied behind, it covered her from throat to waist.

She knew her modesty was appreciated. One day while in the back room of Tresidder's grocery store collecting the books, she heard two women enter the shop talking in shocked tones.

'Some beauty she is,' one sniffed. It was clear from her tone that this was not a compliment. 'Near 'nough falling out of 'er bodice she was, and in church too.' She made a sound of disgust. 'All prinked up like Lady Fan Tod.'

''Tis the latest fashion,' the other said.

Discerning a note of envy Jenefer compressed her lips on a smile.

'You can't make a silk purse out of a sow's ear. It might be *fashion*, but she 'aven't got a ha'pporth of *style*. You'd never see Miss Trevanion making a show of 'erself like that.'

'That's true,' the other agreed. 'Always dress fitty and proper she do. All right, Hannah? How 'ee doing?'

As Hannah returned their greetings, Jenefer had gathered up the books and slipped quietly out through the back door, amused that the villagers would happily accept her involvement in matters normally considered men's business, yet took offence at revealing gowns.

With a satisfied nod at the image in the mirror she turned away, picked up the slop bucket and carried it carefully down the wooden stairs. She liked knowing she could afford silk and velvet. But gauze and muslin were far less trouble to keep clean.

Leaving both halves of the door wide open to admit light and fresh air, she tied a coarse hessian apron over her gown. She emptied the slop bucket down the privy and rinsed it with rainwater from the barrel. After cleaning out the ashes from the range, she brushed up the hearth and refilled the coal bucket. Scrubbing her hands free of dust and soot, she changed her rough apron for a clean one of starched white cotton. She washed and dried her breakfast dishes, made her bed, then took ironed linen from the wooden airing frame above the range and put it away in the chest of drawers and closet.

Hanging her white apron on the hook beside the door, she pulled a wooden chair up to the table and drew the neat pile of ledgers and folders forward.

She re-read the letter. Signed by Edward Barton, it requested her most earnestly to consider transferring her financial affairs to Barton's Bank in Helston. Were she to do him the honour of calling in to see him the next time she was in town she would, Mr Barton promised, be assured of his immediate and personal attention.

Re-reading the letter, Jenefer rubbed her forehead. *Why?* During her first year in business, Mr Barton had been the most vociferous of her critics, telling anyone who would listen that her financial dealings, matters for which she was unqualified and, by nature of her gender, totally unfit, should cease immediately.

She knew that the way in which she had dealt with her dramatic change in circumstances had upset many people. But her choice had been stark: find work or starve. She had faced insults and criticism with a polite smile, biting her tongue till it bled. She had sobbed herself to sleep from exhaustion and loneliness, then forced herself to get up next morning and go calmly about her business.

Though Mr Barton's change of attitude was in some ways a relief, she had no idea what had brought it about. Had she failed, she would have proved him correct. How he would have crowed. Instead she had prospered. People were attracted to success. Hoping, perhaps, to learn the secret. Maybe that was sufficient reason for his interest.

Refolding the letter she set it aside. She could see no benefit in moving her account from the Helston branch of Praed's Cornish Bank. The bank's connection with William Percival in Lombard Street, London, was convenient for her as Mr Lukis, the Guernsey merchant for whom she was an agent, also had links with William Percival. Opening a ledger she started work.

'Dear life, maid. Look at you.'

Jenefer raised her head as Lizzie Clemmow's voice broke her concentration. Holding a tray Lizzie stood in the doorway deliberately blocking the light.

'Hello, Lizzie.' Jenefer straightened up, wincing at the stiffness in her neck.

'Hours you been sat there.'

'You don't know that,' Jenefer said. Lizzie fussed over her like a hen with one chick. 'I might have just—'

'Don't you spin me no yarns,' Lizzie scolded. 'Been bent over they books all morning you have. I know because I been to the pump twice and looked in. 'Tidn no good for you.'

Setting down her pen, Jenefer flexed her shoulders and arched her back. 'I know,' she admitted. 'The trouble is—'

'Last half of the month you always got more to do,' Lizzie recited the familiar excuse. 'Maybe so. But 'tis time you stopped for today. You going to shift they papers?' Waiting while Jenefer moved the pile aside, she set the tray down and whipped off the covering cloth.

'Oh Lizzie,' Jenefer's mouth watered as she looked at the steaming plate of roast lamb, roast potatoes and green beans in rich gravy. Beside it was a small dish of blackcurrant pudding topped with clotted cream. 'That looks wonderful.' Her empty stomach gurgled. 'If you keep feeding me like this I shall soon be as fat as one of Mr Rollason's pigs.'

'Get on,' Lizzie scoffed, folding the cloth. 'There's more meat on his apron than on your bones.'

Jenefer eyed her. 'You're all flattery.'

Snorting, Lizzie flapped a hand. 'I worry 'bout you, bird. All this work.' Her gesture encompassed the ledgers and account books, the piles of invoices, receipts and correspondence.

'I'm fortunate to have it.' Turning to the dresser Jenefer reached into the drawer for a knife and fork.

'I won't argue with that,' Lizzie said. 'You do some fine job too. But 'tidn enough.'

'I suppose I could accept more,' Jenefer said. 'But I enjoy my afternoon walks, and your brave attempts to teach me to cook.'

'That's not what I meant, as you well know,' Lizzie said. ''Tis time you was married.'

'Not you as well.' Jenefer sighed, and began to eat.

'Someone else been telling you? Your sister is it? Some happy little soul she is. She and Jared are a lovely couple. I never see her but she got a smile on her face.'

'No, not Betsy.' Jenefer swallowed a mouthful and groaned with pleasure. 'Lizzie, this is delicious.'

'There's plenty on the joint to have cold tomorrow. Who was it then?'

'Tamara, Roz—'

Shaking her head, Lizzie sighed. 'That Tamara. Wild as a hawk she was. Mind you, her mother was a good part to blame. Always fussing and fretting. 'Tis no wonder the dear maid spent her days out riding or walking on the moors. But since she married she've settled down lovely. As for Miz Casvellan, a proper lady she is now, dear of her.'

'So you think I need settling down?' Jenefer teased, forking up another mouthful.

'What you need,' Lizzie retorted, 'is a man who'll look after you like you deserve, but leave you be yourself.'

Surprised and deeply touched, for she knew her neighbour had been brought up with very traditional views, Jenefer smiled. 'Lizzie, that's the nicest thing anyone has ever said to me. But with your Sam and Tamara's Devlin already spoken for, I fear I am doomed to disappointment.' Even as she spoke a vivid image of Charles Polgray sprang to mind: his unusual grey-green eyes, straight nose, sculpted mouth, and firm jaw. She recalled the way the sun glinted off strands of gold in the brown hair that sprang in unruly waves from his deep forehead and curled on his collar. She blinked, her skin tightening in a shiver.

Since parting from him she had relived their ride countless times, unsettled by her response to a total stranger.

'Get on. You don't mean that.' Lizzie was brisk. 'I got eyes. And I aren't the only one.' She nodded meaningfully. 'We seen the way Mr Ince do smile at you.'

Mr Ince. William. 'Lizzie, he smiles at everybody. He is a very amiable man.'

'That's as may be. And you can say being polite and pleasant is part of his calling. But whenever he look at you he do colour up. I never seen him do that with anyone else. Anyhow,' – she gave Jenefer no chance to respond – 'I'll leave you finish your dinner. Mind you don't move till you've et all that pudding.'

Jenefer picked up her spoon. 'Not so many years ago,' she said darkly, 'you would bob a curtsy when we passed in the street. Now you scold and bully me—'

'Some state you'd be in if I didn't,' Lizzie said, not the least bit cowed. 'With all this work you got, who else is going to make sure you eat reg'lar?'

'I don't know how I'd manage without you,' Jenefer admitted.

Lizzie waved away the gratitude. 'My Sam says you moving in here was handsome for us. You had that lovely great range put in my kitchen—'

'That was for my benefit,' Jenefer interrupted. 'You're a far better cook than I am. And if you're cooking for me, it's only right that you eat the same.'

'We've never et so well, and that's God's truth,' Lizzie said. 'I remember when all we had on a Sunday was taties and point. The bit of meat so small you had to point to see 'n.'

Jenefer smiled. 'I love this pudding. Will you show me—'

'After we've finished all the jam. When are you going to get they broad figs and quinces?'

'I thought – as I'm going up there anyway – this afternoon.' Another shiver danced over Jenefer's skin and anticipation quaked inside her.

'That's more like it. Do you good to be out.' Lizzie paused in the doorway. 'I know what I was going tell you. Old Mr Kneebone passed away last night. Janie Couch told me when I was up the pump.' Lizzie shook her head. ''Tis a blessing really. He was never the same after Minnie died. 'Twas like as if part of him went with her. Fifty years they was married.'

'Cora will miss him.'

Lizzie nodded. 'That's her mother, her father and her husband all in two years. Poor soul. It don't bear thinking about. There'll be a big turn out for the funeral.'

Jenefer nodded. 'Will you cook a joint of topside to slice cold? I

27

daresay Mr Rollason might have a nice ham as well. We'll need extra flour for bread.'

'Wheat or barley?'

'Both. And butter. Tell Hannah and Mr Rollason what it's for. I'll settle up as usual at the end of the month.' She stood up, smoothed her gown then raised her hands to the thick tresses coiled high on her crown, suddenly and unaccountably nervous. 'Perhaps I should stay here this afternoon.'

'What you talking about? Pednbrose was your home. 'Tis only right you should be there when he look round. Any'ow, you told me Mr Casvellan was proper friendly with him.'

'I *know.*' Jenefer was in an agony of indecision. 'He seemed very pleasant, but—'

'Fer goodness sake!' Lizzie threw up her hands. 'You aren't still fretting? Turned out for the best, didn't it? Martin Erisey was never right for you. You can't be dragging the past around with you like some old sack. It happened, it's over. Now leave it go.'

'You're right. I know you're right.'

'I am too. Now, you know you said mister was looking for a house to rent? I b'lieve there's one going up on The Terrace. Mrs Avers' mother's place? Ruth who works for Mrs Avers was telling me they don't want to sell so they're looking for a tenant.' She handed Jenefer her bonnet. 'You tell 'n. He'll be some pleased. And he'll owe you for that.'

Jenefer threw her arms around her neighbour and hugged her. 'Thanks, Lizzie.'

'Get on,' Lizzie shooed her out.

Chapter Four

A straw bonnet shading her face from the bright sunshine and a basket swinging from one hand, Jenefer strolled down the main street. She returned greetings, stopped to ask after an ailing parent or a sick child. She sympathized with complaints about prices and their effect on business. And all the while her thoughts kept leaping ahead to her meeting with Charles Polgray. She barely knew him, yet anticipation fluttered in her stomach.

She couldn't ever remember feeling like this about William though she had known him for two years. Yet less than an hour spent in Charles Polgray's company was long enough to convince her the two men were as different as limestone and granite.

William was steady, dependable: devoted to his calling and his parishioners. It had taken him months to convince the well-to-do in the village to support his plan to start a school for poor children, and almost as long again to persuade them to contribute to the cost of slates, chalks, a blackboard, pencils and paper. How could one not admire such a man?

Yet despite his bold new ideas and forward thinking he could not – or would not – accept that she might feel about her work the way he felt about his. As he never tired of telling her, a woman's greatest happiness would be found in the role for which God and nature had created her: a comfort and support to her husband and a loving mother to his children. Anything else was self-indulgence.

She doubted he had offered this opinion to the elderly unmarried ladies in the parish. He would not wish to offend the most loyal members of his congregation. That his lofty pronouncement might offend *her* had apparently never occurred to him.

The trouble was, part of her believed him: the part that yearned to love someone who would love her in return. Yet hearing him condemn as *self-indulgence* the business she had worked so hard to establish infuriated her. He had not lived her life, suffered her losses. Yet he was utterly convinced he knew what was best for her: that his way was the right way, the *only* way.

At least Charles Polgray had not patronized her. She had prepared for it, made wary by his coolness during their introduction. So she had tested him, surprised and delighted by his dry response to her teasing and irony. But the directness of his grey-green gaze and the powerful tug of attraction had caught her off-guard.

From his questions it appeared he was as curious about her as she was about him. Why else would he have manoeuvred her into accompanying him on his search for a house? Tremors radiated from the pit of her stomach.

At the bottom of the street she entered the builder's yard. Lifting a new coffin from two saw-horses in his workshop, Eddy Barnicoat laid it on the bed of the waiting cart.

'Good afternoon, Mr Barnicoat.'

Glancing round, he came towards her, raising a finger in salute. 'Miss Trevanion.'

She indicated the coffin. 'Is that for Mr Kneebone?'

He nodded. 'I'm taking 'n down there now.'

Removing coins from the stocking purse in her basket, Jenefer dropped them onto his callused palm. 'Cora told me her father wanted to be laid to rest beside his wife. Is this enough to pay for the coffin and the grave to be opened?'

Eddy glanced at the money and nodded. Beneath bushy brows his gaze was sharp. 'Cora never gave you this, and I'll tell you how I know. Because last week she told my missus she was going up the farm to get harvest work. 'Course, then her father took worse and she couldn't leave 'n.'

'Ah.' Jenefer caught her lower lip between her teeth.

'So when I tell her she don't owe me nothing, she's going to ask where the money come from. What am I s'posed to say then?'

Jenefer thought for a moment. 'Perhaps Mr Kneebone gave you the money when you used to keep him company on a Saturday afternoon?

You didn't mention it to Cora because you didn't want to upset her.'

Pushing his cap back, he scratched his head. 'I dunno.'

'Mr Barnicoat, if you tell her the truth, she will feel obligated to repay money I don't need and she cannot afford.' His glare told her he wasn't comfortable taking credit for her actions. 'You know I'm right.'

He blew a sigh. 'Don't have much choice, do I?'

'Thank you.'

'Nothing to thank me for.'

Jenefer touched his arm. 'Even so, I am grateful.'

'Get on with 'ee,' he muttered. 'If this village knew the half of what you do—'

'But they don't, and I prefer it that way.'

Clicking his tongue he raised his eyes heavenward. 'If you say so.' He nodded a farewell.

A few minutes later Jenefer climbed the hill leading towards the headland, her boots stirring puffs of dust from the dry dirt road. On her left a high stone wall hid a hillside house and garden from prying eyes. As she approached, a gate in the wall opened. A tall, slim figure clad in clerical garb of black coat and breeches emerged, his back toward her as he fastened the latch.

All-too-familiar conflict erupted within her. While not exactly handsome – a point in his favour for she had noticed that such men often treated everyone they met as a mirror, expecting their high opinion of themselves to be reflected back at them – William Ince possessed an open countenance and pleasing manner.

'Good afternoon, William.'

He looked round, his pale cheeks turning pink and pleasure crinkling the corners of his blue eyes. 'Miss Trevanion! Jenefer.' Whipping off his round wide-brimmed hat he bowed, fair hair flopping over his forehead. 'This is an unexpected pleasure. How are you?'

'I'm well, thank you. You may not have heard, but Mr Kneebone died last night.'

His smile faded. 'I will call and offer my condolences to Mrs Eustace. I assume the Methodist minister will conduct the funeral?'

Jenefer nodded. 'Mr Barnicoat is on his way there now. The coffin and grave have been paid for. But should there be any additional expenses please don't say anything to Cora. I will settle them.'

'Your generosity is truly admirable.'

'I prefer anonymity to admiration,' she replied. Then added, 'I am fortunate my work enables me to make such gifts.'

'Is that a hint of pride I hear?' He wagged a chiding finger at her. 'A sin against which we must be ever on our guard.'

She inhaled slowly. 'You are missing the point, William.'

'Am I? I don't think so. You have a talent for figures. Talents are a gift from God and, as the parable tells us—'

'They should be used,' Jenefer interrupted, failing to curb both her impatience and her tongue. 'Which is exactly what I am doing.'

'There are other ways,' he said with quiet conviction. 'Better ways. As a teacher for example.'

'I already—'

'Forgive me.' He raised one hand, cutting her short. 'This is not the time or place.' His sudden grin was transforming. 'I shall convince you, you know.'

Trying to ignore her residual frustration Jenefer returned his smile. 'Perhaps I will convince *you*. I perform a valuable service for village businesses, William. I say that not in pride, but as fact.' Having made her point she would not labour it. 'Still, as you say, this is not the time.'

He cleared his throat and his flush deepened. 'Will you permit me the honour of escorting you home?'

'That is most kind. But I'm not going home. I have spent the morning indoors and feel in need of fresh air and exercise.'

'Then I wish you an enjoyable afternoon.' He hesitated. 'When may I call on you? There are several parish matters we need to discuss.'

Despite their differences she was fond of him. And, unlike most of the Overseers, he did not hold the poor responsible for their poverty. 'Shall we say the end of next week?'

Disappointment flitted across his face and was valiantly suppressed. 'I shall look forward to it.' Smiling, he bowed. 'I daresay our paths will cross in the village. Good day, Jenefer.'

She bobbed a curtsy. 'William.'

She walked briskly, trying to shake off conflicting emotions. He was a good man, a man of principle who lived by his beliefs. She accepted that. So why could he not accept her as she was? Why was he courting her at all? His constant gentle scolding – his accusations that in clinging to her work she was turning her back on God's purpose – upset and confused her. She enjoyed her work and it benefited others. How could that be wrong?

Dog roses and honeysuckle festooned the stone walls on either side of the entrance to Pednbrose. The wooden gate stood open for there was nothing left to protect. Grass grew through the lower bars. At the top of the short driveway she followed a flagged path patched with moss and lichen around to the front of the blackened ruins.

What had once been a lawn now resembled a hayfield. Scarlet poppies nodded amid long grass. Beyond the bottom hedge and cliff path, the sea glittered like polished silver. A breeze sighed and whispered through trees on the hillside behind the property, their leaves just starting to turn yellow-gold, orange and brown.

Jenefer reached the arched doorway that led into the walled garden. Seeing it as a stranger would, she noticed how badly the dark-green paint had cracked and peeled, revealing bare wood beneath. Lifting the rusting iron latch she opened the door.

Within the tall stone walls the air was still, heavy, and much warmer. Instead of wind and sea she heard bees and birdsong, and inhaled the rich scent of warm earth and ripe fruit.

Propping the door open with a large stone so he would know where to find her *if he came*, she followed weed-choked paths to the top right-hand corner. There, where west and south-facing walls joined, protected from wind and frost, a gnarled tree with large glossy leaves was heavy with greenish purple pear-shaped fruits the villagers called *broad* figs to distinguish them from raisins which, for reasons lost in the mists of time, they chose to call figs.

When she had half-filled her basket with the ripest, she covered them with a folded cloth and moved towards the spreading twisted branches of the quince tree. Lack of feeding and pruning meant the crop wasn't large, but there were enough vivid yellow fruits to fill her basket to the top.

Each time she visited she was saddened by the worsening neglect. Until a few days ago Charles Polgray's lack of interest in his inheritance had annoyed her. But his arrival signalled more far-reaching changes than she had envisaged or was ready for.

*

Leaving The Standard, Charles nodded politely to people he passed, feeling their eyes on his back. Curiosity and suspicion were inevitable. He had to accept that. He didn't have to like it.

Fifteen minutes later he reached Pednbrose, walked round the front of the ruin and saw the wooden door propped open. He paused beneath the stone arch, surveying vegetable beds choked with crops left to rot and re-grow amid encroaching weeds. Clumps of yellow buttercups and patches of small white daisies had colonised the paths. Thistledown and dandelion seeds drifted on the warm air. But beneath the neglect was a large, protected, well-planned garden.

Then he saw her. She was on the far side, her back to him as she picked fruit. He felt a tightening in his gut. *Had he learned nothing?* This was different. *She* was different. He watched as she raised one of the bright yellow quinces to her nose and inhaled its scent. Dropping it in the basket she lifted her face to the sun.

At any moment she might turn *and catch him watching.* He cleared his throat to announce his presence. 'Good afternoon, Miss Trevanion.'

She whirled round. 'Mr Polgray!'

He shouldn't have come. He needed her help. Deliberately deaf to the conflict raging inside him, he started forward.

Her warm smile had the impact of a blow. 'I didn't—'

'Think I'd come?'

Shock and chagrin eclipsed her smile and, blushing, she looked away. He wished he hadn't said it, hadn't embarrassed her. Since leaving her after their ride from Trescowe he had been arguing with himself. Making use of her position and contacts in the village was justifiable as a sound business move. Wanting to spend time in her company, and thinking up ways he might achieve this, was not only inexcusable it was dangerous, and precisely the reason he should have sent his apologies. He knew that. Yet nothing would have kept him away. He had looked forward to it all morning, knew himself to be all kinds of fool, and felt ridiculously nervous.

She lifted one shoulder, still not meeting his gaze. 'No, what I intended to say—'

'Before I so rudely interrupted.'

'Was that I didn't hear you arrive.'

He gave her credit for a quick recovery, but knew he had guessed correctly.

'Though had something prevented you from coming,' she said carefully, 'I would not have been too surprised. From the little you told me I can see yours is a very demanding life.'

She had no idea. 'So is yours,' he replied. 'Yet *you* came.'

'That's different. I had an additional reason.' She held up the basket. 'Of course, in law the fruit belongs to you.'

'True,' he agreed. He knew what she was doing. She had inadvertently revealed too much. Wanting her slip forgotten, she was deflecting him with a challenge. His uncertainty dissolved. At this moment there was nowhere he would rather be, and no one he would rather be with. As for the rest – *to hell with it.* 'But if I give you retrospective permission, no crime has been committed. However—'

'Let me guess. Your generosity has a price?'

He felt a dart of admiration. 'Mr Casvellan was right.'

'He usually is. But about what in particular?'

'That you have a shrewder grasp of finance than many men of his acquaintance.'

Though she blushed, she held his gaze. 'He flatters me.'

Charles shook his head. 'Unlikely. He struck me as a man of clear vision and forthright speech. But while I have no reason to doubt his opinion of you, I'm sure that as a woman of business you will understand I require proof.'

'Naturally.'

Seeing her soft lips compress to hold back a smile, Charles kept his expression solemn. But inside him pleasure leapt, bright and hot as a flame. *She understood.* 'So in return for all the fruit you have *rescued*, my price – in full and final settlement – is two jars of quince jelly.'

'Two?'

'I'll take another if you insist. I admit it's a particular favourite of mine and one I enjoy all too rarely.'

Her cheek dimpled as she tried not to laugh. 'And I am expected to make it?'

He looked down his nose at her, one dark brow lifting. 'Of course.'

'You drive a hard bargain, Mr Polgray.'

'Do we have a deal?' He extended his hand.

'I should explain—'

'Excuses already?'

'No! It's just I am not yet as proficient—'

'Do we have a deal?'

'Do I have a choice?'

'Absolutely not.'

'Don't ever complain that I didn't warn you.' With a mock glare she took his hand. But as their palms touched and his fingers closed around hers his breath caught. She had felt it too, for shock and vulnerability were naked on her face.

Releasing her hand he pretended to survey the garden. He hadn't expected— *Too late.* He risked a sidelong glance. Her head was bent over the basket, her eyes hidden by the brim of her bonnet. But the delicate nape of her neck and what little he could see of her face had flushed deep rose. His heart contracted. *Tell her.* He couldn't. He had given his word.

'I—' His throat was dry, his voice a croak. He swallowed. 'If you have all the fruit you need, will you show me the rest of the property?'

'Yes, of course.' He read gratitude in her shy smile.

He gestured for her to precede him along the narrow path. Walking close behind he caught a hint of her fragrance, something light and floral, summery. He forced himself to concentrate. 'I met the curate on my way here. Has he been long in the village?' The effort of keeping his tone casual made him sweat. He could only hope that if she noticed she would think it due to the heat.

'Two years.' She glanced back. 'It has not been easy for him.'

'How so?'

'Doctor Trennack, our parish priest, introduced Mr Ince to the congregation at matins one Sunday morning. Within the month Mr Ince found himself solely responsible for the parish's spiritual welfare. I suppose I should not say so—'

'Indeed you should,' Charles urged. 'It is only right and proper that I know the terrible truth.' Guilt loosened its grip slightly as he saw the corners of her mouth tilt upward.

'If you insist.'

'I do,' he stated.

'Well, the *truth* is that Dr Trennack has always preferred his books to his parishioners. Which meant that lacking the guidance he should have expected from his mentor, William – Mr Ince' – she corrected quickly, 'had to find his own way. Fortunately he learned fast and soon settled into village life. Because he was so obviously sincere, the village made allowances for some of his more' – she hesitated, clearly seeking the right word – 'progressive ideas.'

'Is he a particular friend of yours?' Driven by jealousy to ask, Charles wished he hadn't.

'We are friends, yes,' Jenefer replied. 'I help at the school he set up for the village children – those who are not tutored at home or sent away to board.'

'But?'

She threw up a hand, blushing. 'Really, Mr Polgray. You are quite the inquisitor.'

'Forgive me. It is force of habit. When I take on a new project I try to find out as much as possible about the area and the people with whom I'm likely to come into contact. Every detail adds colour to the overall picture.' What he'd told her was the truth: just not *all* of it. He saw some of the tension leave her shoulders. 'I assumed, when you agreed to assist me, that you would expect me to ask about the village and the people who live here.'

'Yes, of course. It's just— William has many good points. I would not want you to think otherwise. And I have the greatest admiration for him regarding his insistence that poor children are as deserving of education and a chance to better themselves as those from wealthy families.'

'Some would call that heresy.'

'Many did – do,' Jenefer agreed. 'Yet with patience and perseverance he got his way. Unfortunately, he shows less understanding regarding my business. He believes I should give it up.' She caught her breath. 'I beg your pardon. That was – I should not have said. . . .'

'We made an agreement, did we not?' he reminded. 'Whatever we discussed was to remain between us?'

'Yes, but . . . when you said that you were referring to the harbour project.'

'True. But if the agreement is extended to cover all our conversations you need not feel constrained.' He didn't wait for her reply. 'Tell me, do you consider your business to be less important than mine?'

'No, not to me.' There was pride in her voice, and her chin lifted. 'Nor to those who are my clients.'

'Then no apology is necessary. As for Mr Ince's wishes, what are your thoughts on the matter?'

She hesitated. 'I'm sure *he* believes he has my best interests at heart. But were I to do as he asks I think – I fear – I would not be happy.'

'Then you mustn't.'

'If only it were that simple,' she murmured, walking on before he could respond.

Kicking away the stone with his dusty boot, he pulled the wooden door closed and followed her, stopping in front of the burned-out shell.

'What happened here?' he asked quietly. 'How did the fire start?'

She returned to his side. 'Two men broke in. They believed my father to be in possession of a hoard of gemstones brought back from India. What they didn't know, and refused to believe when I told them, was that the stones had all been sold and the money used to buy free-trade cargoes. One of them had a gun and threatened to hurt my sister, so I shot him. I didn't intend to,' she added quickly. 'He frightened me and the pistol just went off. The ball pierced his arm and he dropped the lantern. My father had spilled some brandy earlier in the evening and the candle rolled into it.' Her voice faded to a whisper. 'The flames spread so fast.'

Though she was staring at the ruins he knew she wasn't seeing blackened stone and charred wood. Her knuckles gleamed, bone-white as she clutched the basket's handle, reliving the horror. The urge to put his arms around her and hold her close was overwhelming. It took every ounce of his strength to resist. He wanted to protect her, comfort her. *He had no right.* Instead, needing to touch, he laid his hand on her shoulder for a moment, then made himself step away. 'I'm so sorry.'

'We tried, but. . . .' She gave a brief helpless shrug. 'My father died in the fire. At least Betsy and I got out.'

A frown tightened his forehead. 'But . . . I understood your sister is unable to walk.'

She nodded. 'I carried her on my back down the kitchen stairs. It's funny,' she went on, before he could respond, 'I used to run up and down those stairs in seconds and think nothing of it. But that night, in the dark, with thick smoke making it hard to breathe and impossible to see despite the glow of the flames, it seemed to take forever.'

'You lost everything?'

'Almost.' Her shoulder moved again. 'Maggie – she was our house-keeper – helped me empty each of our closets onto the bed. We tied everything into bundles. Then we threw them out of the window. So at least we had clothes, sheets and blankets. But precious little else, apart from some old furniture, crockery and other bits that had been stored in one of the outhouses.' Her quick smile was full of humour. It pierced his heart.

'That junk furnished my cottage. And for my first job as a book-keeper I asked to be paid half in cash, half in groceries. I learned how little I really needed in order to be comfortable.' She glanced up at him. 'If you remain long in Porthinnis, Mr Polgray, you are sure to make the acquaintance of the village's well-to-do families. They will consider it their duty to warn you of Miss Trevanion's peculiar ways.'

Recognizing her wry tone as a façade behind which she hid the scars of that night, and those she had suffered since while trying to build her business, he knew she was one of the bravest people he had ever met. But this was not the time to tell her so.

'Indeed?' His features hardened. 'I form my own opinions, Miss Trevanion, and have no need of others to do it for me. As they will learn.' He relaxed and a smile tilted the corners of his mouth. 'On our ride from Trescowe I asked you about houses to rent. Have you had time—?'

'I haven't, but Lizzie – my neighbour – was in the butchers and learned of two properties.' Opening her purse Jenefer drew out a scrap of folded paper. 'These are the addresses.'

He shook his head. 'It would take me far too long to find them by myself. Besides, you cannot have forgotten you promised me your assistance in return for a generous donation to your chosen charity.' Her cheeks grew pink, but her gaze met his.

'Forget such *persuasion*, Mr Polgray? How could I? I simply thought you might prefer to—'

'Then you thought wrong.' He wanted to offer his arm but resisted. Instead he took the basket from her. 'Allow me. It looks – it *is* heavy. And before you tell me that you are used to carrying such weights, I have no doubt you are perfectly capable. But this afternoon it is my privilege. Do not deny me.'

'You are a difficult man to refuse, Mr Polgray.'

He smiled down at her. 'I try.'

Chapter Five

'No, I'm afraid this will not do at all.' Charles turned away from the elegant townhouse in the middle of a terrace two streets above the eastern side of the harbour. 'It opens directly onto the road.'

'Had you mentioned that proximity to the road was undesirable,' Jenefer said, 'I would not have brought you here.'

'I like the house very well, but not its position. Do you know of another, perhaps with a small area or garden in front?'

She shook her head. 'This terrace was built during the reign of Queen Anne. It is the only one in the village.'

'A pity. However, as I have no desire to be choked by dust in summer, or descend from the step into mud each time it rains, we must look elsewhere.' He started walking, then realized she was not with him. He glanced back.

'Mr Polgray, we have visited both the addresses and you have not liked either of them. Perhaps if you could tell me what it is you are seeking.'

'Surely it's obvious? To find the property that best suits my needs.'

'Right now I know of no others available.'

'Perhaps because you've had so little time to make enquiries. I'm sure something will turn up.'

'I think you would have more success with an agent.'

'We have already had that conversation. And I have asked enough of you for one day. I will escort you home.'

'There's really no need—'

'It would be my pleasure.'

They walked down a cobbled alley that opened onto the street behind the harbour.

'It's very quiet,' he observed. 'Where is everyone?'

'It's harvest time, Mr Polgray.' Her tone was dry. 'They are in the fields.'

He should have realised. 'Of course.' He caught her sidelong glance, sensed she was going to ask him something important. He braced himself, dreading—

'Why did you choose Porthinnis?'

Anxiety receded like an ebbing tide. 'We – the company of Kerrow & Polgray – have always used Hayle harbour to import and export our cargoes. But harbour dues and transport costs have become prohibitive. I did consider other harbours. But Porthinnis is much closer to our mine and with a few alterations will suit very well.'

'What kind of alterations?'

'Lengthening the western quay to form an arm. This will increase protection of the inner harbour while allowing bigger ships to tie up alongside. I also plan to construct a mole – a massive free-standing stone breakwater – fifty yards to the west of the harbour.' He saw her frown as she tried to picture it.

'For what purpose?'

'To absorb the force of storm waves that might otherwise damage the quay. In fact that will be the first work undertaken. I want it in place before the winter.'

'What an excellent idea. Perhaps if such a structure had existed three years ago—' She stopped, shook her head. 'Such thoughts are pointless. One cannot undo the past, only repair the devastation and move on.'

Wincing inwardly, his throat was suddenly, painfully, dry. He swallowed. 'The cargo brigs should not be too much inconvenienced by construction work.'

'Those reliant on the goods they bring will be relieved to hear it,' Jenefer said. 'But what about the crabbers and lobstermen who set their pots close inshore?'

'For a short period they may have to drop their pots a little further along the coast.'

'And the seaweed cutters? The local farms rely on oreweed to fertilize their fields.'

'They too might need to venture a little further than usual. But you

42

and I both know that after two or three days of easterly wind every beach and cove along this coast is knee-deep in kelp and bladder-wrack.' He saw her cheeks grow pink.

'I didn't – I'm just—'

'I know.' He smiled at her. 'You are concerned about protecting the interests of the villagers. But might I suggest that instead of focusing on problems – which I will do my best to keep to a minimum and deal with as they arise – you consider the benefits?' The basket of fruit in one hand, he gestured with the other. 'Months of employment for any man who wants it during the construction phase. Then continuing employment for those with strong backs and willing hands once we start shipping cargoes.'

'I agree it all sounds—'

'The pilchard cellars are empty,' he reminded quietly. 'Fishermen venturing into deep water after mackerel shoals run a very real risk of being taken by press gangs. I, on the other hand, will need masons and labourers, men to site and operate cranes, builders and carpenters to erect storage sheds, and a team to build a new road.'

Jenefer looked up quickly. 'What new road? Where?'

'Cutting through waste ground at the back of the quay to join the main road beyond the village boundary. Why?' he said, before she asked. 'There will be a vast increase in traffic coming to and from the harbour during the next few months. Though much will arrive by sea, the rest will use the new road, so keeping the strings of pack-animals and heavy carts out of the village centre.'

'That's a marvellous idea. Yet I fear you will still face objections.'

'Despite the benefit to local businesses?' He heard the impatience in his voice. About to apologize and make clear it was not directed at her, he saw it wasn't necessary.

'People fear what they do not understand,' she said. 'They cling to familiarity and feel threatened by change. You must have encountered this before.'

He nodded. 'You too, I imagine,' he murmured. 'Your whole life was altered by tragedy.'

'Some changes were forced upon me,' she allowed. 'The rest have been my choice.' She lifted her chin. 'I would not wish you to think me a victim, Mr Polgray.'

'Believe me, Miss Trevanion, nothing was further from my mind.'

She stopped at the entrance to a short alley between two cottages. At the far end he could see a narrow path between a thick hedge and a productive vegetable garden. It led from the cobbles to a stone-built privy shrouded in ivy. 'Thank you for seeing me home. And for the fruit.'

He wanted to see where she lived, wanted to ask when he might see her again. Instead he handed her the basket, and matched her formality with a bow. 'It was my pleasure.'

She dropped a curtsy, and turned away.

'Miss Trevanion? When may I hope to receive the quince jelly?'

'When I have time to make it,' she called over her shoulder.

Smiling at her retort he watched until she disappeared.

*

Seeing the crowd gathered outside Cora's father's cottage, Jenefer glanced down at the laden baskets she and Lizzie carried. 'Cora will be glad of the extra bread.'

'Dear life!' Lizzie whispered. 'I never thought to see so many. 'T will be a comfort to Cora, mind.'

Dressed in their Sunday best, dark coats shiny with age and wear, men had gathered round the simple coffin that rested on trestles set up in the street. An old plank door, now devoid of hinges and latch, leaned against the cottage wall.

Nodding politely the men stepped aside. Eddy Barnicoat caught Jenefer's eye and touched his hat in salute. The fact that all the men were freshly shaved on a weekday signified their respect for the occasion.

Tapping on the open door, Jenefer passed from the bright sunny morning into a dark kitchen fragrant with the smell of baking. A dish of butter and a large hunk of cheese were flanked by a plate containing squares of *hevva* cake stuffed with raisins and peel and sprinkled with sugar, another of saffron buns, a pot of blackcurrant and a pot of gooseberry jam. A score of small pasties baked golden brown were piled on a large oval platter.

'Miss Trevanion!' Cora wiped her hands on the apron that covered her black gown.

'Good morning, ladies.' Setting one basket on the floor, Jenefer pulled back the crisp white cloth covering the other and lifted out a large blue and white plate piled high with slices of cold roast beef and another of sliced boiled ham.

Cora gave a soft gasp, her eyes widening. 'Oh my dear lord! I – I dunno what to say, miss.' The other two women were already moving dishes around to accommodate the plates.

Jenefer emptied her baskets of jars of chutney, a block of butter and two more loaves. 'There's a slab of *hevva* cake as well. But I see you already have one. Perhaps mine should stay on the dresser for now?' Setting it down, she stepped away from the table so Lizzie could take her place.

'Where d'you want these, bird? There's a mutton pie, a couple of damson tarts and another two loaves.'

'Oh, Lizzie, 'andsome that is. Put them over there.' Cora pointed. Then, surveying the laden table, she shook her head. 'Look at that.' Her mouth trembled and her eyes were bright with unshed tears. 'Fit for a king that is.'

'And will be gone in a trice once the men come back,' her friend announced.

''Tis a brave walk up to the churchyard,' the other said over her shoulder while filling the soot-blackened kettle from a tall brownstone ewer. 'Time they've seen Mr Kneebone laid to rest, God bless 'n, they'll be chacking for something to eat and a cup o' strong tea.'

A man poked his head around the door. 'Minister's come, Cora.'

Wiping her eyes, Cora dropped her apron onto the wooden chair, took a deep breath and quickly raised her hands to her frilled cap, tucking escaped strands out of sight. She turned to Jenefer. 'Want to stay, do you? Minister do a lovely funeral.' Her breath caught and one of the women laid a comforting hand on her shoulder.

'I'd be honoured,' Jenefer said. Outside, the crowd had swelled to fill the street. As she emerged from the house after retrieving the baskets she saw people nudge each other and whisper. *Miss Trevanion had been seen with a strange man.* It struck her as both amusing and rather sad that this should be newsworthy.

Murmuring greetings she eased through, Lizzie behind her, until she reached the rear where her presence would not be a distraction.

After leading them in prayer, the minister spoke of Isaac Kneebone as a man liked and respected in the community, and paid tribute to Cora's devoted care. The crowd stood bare-headed and silent in warm sunshine while gulls wheeled and screamed overhead and white puffs of fair weather cloud sailed across a sky the colour of bluebells.

Hearing Cora's muffled sobs Jenefer thought back to her own father's funeral. In a state of shock at the time, her recall of the event was fragmented. She remembered Jared and his parents grouped behind Betsy's wheeled chair; housekeeper Maggie clinging to her husband Treeve's arm while he – sober for once – appeared stunned and lost. Her overriding memory was of feeling totally alone.

Her throat stiffened and she swallowed hard. That was the past. She had come a long way since then, making new friends, building a business. She had much to be grateful for.

After the final prayer the bearers arranged themselves in order of precedence: relatives in front followed by friends and volunteers willing to share the task of carrying the coffin to the churchyard. Only men were involved now.

Bearers in position, Mr Rogers, the chapel steward, announced the hymn. The coffin was lifted onto shoulders, the singing began and the cortège moved off.

''Andsome that was,' Lizzie sniffed, as they headed home. 'Minister got a lovely way with 'n. Not like Moses Carthew. Remember old "Holy" Moses, do you?' She shook her head. 'All hellfire and damnation he was. Well, you don't want it, not when you're grieving. 'T was bad enough Sundays. Rant for an hour without drawing breath he could. I seen 'n the night of the great storm, striding up and down the beach all by hisself, clutching a Bible in one hand and waving the other like he was preaching to hundreds. Off his head he was, poor soul.'

Beside her Jenefer remembered. 'I believe Dr Trennack arranged for someone to take him to his sister in Truro.'

Lizzie sighed. 'We seen some changes these past few years.'

'We have indeed,' Jenefer agreed. And Charles Polgray's arrival threatened more. *Was that why he prowled her thoughts and haunted her dreams?* 'You go on, Lizzie. I'll pick up the sugar.'

'I'll boil up the kettle for when you get back.'

Pushing open the shop door, Jenefer heard the bell jangle, and inhaled the familiar aroma of cheese and roasted coffee. Hannah Tresidder was behind the counter cutting a wedge from a large wheel of cheddar.

'All right, Miss Trevanion? I just seen Mr Kneebone carried up through. Least he got a nice day for it. Cora all right is she?'

'She's coping well. Her neighbours are helping prepare everything for when the men get back.'

''Tis hard to know whether to be glad or sad that he've gone. Cora have had some awful time of it this past two years. Now she'll have to move again.'

'Move?' Jenefer was surprised. 'Why?'

'Her father's was the last life on the lease. Now he's gone she won't be able to stay there no more.'

'I didn't know. Four pounds of loaf sugar, please. On my account.'

'More jam, is it?'

'Quince jelly.'

Hannah lifted two sugar cones wrapped in blue paper from the shelf behind her. Placing them on the wooden counter she leaned forward, lowering her voice though there was no one else in the shop. 'Don't mind me asking, but who was that gentleman I seen you out walking with?'

The shop was the hub of the village. Nothing happened without Hannah hearing about it. Expecting the question, Jenefer had prepared an answer that was truthful but did not betray any confidences.

'His name is Mr Charles Polgray. He's my father's heir.'

'Come to inspect his inheritance, I s'pose. Took his time about it, didn't he? Not that there's much to see, begging your pardon, Miss,' she added quickly.

Janefer waved the apology aside. 'I can hardly take offence at the truth. I understand he was abroad on business and has not long returned.'

'Abroad?' Hannah's thick brows rose as she tucked her chin against the billowing kerchief below her throat. 'Fancy. So now he've seen the place, what's he going to do with it? Think he'll rebuild do you?'

'I don't know. He didn't say. As the property belongs to him now, it's really none of my business.'

'You'll miss the fruit,' Hannah sighed.

Picking up the basket, Jenefer nodded at the sugar loaves. 'Perhaps you should reduce your order.'

Hannah sucked air through her teeth. 'Oh no, I can't be doing with that.' Her face brightened. 'Here, thought of making bramble jelly, have you? Esther went by yesterday with a great bowl of blackberries.'

Jenefer turned at the door. 'What an excellent idea. You could pick the fruit and I will make the jelly.'

'I haven't got time—' Hannah began. Seeing Jenefer's smile she threw up her hands. 'All right, you haven't either.'

''Bye, Hannah.' Closing the shop door, Jenefer hurried home.

Chapter Six

Reassuring Lizzie that she would do very well on her own, Jenefer pared and sliced the quinces then dropped them into her large copper preserving pan with enough water to float them. Then she put the pan on the slab over the fire.

'Everything all right?' Lizzie asked.

'You tell me,' Jenefer gestured towards the range.

Lizzie peered into the pan. 'Looking handsome it is. It'll take about three hours for them to be properly tender, so you got plenty of time to eat your tea then get the jars and oiled papers ready. Right, I'll leave you be.'

Jenefer frowned. 'What's that on your sleeve and the front of your apron?'

Lizzie clicked her tongue. ''Tis the figs. They do splatter something awful. First time I made fig jam and it splashed up, I wiped it off quick as I could, but it took the skin as well.' She clicked her tongue. 'In some mess I was. Now I always keep my sleeves rolled down and use my longest wooden paddle. I'd best get back.' She paused at the door. 'You sure you don't need—?'

'Lizzie, I'm managing very well. Didn't I have the best teacher?'

'Get on with you,' Lizzie flapped a hand at her. 'Right, I'm gone.'

While she ate cold ham with apple and ginger chutney followed by two raspberry tartlets, Jenefer tried to rationalize her reaction to Charles Polgray. She understood his initial coolness. In his place she would have felt the same. Branoc Casvellan's recommendation of her might have helped, but she sensed strongly that Charles Polgray preferred to rely on his own observations and instincts. He had trusted her with confidential information. How could she not feel flattered, and proud that she had won his respect for her accomplishments in business? Yet in her secret heart she longed for him to see her as an attractive woman. *Why?* When she had no such thoughts about William, with whom she had been acquainted far longer and knew to be an upright, honest and caring man.

Her shame and confusion only deepened the conflict between her need to retain her independence – a need she recognized was rooted in fear – and her growing desire for love, marriage and children.

Angry at what she considered weakness, she pushed away from the table and carried her dishes to the sink. After checking the boiling quinces she washed and dried the jars and cut out a dozen circles of paper and brushed them with oil then measured and warmed the sugar.

Glad to be busy, for it allowed her no time to think, she strained off the clear juice, added one pound of sugar for each pint and set the syrup to boil, carefully skimming off the scum as it formed. Sieving the quince pulp, she poured it into a clean pan, added three-quarters of a pound of sugar for each pound of pulp and set it on the slab, remembering Lizzie's warning to constantly stir it from the bottom with a wooden spoon to ensure it didn't burn or stick.

During half an hour of stirring and skimming she planned her work for the week ahead, and in mingled hope and shame wondered if Charles Polgray might have need of her. Then she put the tray of jars into the oven. Fifteen minutes later she spooned a little of the bubbling mixture from each pan onto a saucer. As it instantly firmed to jelly she let out her breath, smiling with pride and delight.

Moving the pans off the fire, she carefully lifted the jars from the oven. Setting them upright she ladled clear jelly into half of them, the marmalade into the rest.

After she had washed and dried the pans, spoons and ladles, the jars were cool enough for the oiled papers to be placed in each one. Her final task was to brush white of egg onto both sides of larger circles of tissue paper. Pressed over the mouths of the jars they would dry hard to create an airtight seal. Leaving them on the table, she went upstairs to bed. It had been a long day and she was very tired. But she had fulfilled her part of their bargain: Charles Polgray would receive two jars of perfect quince jelly.

*

Up since daybreak making a copy of the drawings and detailed list of all the costs, Charles planned to post them to Mr Daniell at the Cornish Bank in Truro with his request for an appointment. The task had taken longer than expected because his thoughts continually strayed to Jenefer Trevanion.

Meeting her at Trescowe he had been misled by her drab coat and plain bonnet. Within minutes he had realized his mistake. Initially reserved, matching his skill at deflecting questions she was not willing to answer, she was surprisingly free of artifice. Devoid of coyness and making no attempt to flatter, she possessed a quick dry wit he found captivating. He had never met anyone like her. Each time he saw her the magnetic attraction between them strengthened. She felt it too. He read it in her eyes, saw it in her heightened colour.

This was not the time. Propping his elbows on the table he pushed his hands through his hair then rubbed his face. Inconvenient it certainly was, but it had happened and he could not wish otherwise. Meeting her was a precious gift: one to be protected at all costs.

A knock on the door made him look up. 'Come in.'

The door opened and the maid entered carrying a large jug of hot water and fresh towels. Putting them on the washstand she bobbed a curtsy and hurried to the door.

'Kindly tell the groom to have my horse saddled. I'll be down in half an hour.'

'Sir.'

Washed and shaved, he put on a clean shirt and neckcloth, fawn pantaloons and gleaming boots, buttoned his waistcoat, and shrugged into a brown tailcoat. Packing all he needed for an overnight stay into a saddle-bag, he picked up his hat and clattered downstairs.

Riding hard, he arrived in Helston two hours later. He left his horse at The Bell and walked up the street to his attorney's office.

'Good morning, Steven.' Charles dropped his hat on one corner of a large oak desk on which papers and documents tied with red ribbon were arranged in neat piles.

'Charles, my dear fellow.' Steven Vincent rose from his chair and leaned across the desk to shake hands before resuming his seat. 'Do sit down. This is most fortuitous. I was about to write to you.'

Crossing one leg over the other, Charles pulled off his gloves. 'You've drawn up the necessary documents for the new company?'

Steven reached for one of the folders bound with ribbon. He looked up, his expression concerned. 'You're aware you'll need Samson Kerrow's signature?'

Charles nodded. 'I do not relish the meeting, but it cannot be avoided.'

'Unfortunately I doubt you will find him in his office. One of my clerks informed me that according to Gilbert Voss, Mr Kerrow's man of business, Mr Kerrow claims to be suffering congestion of the lungs.'

Charles blew a sigh. 'Then I must call on him at home.'

Steven hesitated. 'Do you think, given the current situation, you will persuade him to sign?'

Charles's smile was bleak. 'Samson Kerrow is a businessman to his bones. Balance sheets are his preferred reading. He cannot fail to recognize how much money will be saved by moving our business from Hayle, not to mention the potential revenue from increased trade as a result of expanding the harbour.'

'I hope you are right. You know him better than I.'

'I thought I did,' Charles murmured.

'Will you stay here in town tonight?'

'If I must.' He rose to his feet. 'As soon as I have his signature on the documents, I will go directly to Barton's and transfer funds to the new company.'

'Charles, while you are with Mr Kerrow will you try to find out when he plans to return to the office? It is four weeks since he last put in an appearance. Mr Voss is feeling the weight of responsibility, especially as the Porthinnis expansion requires you to be absent from the office as well. Do not be anxious,' Steven added quickly. 'Gilbert Voss is a most able man, and utterly trustworthy. But I believe he would sleep better if he knew there was an end in sight.'

'Wouldn't we all?' Unable to keep still, Charles walked to the window. He ought not to see her, not until he was free. But that was impossible. The expansion had to be underway before winter storms arrived. And for that to happen he needed help only she could provide. He forced his thoughts back to the matter in hand. 'Does Mr Voss have a particular concern?'

Steven nodded. 'The engine dues. Though they were halved during the worst of the depression to keep as many mines as possible in work, now the price for copper ore is climbing again Boulton & Watt want the dues increased as well so they can recoup the money they are owed.'

'I'll be sure to mention it to Samson. Clearly we cannot refuse an increase. But we might be able to negotiate on both the rate and timing.' Returning to the table he reached for his hat. 'At least both our mines continued in work. Those that shut down and were allowed to fill with water will need weeks, maybe months, of pumping out. That means rising expenses and no income for their investors.' Reluctant to ask, dreading the answer, he braced himself. 'Steven, about the annulment—'

'No word as yet. I did warn you it might take several months.'

'I know. But that was in June and we're almost into October. I need it ended.' Tempted for an instant to tell his friend the reason, he clamped his lips together. He trusted Steven absolutely. But confiding would be self-indulgence. Besides, he had given his word. Others might break promises: he would not.

Eve's treachery had hit him hard, shaking his confidence and battering his pride. He had dealt with both by throwing himself into work. Steven's reminder of his inheritance, and their visit to Porthinnis which confirmed the harbour ripe for expansion, had been a happy coincidence.

His decision to base himself in the village made economic and practical sense. He had certainly not expected – would never have imagined – but within half an hour of meeting Jenefer Trevanion he knew. She was *everything*. He had been missing her and not even known it.

Fighting a powerful urge to smash something, he paced, slapping his gloves against his thigh. 'Damn it, *how much longer?* I am the victim in this whole wretched mess. Eve married me knowing she was carrying another man's child. Those are unequivocally grounds for annulment. Why should it be taking so long?'

Having to write in detail about how he had been deliberately duped and used by people he trusted, people he had known all his life, had been one of the hardest things he had ever done.

A proud man, he knew his was no false pride, but justified by achievements attained through his own hard work. The knowledge that in reading the story of his ill-fated marriage other men would judge him a blind fool was hard to stomach. *Yet how could he have known?*

'There is always—'

'No.' Charles was shaking his head before Steven had finished. 'No divorce. Quite apart from the fact that it would require an Act of Parliament and cost a fortune, I gave Samson my word. Not for his sake,' he added before Steven could speak, 'or to protect Eve and her mother.' His stomach tightened as remembered shock and painful memories surged through him like a breaking wave.

Sweat dampened his skin. He fought the flash of rage and burning self-reproach at his own part in the terrible charade. He could have – *should* have – taken time to know his own mind instead of yielding to the demands of his body. But Eve had seduced him with an irresistible blend of innocence and guile. And, fool that he was, he had believed.

Experienced with women, he had never lost his heart. Never, since his mother's death when he was nine years old, experienced affection inspired by genuine love. He had assumed Eve's deliberate closeness, the frequent brush of her fingers against his, her hand resting lightly on his arm as she made some point, signalled true affection. Solitary for too long, he had fallen into the trap.

'But Susan had no part in it. Divorce might afford me revenge, but it would destroy her life. She's not yet eighteen and was away at school when I returned from Mexico. The inevitable scandal would wreck all hope of her making a good marriage. I cannot do that.' His gesture betrayed both anger and helplessness. 'I just want the whole sordid episode erased as if it had never been. So' – he sucked in a deep breath – 'If I must, I'll wait.'

Steven nodded. 'I'm sure Susan will appreciate—'

'I would prefer she never know.'

'Shall I send a letter enquiring about progress? It can do no harm, and may possibly speed the matter.'

'I would appreciate it.'

Charles walked briskly down the hill and up Church Street, hoping the exercise would rid him of tension that lay like a yoke across his shoulders. He turned left onto the tree-shaded thoroughfare of Cross Street. Lawyers, bankers and businessmen like Samson Kerrow had built homes here, the grandeur of their houses displaying their power and status.

Number 5, known as the Great Office, housed several banks, one run by Edward Barton on whom Charles planned to call as soon as he had Samson's signature on the documents.

The maid who opened the door to him flushed scarlet as she bobbed a curtsy.

'Is Mr Kerrow at home?' Charles enquired.

'Yes, sir. He's in his study. Got some awful cough he have. But he won't stay over stairs.'

'And Mrs Kerrow?'

'Out, sir. She and Miss Susan have gone to see—' She stopped suddenly, her colour deepening.

'Friends?' Charles suggested, sorry for the girl despite the sting of knowing his private business was servants' gossip.

'Yessir.' She hurried ahead of him, almost running, and knocked on the study door.

'What?' Samson's growl ended in a fit of coughing.

'You can go now,' Charles told the maid. As she scuttled away he opened the door and was met by a gust of warm stale air.

'Charles!' Seated in an armchair by the fire with a plaid blanket over his knees, Samson Kerrow wore a banyan of quilted maroon with gold buttons and a maroon velvet cap. He was pale and lined, and there were dark shadows under his eyes. He leaned forward as if to get up.

'No,' Charles waved him back. 'Stay where you are.'

Samson slumped against the cushions, clearly relieved to be spared the effort. 'My dear fellow, it is such a pleasure to see you. I had so much hoped you might – and now here you are. I can't tell you how glad— Madeleine and Susan are out but will be back soon. Then perhaps—'

'This is not a social call,' Charles interrupted, averting his gaze from the hope and desperation on Samson Kerrow's haggard face. Had he desired revenge, the sight of this broken man must surely have satisfied it.

'I am here about a company matter. Had you been in your office I should not have needed to trouble you at home.'

'I've not been well.' Samson's struggle for breath triggered a coughing fit: a wet gurgle that sounded as if he were drowning.

'You've had the doctor?'

Samson nodded, indicating several small dark bottles on the round table beside his chair. 'For all the good he does.' His eyes opened. 'But seeing you—'

'As I said,' Charles cut him short, refusing to be manipulated; he'd had his fill of emotional blackmail. 'I am here on a company matter. No doubt you will recall your frequent insistence that personal matters must never be allowed to interfere with business?' He watched Samson's gaze slide away. 'You cannot have failed to notice that using Hayle harbour for our import and export trade is costing the company money we can no longer afford.'

Samson shifted uncomfortably. 'I'm not well. Voss is perfectly capable—'

'Indeed he is,' Charles snapped. 'He has kept the office running and shouldered responsibilities that should not have been asked of him. This is grossly unfair and cannot continue. If you intend retiring then we must seek a new partner.'

Samson sat bolt upright. 'I never said I was retiring. I've been ill.'

'That is my point. The Cornish end of the business will not run itself.'

'But you can—'

'No, I can't. A new project means that for the foreseeable future I shall be working elsewhere.'

'What new project? I knew nothing of this.' Resting his elbows on the chair arms, Samson gripped the plaid blanket. His narrowed gaze was bright and sharp.

'Only because you have not bothered to read your mail, or the reports Mr Voss has been sending you. Please,' – Charles raised a hand before Samson could speak – 'you have already claimed illness as your excuse. Yet far from being confined to bed, I find you dressed and sitting by a fire.' He paused. 'Clearly you are not dying. You merely have a cough.'

Twin patches of dull red replaced Samson's pallor. His tongue snaked out to moisten dry cracked lips. 'I could not go down there. I could not face— Charles, I swear to you by everything I hold dear, I didn't know.' He gestured helplessly. 'When I did find out, you and Eve were already married.'

'And that is supposed to make me feel better?' Charles turned away, fighting for calm, angry at his loss of control. Rage achieved nothing. It merely wasted energy. He took a slow deep breath then turned.

'As I was saying, I have been seeking an alternative to Hayle for our trade. Porthinnis is a small harbour and village on the eastern side of Mounts Bay. These are the drawings and an estimate of costs for the work required.' Drawing up a low table, he unfolded the drawings on it. Immediately Samson leaned forward, frowning in concentration as he examined them.

'My attorney has already secured a twenty year renewable lease from the Berkeleys who own the harbour and land behind it,' Charles continued. 'With Porthinnis so much closer to our mines, the transport costs will be less than half what they are now.'

Samson glanced up. 'The voyage to Wales will take two days longer.'

Charles nodded. 'Yes, but additional cargoes traded through the port will more than compensate.' Unfastening the ribbon he opened the folder. 'To protect Kerrow & Polgray, I propose setting up a separate company for the Porthinnis project. My attorney has prepared all the necessary documents. All that's needed is your signature.'

Sitting back, Samson looked up at him. 'How do you intend to fund it?'

Charles set a sheet in front of him. 'That is my estimate of the overall cost. It includes construction of the new road, alterations to the harbour, and working capital to keep us going until we start generating revenue. I'm looking for fifty per cent from Kerrow & Polgray.'

Sucking air through his teeth, Samson shook his head. 'Forty is more—'

'Not enough,' Charles snapped. 'Forty-five is the minimum if we are to maintain overall control.'

Samson squirmed then gave a reluctant nod. 'All right. Forty-five it is. Where will you raise the rest?'

'From Mr Ralph Daniell in Truro.'

'Guinea-a-minute Daniell? He's a hard man.'

'And this is an excellent proposition.' Fetching an inkstand and pen from the bureau, Charles opened the lid and offered the pen.

Slumping back in his chair, Samson gestured weakly. 'All this – I'm tired. Leave the papers with me tonight. You can come back in the morning.' His gaze met Charles's and skittered away. He swallowed. 'Eve is in a terrible state—'

'Don't!' Charles warned. 'Had I brought this proposal to you four months ago, you would have signed immediately and sent me on my way. I expect no less now.'

Samson's face flushed crimson. After a moment's silence he raised his eyes. Seeing how encroaching age, illness, and the weight of guilt had taken their toll, Charles felt fleeting pity for a man he had once respected. But it was swiftly gone leaving only bitterness, anger and disgust.

For twelve years he had worked hard learning every aspect of the business. He travelled wherever the company needed him, earning a reputation for finding solutions to problems that would otherwise have proved costly. Samson had never made any secret of his hope that one day, when Eve was old enough, she and Charles would marry. So who better to solve Eve's little problem and ensure there was no scandal?

Had they really believed he would not find out? And that if he did, that he would simply accept being made a fool of? Do nothing?

Refusing to acknowledge the depth of his hurt for that was weakness and they were not worth it, he proffered the pen once more and pointed.

'I know, I know,' Samson was testy. 'I'm not in my dotage yet.' The pen scratched as he scrawled his signature on each of the papers placed in front of him.

'I'm delighted to hear it. No doubt Mr Voss will be equally pleased. I'll tell him he may expect you back in the office very soon.'

'I need a few more days.' Thumping his chest Samson coughed.

'The end of next week?'

'If I must,' Samson muttered.

Checking the ink was dry Charles gathered the documents and drawings into the folder and retied the ribbon.

'Stay and have a bite of dinner with me,' Samson urged.

'Thank you, but no.'

'Then at least take a glass of brandy. Surely you can spare time for that? To toast the success of the new company?'

Shaking his head Charles picked up his hat and gloves. 'I told you this was not a social call.'

'Go, then,' Samson snarled. 'Get about your business if it's so important.'

Charles bit his tongue, refusing to be drawn. He had lost too much to this family. He would not sacrifice his dignity to angry argument. 'Good day to you.'

He closed the door on the sound of a muffled sob. Was it prompted by regret or by frustration at his refusal to forgive? He would never know and could not bring himself to care.

Chapter Seven

Wearing a short jacket of dark-green velvet and a matching hat over her gown of primrose muslin, Jenefer reached in to knock on the open upper half of the two-part door common to many cottages in the village.

'Good morning, Miss Laity,' she greeted a short, plump woman dressed in blue with a white gauze kerchief about her shoulders, her hair covered by a neat cap.

'Come in, Miss Trevanion.' Louise Laity bobbed a curtsy and opened the lower half of the door. ''Tis good of you to come so quick.'

'Your note implied some urgency.' Seeing Louise's gaze flick to her hat, Jenefer smiled. 'It looks well, does it not? And is so comfortable. I'm sure all your customers are equally delighted.'

Following Louise into the room that had once been a parlour and now served as shop, display and workroom, Jenefer pulled off her gloves. She noted three chairs carefully placed to allow anyone wishing to sit room to do so without hindering others who preferred to walk round the centre table. Two earthenware chills, shaped like heavy candlesticks stood at either end of the mantelpiece. But as there was no lingering smell of burned train, the oil from pressed pilchards, Jenefer realized they were no longer used.

'How do you manage for light in the dark evenings?' she asked.

'I don't do no sewing by night, miss. I catch up on baking and ironing, jobs like that. Then by time I got Mother up over stairs and settled, I'm ready for bed myself.'

'I've always thought this an excellent idea.' Jenefer indicated a small table spread with a white cloth beneath the window. On it a bonnet of black velvet and rose pink satin was nearing completion. An elaborate trim of matching pink ribbon had been made into a large multi-looped bow in front. Another pink bow, partly completed, lay next to a black ostrich plume. 'It allows customers to see the different stages of creation.'

Louise rubbed her hands. 'I don't know that everyone like it. I did think about putting up a curtain to cut the room in half. But with only the one window . . .' She shrugged, then said quietly, 'I tried working in the kitchen. But if a customer called and we come in here, Mother couldn't resist putting in a few stitches. She didn't mean no harm. She just wanted to help. But I'd have to unpick it all and she'd get upset.' Louise rolled her eyes. 'So in the end 'twas easier for me to keep everything in here. I keep popping through to make sure she's all right. And if she need me she only got to shout.'

'I think you have it exceptionally well arranged,' Jenefer said. To one side of the worktable stood a sewing box, the lid raised to reveal a tray of multi-hued silks and cottons. Beside it, in the open top drawer of a small chest, a rainbow of ribbons and braids lay in neat rows. But a swift glance told Jenefer that both tray and drawer were missing several colours, and of others there was little left on the reel. She turned to the centre table.

'I see you have a new display stand.'

Louise beamed. ''Tis just three shallow wooden boxes Eddy Barnicoat made up for me. With them set crossways on top of each other like that, each bonnet got its own triangle of space. I keep the top for something special.'

'The pale-blue velvet makes a beautiful backdrop.'

'A bargain it was, 'cos one edge had a water stain. I trimmed off the worst and with the folds arranged like that you'd never know.'

'It's very impressive, Miss Laity, and shows great artistry.'

Louise blushed deep rose. 'Good of you to say so, miss.'

Jenefer leaned forward to look more closely at a turban of fluted silver gauze over midnight satin. 'This is both striking and elegant. Are those egret feathers?'

Louise nodded, indicating a neat pile of magazines. 'I keep up with all the new fashions so my customers can have exactly the same as the ladies up London.' She twisted her hands. 'See, what it is, why I asked you to stop by, I got plenty of orders. Truth is, I can't keep up with them all. I'd like to take on a girl apprentice. But the way things are I haven't got the money to pay her.'

Jenefer knew then that her assumption on receiving Louise's note had been correct.

'Like I say, I got enough work for two. But when it come to paying . . .' She sighed and clicked her tongue. 'I send out accounts at the end of each month. But half just ignore them. One lady come in and ordered another bonnet, promising to pay the whole lot when 'tis ready.' Her opinion of that tactic was plain. 'I don't want to lose custom, but I can't go on like this. I need stock: velvet, satin, lace, silk flowers, feathers, ribbons and braid.' She ticked them off on her fingers. 'Will Prowse said he can get me fine French lace for half the price I'd pay in Helston or Penzance. Trouble is, he want money up front. But until I get these here accounts settled I can't pay 'n 'cos I haven't got it.'

'I see.' Jenefer understood only too well. She remembered being unable to pay bills because her father had drunk the housekeeping money. She quickly learned to hide it. Soon after that he had allowed her to take charge, first of the domestic accounts, then his smuggling investments. In return, he demanded a keg of brandy from each cargo, deaf to the doctor's warnings and her pleas. He had been drunk on the night of the fire, unconscious in his bed, unaware of the wall of flames that had prevented Treeve reaching him while she carried Betsy down the back stairs.

When she first set up her bookkeeping business, two customers delayed paying her for work she had done, money she needed to buy food and fuel. In desperation she threatened to make their behaviour public as a warning to others. Furious, they had paid up and she had refused to work for them again. Yes, she understood.

Louise opened the bottom drawer of the chest and drew out two ledgers. 'Here's my books, miss. You see for yourself. Every penny accounted for. I'm very partic'lar like that.' She held them out.

Opening the top ledger halfway through, Jenefer turned several pages, noting the careful copperplate handwriting, dates and details of materials purchased, and prices paid. Closing it she opened the second one, saw pages showing the name of each customer, details of what they had bought, the price and the date the item was collected. But where settlement dates should have been entered there were too many spaces. Convinced Louise Laity was as painstaking with her books as she was in creating her hats, Jenefer handed the ledgers back. 'So what you are seeking is a short-term loan with which to buy materials?'

Louise's shoulders dropped in relief as she clasped the books to her gauze-covered bosom. 'Oh, miss. I'd be some grateful. At my wits' end I am.'

'I'll be happy to advance you what you need, Miss Laity, but that only solves half of the problem. We also need to settle the other half. I don't suppose you have a list of—?'

Opening the cover of top ledger Louise removed a sheet of paper and offered it. 'I put down the name, what they bought, the price agreed, and the date they took delivery.'

Jenefer smiled at her. 'I wish all my clients were as well-organized.' As Louise's blush deepened, Jenefer read down the list, noting the amounts owed by Mrs Penkivell, wife of the notary, and Mrs Avers. 'I don't see Mrs Casvellan's name on here.'

Shock rounded Louise's eyes. 'Nor will you, miss. Like you, Mrs Casvellan is. She don't even wait till the end of the month. Always pay the week she take delivery. Most partic'lar about it.'

Jenefer nodded. Though she'd never had cause to doubt Louise's honesty, she'd needed to be sure. Now she was. Having known terrible poverty herself, Roz never kept any tradesman or woman waiting for payment.

'Then with your permission I shall write to everyone whose account is more than two months overdue.'

Louise's face lit up. 'Take some load off my mind that would, Miss, and that's God's honest truth.' She chewed her lip. Wanting to say something, she was clearly wary of doing so, anxious not to offend. Jenefer guessed what was troubling her.

'Please don't be concerned, Miss Laity. I am the soul of discretion.'

'I didn't mean no offence.'

'I know you didn't. You may be more comfortable if I tell you what I intend. In my letter I shall explain that as you are so overwhelmed with orders you have asked me temporarily to take over the book-keeping side of your business. As I already perform this service for a number of village businesses no one will think it at all strange. I shall then politely point out that the account is overdue by however long.

Immediate settlement would be greatly appreciated and should be sent directly to me. I think we may be confident my signature will ensure a reasonably swift response. You have my word that only I, you, and the recipient of each letter will be aware of its content.'

Louise's relief widened her smile as she bobbed a curtsy. 'I should've known you'd do it right. God bless 'ee, Miss Trevanion. I'm some grateful.'

Folding the list, Jenefer tucked it deep into her basket, then lifted out a stocking purse that clinked. 'Here is five pounds. When you prepare your list, will you also make a copy for me? Our merchant in Guernsey appreciates detailed accounts. And may I suggest you start interviewing prospective apprentices?'

'Oh, miss!' Louise breathed. 'You don't know how much this mean to me.'

'It's my pleasure, Miss Laity.' After they had agreed terms, Jenefer drew on her gloves.

'How's your sister, miss?' Louise asked as they walked to the door. 'And that dear baby of hers?'

'They are very well, thank you. I'll tell her you asked.'

*

Edward Barton paced his office, mopping his face with a handkerchief already damp. His gut churned. 'More money? What does he need it for?'

Seated in his father's chair, behind his father's desk, John Barton shrugged. 'I'd guess it's taking longer and costing more than expected to pump the mine out. But Kestle is certain the copper is there. Once the new lode is found all the money can be paid back with no one any the wiser.'

'He's been saying that for weeks. I'm not happy about it, John.'

'Nor am I. But what choice do we have? We're in too deep and have risked too much to stop now. And what about the money we've already taken? How would we explain the discrepancies?'

Edward Barton grimaced and pressed his fingers to his stomach as pain stabbed. He turned a haggard face to his son. 'What have we done?'

'What was necessary.' Rising from the chair, John Barton came round the desk and draped an arm over his father's shoulders. 'Courage, Father. Since the Anglesea mines failed, the price of Cornish copper has been

steadily rising. It's almost double what it was ten years ago. And we're so close. A week or two more to finish pumping out, that's all. As for the money—'

'It's hundreds of pounds, John.'

The younger man's gesture was careless, dismissive. 'A pittance compared to what we stand to make. Look, we haven't stolen anything. We've simply borrowed it. Money that just was sitting there, doing nothing. Who's to know? Besides, isn't this what banks are for?'

Edward Barton would not allow himself to think about trust betrayed, integrity forfeited, honour lost. He wiped his upper lip, trying to convince himself there had been no alternative. John was right. They had come too far to stop now. 'If by some misfortune an alarm is raised—'

'It won't be.'

'I would need to put it all back before an audit could—'

'And you will.'

'How? Where can I possibly—?'

'Be quiet!' John's voice was harsh, his expression threatening. 'Enough of this guilt and anxiety. Pull yourself together, Father. Unless you want to see everything we've worked for slip through our fingers. The mine is sound. The copper is there and Kestle will find it. This time next week we'll be celebrating.'

Edward Barton nodded. 'Yes. You're right.' Perhaps if he said it often enough he would believe it. He glanced at the Dutch clock on the wall. 'You should go. I'm expecting Charles Polgray.'

'From Kerrow & Polgray? Have we drawn—?'

'No. Not yet.' Closing his eyes, Edward Barton swallowed audibly. 'And I'd prefer we didn't.'

'With luck we won't need to,' John comforted. 'But if it's necessary, the money will be repaid within a week or two and everything will be as it was.' John picked up his hat from the table. 'Still, it would be better if he didn't see me. Remember, Father, all that's occurred is a temporary transfer of assets, an emergency business transaction. It's done all the time.'

'Yes. Yes.' Edward Barton stood straighter, adjusted his cuffs. If he viewed it like that— He bit his lip as pain pierced his gut like a shard of glass.

*

Removing his hat and gloves, Charles followed the clerk into Edward Barton's office. Brown furniture, ochre walls, a cluttered desk and dusty window, it looked unchanged from his last visit. And yet there was something in the atmosphere.

Rising from his leather chair behind the desk, Barton bowed. 'Good afternoon, Mr Polgray. Mr Vincent sent word that I might expect you.' He cleared his throat. 'Do sit down.' A smile came and fled. 'How may I be of service?' He resumed his own chair.

Charles laid copies of the documents signed by Samson on the desk, then sat. 'I am setting up a new company and need funds trans-ferred from Kerrow & Polgray's reserve account—' He broke off as the banker gave a violent start.

'I beg your pardon, Mr Polgray,' Barton said bending sideways to massage his calf. 'A sudden cramp. Do forgive me.' He straightened up, his face pallid, eyes glassy. 'You were saying?'

'To a new account in the name of Porthinnis Harbour Company,' Charles continued. 'With myself and my attorney Steven Vincent as co-signatories.'

He watched Barton draw the documents towards him with unsteady hands.

'Will' – the banker cleared his throat – 'will Kerrow & Polgray be the sole source of funds for this new venture?' He turned pages, his head bent.

'No, I shall be applying to other sources.'

Glancing up, Barton nodded. 'A sensible move, and one I would have suggested. It is always advisable to spread the risk.'

'This venture is far less risky than some I have heard about,' Charles returned, his tone dry.

Barton's head jerked up. The same glassy smile flitted across his face. 'Quite so.' He moistened his lips. 'Did you say Porthinnis?'

Charles nodded briefly. 'I shall be spending the next few months there.'

'Indeed?' Barton folded his hands but seemed unable to keep them still, flexing and clasping his fingers. 'That being the case, you are likely to make the acquaintance of Miss Trevanion. A most . . .

unusual young woman.'

Charles controlled his response to an expressionless, 'Oh?'

'Perhaps you have heard of her?'

About to say he had not only heard of her but they were well acquainted, curiosity stopped him. 'I was abroad for most of last year. Is there something I should know?'

Laying his hands on the documents, Barton leaned forward. 'It is my understanding she has caused quite a stir.'

'How so?'

'By her involvement in matters many consider beyond her intellect or capability. She calls herself a bookkeeper.' Barton's grimace of a smile and bitter tone betrayed a conflict Charles found intriguing. 'But the truth is, to all intents and purposes she is a banker.' He sat back, clearly expecting a response.

Doubtful that his startled admiration would be appreciated, Charles raised his eyebrows. 'Good heavens.'

Barton wiped his upper lip with a forefinger. 'I admit I was among those who initially harboured doubts. But to the astonishment of all she has prospered. She has even persuaded Mr Lukis of St Peter Port to employ her as his agent, and through him established an accord with William Percival of Lombard Street in London. Such connections confer considerable status.' Despite his attempted smile there was no mistaking the banker's bitter envy.

'And you are telling me this because. . .?'

'Simply to make you aware, Mr Polgray.'

Charles regarded the perspiring man. 'Aware of what, Mr Barton? Surely you cannot feel threatened by *a mere woman*?' Even as he said the words, he could imagine Jenefer Trevanion's response to his words. She would laugh. She might even blush. For beneath the irony she would have heard his admiration. He sighed inwardly as he watched the banker draw himself up. He should have guessed Edward Barton would take the remark at face value.

'Threatened?' Barton's voice rose. 'Threatened? Me? A mine purser and banker for forty years? Of course I don't feel threatened. The notion is preposterous. I have always believed finance to be the province of those with the proper knowledge and experience. Miss Trevanion's *trespass* – for want of a better word – into a world for which she has no training is seen by some as gross impertinence, a – a mockery.'

'I appreciate your concern on my behalf, Mr Barton,' Charles said coolly. 'Allow me to assure you it is quite unnecessary.'

'I am relieved to hear it.' The banker mopped his forehead and upper lip. 'But you did not allow me to finish. I would not have you think I am among those resentful of Miss Trevanion. Nothing could be further from the truth. Indeed, were you, in the course of your business there, to make her acquaintance, I would be most exceedingly obliged if you would tell her that were she to consider transferring her business to this bank, my many years of experience would be at her disposal.'

'Should the occasion arise I will be sure to tell her.' Charles frowned. 'Are you unwell, Mr Barton? You look rather pale.'

'A mere trick of the light, Mr Polgray. I am in excellent health, thank you.' Revealing his teeth in a smile as brief as it was insincere, he tucked his handkerchief up his coat sleeve. 'I shall arrange your transfer of funds immediately.'

Rising to his feet, Charles picked up his hat and gloves. 'Then that is all for the present. Good day to you, Mr Barton.'

Leaving the Great Office, Charles walked to the end of the tree-shaded cobbled street and turned right. On his way down the hill it occurred to him that though Barton's colleagues were clearly offended by the notion of a *woman* banker, what had really shocked them was Jenefer Trevanion's success.

She had every reason to be proud of herself. Charles knew most men of his acquaintance, achieving what she had, would be crowing like cocks on a dung heap. Yet she chose to continue living in a small terraced cottage and was on intimate terms with people whose station in life was far below hers. He had never met anyone like her.

At The Bell he ate steak and kidney pie washed down with a tankard of ale. Though he had achieved all he had come to do, instead of enjoying his success he felt restless, unable to relax.

Sending the boy to order his horse saddled, he collected his bag, paid the landlord, and set off back to Porthinnis.

Chapter Eight

Seated in the wheeled chair her husband Jared had made for her, Betsy lifted her baby daughter from the soapy water and into a warm towel. Watching her sister deftly turn the kicking baby on her lap, Jenefer fought the familiar yearning ache.

'So, what did he come to Porthinnis for? This Mr Charles Polgray?' Betsy asked, her eyes bright with interest, her face flushed from the warmth of the fire as she carefully dried Libby's tiny toes.

Glancing up, Jenefer saw the same interest on Inez's face as she refilled the big black kettle from an earthenware pitcher then bent to lay two more squares of dried turf on the glowing embers.

'To inspect Pednbrose,' she said, unable yet to tell them the other far more important reason: his plans for the harbour.

'There can't be much left for him to look at,' Betsy said, catching a waving fist and kissing it as Libby chuckled. 'And it's certainly taken him long enough.'

'I thought the same,' Jenefer said. 'Until he told me he hadn't been able to come sooner because he was working abroad.'

Tipping her daughter over her forearm, Betsy patted her dry with the towel and gently rubbed damp blonde curls while Libby gurgled and reached for her toes. 'Well?' she demanded. 'Don't keep us in suspense. What is he like? His appearance, his character?'

Hoping the glowing embers might explain the telltale heat in her cheeks, Jenefer lifted one shoulder. 'He's tall—'

'How tall?' Betsy interrupted.

Jenefer recalled facing broad shoulders and having to look up to meet his gaze. 'A head taller than me. He has brown curly hair and grey-green eyes. His manners are excellent, his demeanour pleasant.

Yet there is also a reserve about him.' Too late she realized what she had said, and knew Betsy was certain to ask.

'Reserved in what way?' The towel stilled in Betsy's hand. 'I hope he has not taken it upon himself to pass judgement on your occupation and way of life'

'Not at all,' Jenefer smiled, touched by her sister's readiness to spring to her defence. 'At least, if he does hold critical thoughts he has been polite enough to keep them to himself. In truth, I was surprised at his lack of condemnation. No, it's just' – *he took my hand* – 'his manner will suddenly change.' She smiled and shrugged it off. 'It may be that he is shy. Or simply has a lot on his mind. Did I mention he is employed in the family business?' As Betsy and Inez exchanged a look charged with significance, she glanced from one to the other. 'What?'

'Shall I tell you what I think?' Betsy's eyes reflected the dancing flames. 'Meeting you has thrown him into disarray.'

Jenefer's heart kicked. 'Why on earth would you suppose such a thing?'

'Because you are special,' Betsy said simply. 'And I'm not saying that just because you are my sister. He will not have encountered anyone like you.' She looked across at Inez. 'What say you, Ma?'

Betsy's absorption into her husband's family had left Jenefer feeling even more solitary. Not that she resented it. Indeed, Betsy's transparent happiness with Jared and loving relationship with his parents was a joy to behold. *And had released her from a heavy responsibility.*

'Betsy's right,' Inez nodded, cutting thick slices from a fresh loaf.

Jenefer dismissed their words with a gesture. 'You are both dreadful teases. As for his being *in disarray* as you put it, he demanded two jars of quince jam in payment for the fruit I've been picking.' He had been teasing her. Yet he'd been serious about wanting the jam. 'I'd say Mr Polgray's primary interest is business. Though I will admit I do not know him well.'

Which wasn't altogether true. She knew he was courteous without condescension; and able to laugh at himself – a rare attribute in a man. And if he sometimes appeared aloof, he was never arrogant.

One of the things she liked most about him was his refusal to make assumptions about her morals just because she lived alone without protection of chaperon or companion, and worked to support herself.

But she could not tell Betsy that: not yet. Nor did she dare mention the deeper more powerful attraction she sensed beneath his curiosity: an attraction that mirrored her own feelings.

Betsy shook her head. 'Jenefer, you are the cleverest woman I know. But in certain matters you are as blind as a bat.'

'What do you mean?'

'Has it not occurred to you that by requesting the jam he has an excellent reason to maintain contact?'

Of course it had. And the notion thrilled her. But she was wary of making assumptions, wary of hoping. She feared what she felt for him. It was too much too soon. Yet she hungered for more.

To her relief she heard male voices and the sound of footsteps. The back door opened and Jared entered followed by his father, both carrying that day's catch in two large wicker baskets they dropped on the kitchen table.

'Miss Jenefer,' Jared nodded, then smiled at his wife as Libby raised chubby pink arms, her tiny fingers opening and closing as she demanded her father's attention. 'How's my two best girls, then?' Sweeping the baby up in his huge hands, Jared kissed her curly head.

'Good afternoon, Jared, Mr Sweet,' Jenefer rose from the stool.

'All right, miss?' Arf nodded to her.

Inez took plates and cups from the dresser behind her. 'Put the baskets out the back kitchen, bird,' she directed her husband. 'If there's mackerel I'll souse them in vinegar with a few bay leaves, and salt the rest.' She turned to Jenefer. 'Stay and have a bite of tea with us, will you, miss?'

Jenefer knew the invitation was genuine, and that she would be made welcome. But the kitchen was crowded and she felt very much an outsider.

'That's very kind of you but I'd better get on home. I have work waiting.' Stroking Libby's downy cheek, she kissed Betsy, said her goodbyes, and left.

As she walked home she deliberately counted her blessings. Her days were full and she enjoyed the challenges each one brought. Yet seeing the loving look exchanged between Betsy and Jared, the easy affection between Arf and Inez, she was keenly aware of a void in her life. Something – someone – was missing.

*

Dusk was falling and the day's warmth faded into autumn chill as Charles rode towards the village, weary in mind and spirit from the demands of the day. Trees arched overhead deepening the gloom as the track climbed towards the open moor. With luck he would reach The Standard before it was fully dark. Then tomorrow—

A white shape swooped silently across the track barely six feet in front of him. His horse squealed in fright and reared up. Thrown from the saddle, instinctively clinging to the rein to stop the animal bolting, Charles landed heavily and knocked his head against a rock.

He lay winded for a moment, the rein tight around his left hand while his horse stamped and snorted.

'All right, boy. Steady now,' he muttered. But as he climbed to his feet, stabbing pain in his right wrist made him gasp. Fighting nausea, blood pounding in his temple, he raised his right hand carefully to the lump above his right eyebrow and saw the dark wetness of blood on his fingertips. His head spun. His glove felt uncomfortably tight. If he didn't remove it now, by the time he reached the inn it would have to be cut off.

Looping his left arm through the rein, he gritted his teeth and eased the soft leather from a hand that ached abominably. Moving slowly he picked up his hat and led his horse along the track until he found a fallen tree trunk. Pain and the effort of remounting made him sweat. Sliding his injured hand carefully inside his buttoned coat for support he resumed his journey.

He remembered handing over his horse to the stable boy and walking into the inn. Tom Lawry, the landlord, appeared in the passage. Then everything went dark. When Charles regained his senses he was lying on his bed. He opened his eyes but the candlelight made the throbbing in his temple worse so he closed them again. His wrist felt as if sharp teeth were gnawing on the bones.

He heard footsteps, low voices. A chair scraped on the floorboards, a cool wet cloth bathed his forehead and temple. He winced and opened his eyes. The fog in his head gradually cleared.

'Ah good. You're awake, Mr Polgray. I'm Dr Avers.'

'Why—?'

72

'Am I here?' Mr Lawry was concerned. 'Do you remember sustaining your injuries?'

'An owl—' Charles's throat was dry, his voice hoarse. 'My horse took fright. I was thrown.' His breath hissed sharply as Avers probed his hand and wrist.

'You were fortunate. I can feel no break. But the wrist has been badly sprained. Mrs Lawry will bind it for you. She is familiar with such injuries. I advise that you support it in a sling during the day.'

'Is that really necessary?'

'I would not suggest it if I did not think so,' Avers reproved. 'Unless you keep it elevated and immobile the swelling will increase and healing will take longer.'

Charles levered himself up against the bed head. 'Of course. I beg your pardon.' With his left hand he gingerly explored a lump the size of a hen's egg on one side of his forehead.

Avers put a small brown bottle on the nightstand. 'This will ease the pain and allow you to sleep. Take three drops in a little water.' He closed his bag and stood up.

'My wrist,' Charles said quickly. 'How long—?'

'That depends on you.' Avers was brisk. 'With rest and elevation perhaps ten days. But it may take longer. Good evening.' He opened the door. 'I will send my account in the morning.'

Charles slumped back as the door closed. This could not have happened at a more inconvenient time. With a dozen letters needing to be written how on earth was he to—

Jenefer Trevanion. She was already in his confidence: aware of his plans for the harbour. So who better? But with her own business to run, would she have the time, or the inclination, to help him? The urgency of his need to convince her made him realize that, while he genuinely needed her assistance to avoid losing valuable time on the project, the opportunity to spend more time with her was an equally powerful reason.

*

At ten the next morning he walked through the alley and into a sunny cobbled yard. The drops had helped him sleep and his headache had gone. Even the ache in his wrist had receded after the landlord's wife bound it with a compress of thyme steeped in boiling water. This morning, after the boy helped him shave and dress, she had applied a fresh bandage dampened with witch hazel, and made a sling from a broad strip of linen.

These extras would be added to his account. He didn't mind at all, relieved – and astonished – to be free of pain. But the prospect of depending on others for a week or more horrified him.

Passing the first two cottages he saw the top half of each front door was fastened back to let daylight and fresh air. As he approached Jenefer's door, open like the others, his frustration evaporated, replaced by curiosity and a slight nervousness that surprised him. He was a grown man, not some dreamy-headed youth. But she was no ordinary young woman. He knocked gently on the wooden panels.

He heard her chair scrape the stone floor. Then she appeared, fresh and pretty in apple-green muslin and white kerchief; her honey-gold hair piled high.

'Mr Polgray.' Surprise widened her eyes. As she opened the lower half of the door he removed his hat. Her gaze flew from the sling to the swelling above his eyebrow. Concern replaced her smile of greeting. 'You're hurt.'

'It's not serious. More an inconvenience.' Seeing ledgers open on the table, a list of names beside an unfinished letter and several others neatly folded and sealed, it occurred to him that his request would place even more weight on her shoulders. But whom else could he ask? Whom else could he trust? 'You're busy and I have interrupted you.' He felt foolish for stating the obvious.

Instead of saying it didn't matter which, while polite, would clearly not have been true, she stepped back. 'Please, come in.' Indicating the armchair beside the range she resumed her own seat, turning it to face him. 'May I ask what happened?'

As he lowered himself into the chair he had the strangest sensation of setting down a burden so familiar he had forgotten how heavily it weighed. Gentle warmth emanated from the range and the kitchen smelled faintly of toast and hot chocolate. 'A stupid accident. On my way back from Helston last evening an owl spooked my horse. I was thrown and hurt my wrist when I landed.'

'It is not broken?'

He felt soothed by her concern. Had Eve ever truly cared for him? Or had her interest been just part of the charade? He realised it no longer mattered.

'Fortunately not. Doctor Avers examined it last night.' He saw no reason to mention his loss of consciousness. Such weakness made him feel foolish. 'He says it is merely a bad sprain. Mrs Lawry wrapped it in a thyme compress which, I have to say, made it far more comfortable.'

'She is very knowledgeable about such things. How long—?'

'At least a week, maybe longer.' As her forehead puckered in sympathy he continued, 'It was my intention to write several letters today. All relate to the harbour and are urgent. As you see, I am unable to write. So I was hoping you might be willing to assist me.' When she did not immediately reply he added quickly, 'Naturally I would pay you for your time.'

As she looked away, booted feet approached and someone rapped on the door. Rising quickly she started towards the door as Will Prowse poked his head in.

'Miss Trevanion? You home? Oh, beg pardon, miss.' He snatched his cap off greasy hair that hung in lank locks around his ferret-like face, his narrowed glance darting from Jenefer to Charles and back. A smirk twisted his mouth. 'Didn't know you had company. I won't keep you. I just been in the shop and as I was coming this way I told Hannah I'd bring you the list and the money.'

Jenefer held out her hand for the small drawstring bag. 'Thank you, Mr Prowse.' Despite the anger and dismay kindled by his knowing leer her voice remained cool. 'But in future I would prefer that you leave it for me to collect.' She did not want him coming to her door again for any reason.

'Doing you a favour I was,' he retorted, aggression bubbling to the surface. Behind her, Jenefer heard a soft sound as Charles Polgray rose from his chair. 'Anyhow, seeing I'm here I may as well tell you. I aren't happy. The Brague boys don't have to pay nothing till after they've sold their cargo. And they do more runs, and bring back twice as much each time.'

Jenefer sighed. 'Mr Prowse, the Brague boys are funded by a venturer.' She wondered if he knew the money behind one of the biggest smuggling operations in the area came from local landowner

75

and corrupt justice, Sir Edward Pengarrick. 'The fact that Mr Lukis is willing to give a ten per cent discount for cash with the order means the villagers get more for their money. But they can't afford more than one run a month. No one is preventing you from trading on your own account.' She watched his lips compress in bitter frustration.

'You know I can't, not without a backer.'

'If you wish to join the Brague men – and they are willing to have you – then feel free to do so. I'm sure I'll be able to find another boat—'

'No need to be like that,' he broke in quickly. 'I was only saying—'

'That you could obtain French lace at a special price? Miss Laity wasn't tattling on you, Mr Prowse. We were discussing another matter when she happened to mention your offer.'

His sharp features reddened and he looked away. 'Trying to help, that's all.'

'Of course you were,' she replied without expression. 'However, I think it most unlikely your supplier – whoever he may be – could improve on Mr Lukis's price, quality, or range of merchandise. So—'

'All right! You don't need to go on about it.' Reaching inside his coat he pulled out a grubby handkerchief knotted in one corner. As he pulled the knot loose, coins and a small piece of folded paper fell into his hand. He thrust them at her. 'That's what she gived me.'

'You asked her for payment in advance, Mr Prowse?'

His small eyes glittering, his flushed face tight with anger, he turned and stomped away.

Placing the bag, money and folded paper on the table, Jenefer returned to her chair. 'I apologize for the interruption.'

Charles resumed his seat. 'I have no desire to alarm you, Miss Trevanion, but if that man sees an opportunity to do you harm, he'll take it.'

Having braced herself for questions or criticism, Jenefer was startled. 'Fortunately our paths rarely cross, so—'

'I don't mean physical injury. He's too much of a coward. But his dissatisfaction is obvious. And you caught him out. That is something he will neither forget not forgive.'

Tempted for an instant to make light of his warning she felt uneasy as she recognized the truth in what he said. 'Fortunately I have very little to do with him.'

'May I ask how the business is arranged?'

'Any villagers who want to invest in a cargo take a list of what they want, and the money to pay for it, to Hannah.'

'Why her?'

'For convenience. Everyone uses the shop. It's in the centre of the village. She's happy to do it and I am spared constant interruptions. A few days before a run I collect the list, bank the money in Helston and mail a copy of the list and the bank receipt to Mr Lukis in Guernsey. I give another copy of the list to Will Prowse just in case the mail is delayed or goes astray.'

'So Prowse is not entrusted with money?'

Jenefer shook her head. 'No, because—'

'The villagers' cargo has been paid for in advance.' Charles nodded. 'So what does he get out of it?'

'A fee for the use of his boat for one run a month.'

'Who pays that?'

'I do. I charge each person one per cent of their profit to look after their accounts.'

A quick smile of appreciation crossed face. 'So those who make the most pay the most.'

She nodded. 'The boat fee comes out of that. What?' she said as he shook his head and a wry smile lifted one corner of his mouth.

'Don't you see? You're privy to the financial affairs of half the village and entrusted with large sums of money. You pay him what he no doubt considers a paltry amount while he takes all the risks. I'll lay odds he has been unable to find a merchant willing to let him have goods without payment of a sizeable deposit, or at least a letter of guarantee. Seeing other smugglers making large amounts of money is increasing his resentment. He's looking for someone to blame. Your success would be reason enough. That you are a young and' – colour stained his cheeks but his gaze remained steady – 'a very beautiful woman adds insult to injury as far as he is concerned. You live alone which makes you an easy target. That is why I ask you to be on your guard.'

As her heart tripped on a beat then raced to catch up, Jenefer clasped her hands tightly in her lap. 'Thank you. F–for the warning,' she added quickly in case he thought she was thanking him for his compliment. *He had called her beautiful.* No one had ever done that.

He cleared his throat. 'Regarding my request for help,' – he adjusted the sling supporting his bandaged hand – 'I think that by offering payment I may have offended you. If so, I apologize. But should you agree to help me, and I very much hope that you will, the work is certain to encroach on what little spare time you have. I could not ask that of you without offering recompense.'

'I am not offended,' she replied truthfully. 'And my hesitation was in no way due to reluctance. I was simply wondering how to rearrange my current work.' To confess her hope that he had asked her as a friend while payment implied a business arrangement, would only embarrass them both. 'I should very much enjoy assisting you. To learn how such a project is organized will be fascinating.' Could he tell she hadn't been entirely candid with him? Had he seen her flinch before she looked away?

He inclined his head. 'My apologies for the misunderstanding. However, much as I appreciate your generous offer I cannot accept it. I do want your help. Indeed, there is no one I would rather—' He stopped abruptly and looked away. Then his gaze returned to hers in a silence filled with questions.

When he spoke his voice was harder, more determined. 'However I will not take advantage. I must pay you. Do what you like with the money.' He gestured with his free hand. 'Give it to the poor if you wish. But I will have my way in this.'

He must pay her. Did he fear being in her debt? Was he determined to keep their dealings impersonal? Yet if that was so, why had he cut himself short? *He had called her beautiful.*

'Miss Trevanion?'

To argue with him was not only futile, it would be ungracious. 'You may have your way. I will say no more on the subject, except' – as his chin rose and he started to frown, she smiled – 'thank you.'

'The debt and gratitude are mine.' With a brief nod that declared the matter settled he leaned back in the armchair. 'The sooner I find a house, the more convenient it will be for both of us. I can hardly ask you to come to my room at The Standard. Nor is it convenient to work here.'

Jenefer eyed him, her voice deceptively quiet. 'I manage very well.'

'I meant no criticism of your arrangements,' he said quickly. 'But I see you find it necessary to leave the door open to ensure sufficient light. Also, would I be right in thinking your neighbours interpret the open door as an invitation?'

She couldn't deny it.

He lowered his voice. 'You remember I asked you to treat any discussion between us concerning the harbour as confidential?'

Shock made her heart quicken. 'I have not said a word—'

'Of course you haven't.' His mild impatience was strangely reassuring. 'Nor was I suggesting otherwise. But how can we expect to maintain that secrecy if the open door allows anyone passing to overhear our conversation?'

He was right.

The sound of quick footsteps on the flags outside made them both turn.

Chapter Nine

Rapping knuckles on the door were a mere formality overlaid by Lizzie's voice. 'I tell you, miss, I'll swing for that Annie Rollason one of these days. Just see if I— Oh!' She stopped in the doorway, her bristling anger forgotten as one hand flew to her cheek.

'Oh my Lor'. I'm some sorry. Miss, if I'd known I never would've— '

Charles caught her eye, one dark brow lifting, and Jenefer conceded quietly, 'Your point is made.' She turned to her neighbour. 'It's all right, Lizzie. You remember Mr Polgray?'

Lizzie nodded, curiosity overtaking her embarrassment. ''Course I do.' Turning to Charles she bobbed a curtsy. 'Lovely morning, isn't it?' Then she registered the sling. 'Dear life! Whatever happened to you?'

'Lizzie,' Jenefer interrupted quietly. 'Was there something you wanted to see me about?'

'It'll keep.' She turned to Charles. 'I aren't being nosy, mister, but word is you're looking for a house to rent? Be interested in Mr Trembath's place, would you?'

Charles glanced at Jenefer. 'I have no idea. Would I?'

They both turned to Lizzie and Jenefer asked, 'Is that the one on the far side of the harbour?'

Lizzie nodded. 'Above the Judas heaps.'

'Judas heaps?' Charles enquired.

'Dangerous rocks running from the shore out to sea,' Jenefer explained.

'House is called Kegwyn,' Lizzie said. ''Tis named for the hawthorn blossom that covers the hedges every spring. Lovely 'tis. Look just like snow. Matthew Trembath inherited the place when his father passed on. He's a mine engineer, lost his wife and baby three months back, poor soul. Anyhow, he've gone out to South America. Peru, or some such place. I heard about it while I was in the butcher's. 'T is being let furnished, and Mr Rollason have got the key.'

Charles rose to his feet. 'I am most grateful to you, Mrs Clemmow. I should certainly like to visit the house. I'll go and request the key from Mr Rollason.' He turned to Jenefer. 'Would you be so kind as to accompany me to view the property, Miss Trevanion? I'll need staff and would appreciate your advice.'

Walking with him to the door Jenefer wanted to say she'd be delighted. Instead, while butterflies danced in her stomach and confusion reigned in her head, she matched his formality with a polite nod. 'Of course.'

'I should be no more than twenty minutes.'

As his footsteps receded she returned to the table.

'Honest, miss,' – Lizzie wrung her hands – 'I'm awful sorry bursting in like that.'

'It's all right, Lizzie. Truly.' Slotting the list Louise Laity had given her into one of the ledgers, Jenefer closed them both and gathered the letters into a neat pile. 'What has happened to upset you?'

'Annie Rollason.' Lizzie's voice shook with renewed anger. 'Got some spiteful tongue on her, she have. Going on about all the benefits me, Sam and Billo get because of you living next door.' Lizzie's anger dissolved into distress. 'I don't need she nor anyone else to tell me how much we owe you.'

Grasping Lizzie's shoulders Jenefer shook her gently. 'Stop that at once. If there is a debt, it's mine. Without you to cook my meals and do my washing and ironing, I could never have developed my business. Nor could I continue to run it efficiently, for there are not enough hours in the day for me to do everything myself. Our arrangement is a private matter that suits us both and has Sam's blessing. It's none of Annie's business, which I'm sure she knows. The truth of the matter is that Annie is jealous.'

Sniffing back tears, Lizzie wiped her eyes with a corner of her apron. 'I know I shouldn't take it to heart.'

Jenefer slid an arm around Lizzie's shoulders. 'No, you shouldn't. But that is easy to say and hard to do. If Annie really is upsetting you, the quickest way to stop her is to offer sympathy for her unhappiness.'

'What have she got to be unhappy about?'

Jenefer shrugged. 'How would I know?'

Lizzie thought it over. 'Tell her I feel sorry for her?' As Jenefer nodded, a grin spread slowly across Lizzie's face. 'Oh yes. She'd hate that, Annie would. She 've always fancied herself special. She used to tell the rest of us that she would marry up and have a proper house with a girl to do the heavy work and a maid who would look after her clothes and dress her hair in the latest fashion. Harry Rollason's a good man and a hard worker, but he isn't what she had in mind. Though truth be told, she was lucky to get 'n. He must have some patience, that's all I can say. I s'pose she picked up her grand notions from Mrs Gillis.'

'Mrs Gillis? Tamara's mother?'

Lizzie nodded. 'Didn't you know Annie and Mrs Gillis is cousins?'

Jenefer shook her head. 'Though I don't know why I'm surprised. Half the village appears to be related either by blood or marriage.'

Taking a deep breath Lizzie straightened her back and smoothed her apron. 'I won't go looking for trouble. But next time she start I'll have her. Cut her off at the knees I will.' Emphazising her determination with an abrupt nod she blew out a breath. 'Here, miss, I was just thinking. After you've looked at the house, how don't you invite mister back for dinner? Nothing against Esther, she cook a nice roast at The Standard, but with mister's arm in that there sling he'll feel some fool if he got to have his food cut up for 'n.'

'I don't know, Lizzie.' The idea was all too appealing. 'Someone in my position—'

'There isn't no one else in this village in your position,' Lizzie pointed out.

'Exactly. Which is why I need to be very careful about—'

'What people think? You know as well as I do, you could live like a saint – which you do, near enough – and there'd still be gossip. People will think what they want. So how don't you please yourself for once? Mister have got a nice way with 'n. And he must like you else he wouldn't have come calling.'

If only. Berating herself for wishful thinking, Jenefer moved round the table and squared up the already tidy papers. 'You've got it all wrong, Lizzie. He came because his injury means he can't write and he needs help with correspondence.' *There is no one I would rather—* What? *Ask for help?* That was most probably what he had intended to say. He knew she had business and financial experience, and understood the importance of confidentiality. He simply needed someone he could trust. That was all. So why hadn't he said so? *He had called her beautiful.*

'He did? Well, there you are. You'll have plenty to talk about. Go on, you ask 'n. Do you good to have a bit of company. If he got other things to do he can always say no. You get yourself ready. I'm going in and do extra veg.'

*

Jenefer waited for Charles to close the gate, then walked beside him towards the house. Long and low, it was built of stone with a slate roof and a pillared porch that protected the front door. He followed a flagged path round the side. Multi-paned sash windows gleamed in the sunshine and fragrant honeysuckle scrambled up the stonework to arch over French doors that opened onto wide shallow steps and an area of grass in need of a scythe.

He stood for a moment then turned in a slow circle, surveying the property and the view. 'This is it,' he stated with quiet conviction. 'This is the house I want.'

Startled, Jenefer looked at him. 'Might it not be wiser to wait until after you have seen inside before deciding?'

'I will not change my mind.'

Her amusement was tinged with frustration and, she had to admit, a little envy, for the house was delightfully situated, and the wide windows would let in so much light. She thought of her little cottage with its single kitchen window and the ever-open door. 'Then why, when you clearly have no need of my opinion, did you insist on me coming?'

'For the pleasure of your company,' he replied, his gaze on the house.

On two sides of the property trees provided shelter and privacy. Glossy green holly offered rich dark contrast to the autumn russet and gold of sycamore, elm and ash. The lawn stretched the full width of the house and sloped gently towards to an overgrown hedge. At one end a single Stone pine, with its distinctive forked trunk and broad canopy, stood sentinel. At the other, a small gate was barely visible amid the overgrown sloe and hawthorn bushes. Beckoning her to follow he set off towards it.

Beyond the gate a path ran along the cliff top above narrow coves where waves foamed against jagged black rock, and golden-brown weed ebbed and flowed in the clear water.

As she reached him he said, 'Do smugglers use the path or coves?'

'I have no idea.' His brows rose and he shot her a dry look. 'Mr Polgray, I act as agent for a merchant and keep accounts for the villagers. I take no part in the trade myself.'

He eyed her again then looked out to sea. 'You are too modest, Miss Trevanion.'

'I'm not sure what you mean.'

He turned to face her. 'It is my understanding that you hold a position of great trust.'

'Well, yes, but—'

'That aside, you have lived in the village all your life. You must know at least some of the routes and hiding places.' She nodded. 'And they are – where? Trust me, Miss Trevanion. I have a reason for asking.'

Trust me. His arrival signalled change for the village. Maybe it was an opportunity for her as well. Perhaps it was time she stopped fearing change and embraced it instead. But to do that she would have to release the past and lower her protective barriers. 'I'm aware of paths and tracks leading from coves along the coast from Pednbrose. I have also heard mention of hiding places in barns and wells, in caves, the church bell tower, and certain cellars. But—'

'To the best of your knowledge has any part of this property ever been used in connection with smuggling?'

Jenefer shook her head. 'No.'

'You're certain?'

'I am. The rocks off-shore make this side of the harbour and village too dangerous.'

He smiled. 'Thank you. That was my only reservation. You have laid it to rest. Now, let us look inside.' They returned to the front door and he inserted the key. The door opened silently on well-oiled hinges.

In the spacious hall she inhaled, testing the air for the sweet musti-ness of damp or decay. But all she could smell was beeswax and a hint of lavender. She followed him into the drawing room. The carpet had been rolled up to expose a varnished wood floor. The furniture was draped in Holland covers. Lifting the latches on the shutters he folded them back one at a time. The room faced south and sunlight streamed in, reminding her of Pednbrose when her mother was alive and Betsy could walk and the family held a position of prominence in the village.

She blinked stinging eyes. Then one shrouded shape caught her attention.

He walked round the room and paused in the doorway. 'I'll take a look upstairs.'

Distracted, she gave him a brief smile. After a moment's hesitation when he seemed about to speak, then changed his mind, he left. Alone in the room she lifted the cloth. The pretty walnut-veneered spinet looked similar to the one on which her mother had taught her to play.

But as she raised the lid she saw an immediate difference. On her mother's the keys had been made of wood. These were ebony and bone. Had it been a gift from Matthew Trembath to his wife? Or an heirloom, inherited from one or other of their families? Had Mrs Trembath sat in this sun-filled room, perhaps playing for an hour each afternoon while she looked forward to the birth of her baby? Now she was dead and he had gone to South America. How fragile life was: how swiftly joyful anticipation could shatter into tragedy.

She glanced toward the doorway then, unable to resist, drew out the brocade-covered stool. Sitting down she began tentatively to play a Bach minuet.

As her fingers moved over the keys she recalled her mother playing this same piece, and was suddenly rocked by a sense of loss. Dwelling on what had gone achieved nothing. Nor did wallowing in self-pity. For the past three years she had combated loneliness by keeping busy. But work was no longer enough. Shaking her head to dispel tears that blurred her vision, she switched in mid-phrase to a frivolous air. But lack of practice tripped her fingers and after the third missed note she sighed and gave up. His voice from the doorway made her jump.

'That was pretty.'

Quickly she closed the lid, tucked the stool away and pulled the cloth cover into place, embarrassed by her poor playing. How long had he been watching? 'Either you have no ear for music, or you are being kind.'

'You do me an injustice,' he said mildly. 'I have an excellent ear. And I am not in the habit of saying things I don't mean.'

Shame burned. 'I beg your pardon. That was unforgivably rude.' She forced a cheerful smile, fearing the desolation she had glimpsed and wanting it banished. 'So, is the rest of the house to your liking?'

'I have yet to see the domestic quarters. Would you come with me? You will know better than I what may be required.'

At the far end of the hall Jenefer opened the door into a spacious kitchen. A large window let in plenty of light. The cavernous open hearth had been swept clean. Fire irons, brandis and bellows were neatly placed side by side. An enormous table occupied the centre of the flagged floor with wooden benches tucked underneath and an armchair at each end. Plates, dishes and cooking pots filled two long shelves. A flour hutch and saltbox stood near the hearth where warmth would keep them dry and free of mould.

She was acutely aware of him behind her in the short passage leading to a scullery with a square wooden sink and copper in the corner, and then to the cool dairy with its wide slate shelves and stone trough. He gestured for her to precede him as they retraced their steps.

Between kitchen and scullery, she opened the back door onto a paved yard containing a well and two lean-to shelters still half full of furze and dried turf squares. 'So?' he said. 'What is your opinion?'

This time her smile was genuine. 'It is very well appointed. I think with good staff you will be extremely comfortable.'

'That's settled then. If Mr Rollason is acting as agent for the owner I shall close with him directly.'

They returned to the hall and she walked out into the sunshine, her heartbeat quickening as she silently practised inviting him to dinner.

He locked the door then strode briskly to join her as she started towards the gate. 'Miss Trevanion?' She turned. 'Would you do me the honour of dining with me?'

Taken aback, she hesitated. 'Oh – that is most kind of you, but—' Before she had time to explain he had withdrawn.

'Forgive me,' he made a brief bow, aloof and unapproachable. 'I have already taken too much of your time.'

'No,' she interrupted quickly. 'You misunderstand. My hesitation was because you had taken the words from my mouth. I was about to invite you to join me for dinner.'

Quick pleasure warmed his gaze and softened his features as they started down the hill. 'I have no wish to cause you any inconvenience.'

She smiled. 'You won't. When you went to collect the key, Lizzie informed she was making extra.'

'So it was your *neighbour*'s idea that we dine together?'

She saw amusement behind his bland enquiry. 'No, I had already decided to ask you.' She did not feel it necessary to tell him of her doubts. 'She suggested it before I had a chance to tell her. She was concerned that you might feel uncomfortable about eating at The Standard.'

Bemusement deepened the crease between his brows. 'Why?'

'Because you would need your food cut up for you?' As he glanced down at the sling cradling his bandaged hand, she wondered if she had been tactless.

The corners of his mouth tilted briefly. 'Ah. I see.' As he looked at her, she was aware once more of his reserve. He used it to keep people at a distance. She knew that because she did the same. This recognition of shared experience was part of her attraction to him. She knew only too well the reasons for her wariness. But what had caused his?

'So your motive was pity?' he challenged.

She lifted her chin. 'Certainly not. Was it yours for accepting?'

'No.' He frowned and she realized she had surprised him. 'Why on earth would I pity you?'

His bewilderment was so obviously genuine she had to bite back laughter. Relief lightened her mood as she cocked an ironic brow at him.

'I am not belittling the grievous loss of your father or your home,' he said. 'But others who have found themselves in your position usually seek a governess's post, or throw themselves upon the mercy of relatives. Your response was far less – prosaic.'

'You talk as though I had choices.'

'Did you not?' he challenged. 'I'll wager you could have left the village and gone to live as companion to some elderly female relative.'

'I could. But such an arrangement would swiftly have proved intolerable to both of us.'

'My point exactly.'

'In any case I didn't want to leave Porthinnis. So I simply did what made most sense. I am familiar with accounts, and several businesses in the village needed a bookkeeper.' She shrugged, knowing he was astute enough to realize that her journey from then to now had been considerably more difficult than her words suggested. But she had never sought pity and definitely did not want his.

'I don't know any other woman who could, or would, have done what you did.'

'Perhaps,' she offered, poker-faced, 'you do not know many women?'

'Enough, believe me.'

'Then maybe the ladies of your acquaintance possess a greater sense of decorum.'

'Less courage, certainly.'

'Are you flattering me, Mr Polgray?'

'We have not known each other long, Miss Trevanion. But I believe you have as little regard for flattery as I do. I merely state facts as I see them.'

His words comforted. She glanced up at him. 'Being unable to use your hand must be most inconvenient. But I cannot imagine you being the least bit reluctant to ask Esther or one of the girls to cut your meat for you. So, in answer to your question: I invited you to dine with me because—' her throat dried. But she had come this far and would not fail now. Besides, she thought wryly, had he not just praised her courage? 'Because I rarely have company, and I enjoy yours.'

His gaze held hers: enfolding her in warmth. But conditioned to hearing what was *not* said, she sensed conflict in him and wondered at its cause. Then he smiled, and made a formal bow. 'Thank you, Miss Trevanion. It would give me great pleasure to dine with you.'

They parted at the mouth of the alley. While he continued on to see Mr Rollason, she hurried down the yard past her own cottage to Lizzie's. Savoury smells wafting out of the open door made her stomach gurgle. *What had she done?* Tapping on the door she leaned in.

'Lizzie? He's accepted my invitation.'

Turning from the stove, Lizzie wiped her hands on her apron.

"Course he has. I knew he would. Where's he to now?'

'Gone to tell Mr Rollason he wishes to take the house. He'll be back shortly.'

'Everything's ready, bird. You go on in and soon as I hear'n come, I'll dish up and bring it round.'

Jenefer took off her hat, gloves and jacket, tidied her hair and washed her hands. She set out cutlery and napkins. When she heard his boots on the cobbles her heart leapt. Adjusting the folds of her kerchief she pressed one hand to her fluttering stomach as he tapped on the door. She went to greet him.

'Come in, Mr Polgray. Let me take your hat.' She set it on one corner of the dresser. 'Would you care for a tankard of ale? I keep a keg so I have something to offer my fishermen clients to make them feel more comfortable.'

'I should enjoy that very much, thank you.'

Handing him the pewter tankard, hoping he would not notice the slight tremor in her hand, she was pouring elderflower cordial into a glass when Lizzie appeared on the threshold carrying a tray.

'All right?' she beamed. Her cheeks were rosy, but whether this was due to heat from the stove or the fact she was serving a gentleman guest, Jenefer couldn't be sure. 'You'll be ready for your dinner after that long walk.' Placing the tray on the table, she set the covered plates between each set of cutlery, and a small bowl in the middle.

Removing the tray, Lizzie went to the door. 'Anything you want, just shout. I'll bring your afters d'rectly. Mind that horseradish. He's a bit fiery.'

'Thank you.' Jenefer smiled at her.

With a brisk nod Lizzie hurried out.

Jenefer lifted off a covering plate and saw that thick slices of roast beef, roast potatoes, carrots and cabbage had been carefully cut into bite-sized pieces. She bit her lip as their eyes met.

'Mine, I think,' Charles said, and remained standing until she had taken her seat opposite. 'So, Miss Trevanion,' he smiled. 'I have a house.'

Jenefer looked at him. 'But what of the lease?'

'Mr Trembath had it drawn up before he left. Apparently all that is necessary is for my name to be inserted and the notary to witness my signature. Mr Rollason has agreed to accompany me to Mr Penkivell's office later this afternoon.'

'Heavens, Mr Polgray. You are certainly decisive.'

'It was not difficult. The house . . .' He stopped.

'Felt right?' she suggested quietly. As he nodded, she said. 'I know what you mean. It was the same for me. This cottage offered a safe haven when I badly needed one. I have been – am – very happy here.'

'You mentioned staff?' he said. 'Whom do you recommend?'

Jenefer spooned a little of the sauce onto the side of her plate, then pushed the bowl across to him. 'If you are looking for a housekeeper, Cora Eustace is an excellent cook, utterly trustworthy, and does not gossip. She's a widow and looked after her father until his recent death. So she has no ties.'

'She sounds ideal. Who else?'

'A housemaid. I'm sure Cora will know a suitable girl.' She cut into her beef and found it tender and delicious. But the sauce's bite made her cough. 'Goodness, Lizzie wasn't joking.' Dabbing her eyes with her napkin, she pressed it to her mouth to hide laughter as he she watched him swallowed hastily and blow out a breath.

'That is powerful indeed.'

Jenefer sipped her cordial. 'I imagine you would prefer to choose your own valet? ' When he nodded, his head bent over his plate, she went on, 'Perhaps your man might combine his duties with those of a groom? You'll also need a gardener. I can recommend Harry Tozer. He lives two doors down on the other side of the Clemmows. My neighbours and I have all turned over our gardens to him. He grows delicious fruit and a great variety of vegetables. And for laundry I suggest Lucy Tallack. She lives along Back Row. But neither of those need be full time positions.'

'I'm relieved to hear you say so. It was beginning to sound very crowded.'

Smiling, Jenefer shrugged. 'It's entirely your choice. But good staff will make your life very much easier and allow you to concentrate on your work.'

'You're right of course. Might I trespass even further on your good nature and ask you to speak to them on my behalf? Find out if they would be interested? They might feel more comfortable talking to you rather than me. I am, after all, a stranger.'

'Of course. And if they are interested?'

'I will see them at the house later in the week.' They continued eating in silence. Just as Jenefer was casting about for a topic of conversation that would sound neither banal nor desperate, Charles spoke. 'Apart from your bookkeeping, I believe you also lend money to local businesses?'

How had he found out? *Branoc Casvellan?* Not that it was a secret. 'Yes, I do, and consider it a privilege.' She wondered why he was asking. Then it dawned on her. She dabbed her lips and still holding the crumpled napkin, rested her forearm on the table. 'May I enquire how you intend to finance the harbour expansion?'

Laying his fork on his empty plate he wiped his mouth and sat back. 'I have already obtained a proportion of the funding from Kerrow & Polgray and opened a new account in the name of the Porthinnis Harbour Company. But I'm going to need considerably more. Mr Casvellan has expressed an interest in buying shares.'

Jenefer leaned forward, her fingers tightening on the crumpled damask. 'Would you be willing to sell me some?'

'Of course I would, but—'

'I don't suppose the amount I can spare will make much difference—'

Reaching across the table he covered her hand with his. 'No, that wasn't what I—'

As she raised startled eyes to his, he withdrew his hand.

'I beg your pardon. I – forgive me.'

'Please don't,' she interrupted, acutely aware of the heat that had rushed to her face. Her heart thudded against her ribs. She could still feel the warm weight of his palm, the supple strength in the fingers that had gripped hers. 'No offence was intended and none is taken.'

But a line had been crossed. She saw now that since their unexpected meeting at Trescowe, every moment they had spent together had been leading inexorably to this one. His touch had stirred her, left her wanting more. But memories of Martin's betrayal loomed, dark and threatening as thunderheads. Her throat painfully dry, she lifted her cordial. As she sipped, the glass rattled against her teeth. She heard Lizzie singing.

The singing grew louder. Then there was a knock on the door. 'How're you getting on? Finished have you?'

As Lizzie waited on the threshold, Jenefer caught Charles's gaze and awareness arced between them. She glimpsed impatience at the interruption then saw it soften to amusement. 'Come in, Lizzie,' she called over her shoulder.

'All right, was it?' Placing the tray on the table, Lizzie removed two dishes of golden-crusted apple pie and a small bowl of clotted cream, then gathered up the dirty plates.

'Delicious, Mrs Clemmow,' Charles smiled at her. 'As I'm sure you know.'

'What about the horseradish?' Anxiety edged her smile.

'It's in a class of its own.'

Lizzie beamed. 'Right, I'll leave you get on.' She bustled to the door.

As soon as she heard Lizzie's door shut Jenefer turned to Charles. 'That was well done,' she said softly. 'A class of its own.' Laughter trembled in her voice. 'Indeed it was, bless her.'

'She had gone to considerable trouble.'

'Well, I appreciate your kindness.'

'It is I who am obliged to you. Just think what I might have missed had you not invited me.' He spooned up a small portion of pie and cream. 'To return to your offer. I would be delighted to have you as a shareholder. But I'm looking for additional investment of several thousand pounds.'

'Ah. I'm afraid that's rather more than I can manage.'

'Oh dear.' She caught the gleam in his eyes. 'Then it's as well I have other options.'

Her heartbeat had steadied but awareness of him hummed along every nerve. 'Am I permitted to ask?'

'I was about to tell you. I intend applying to Mr Ralph Daniell at the Cornish Bank in Truro. He already has a holding in K&P's shipping and smelting interests so I am fairly certain he will be receptive.'

Jenefer toyed with her spoon. Though the pastry was feather-light and the clove and cinnamon-flavoured apple was delicious, she could not swallow another mouthful.

As he pushed the bowl containing his unfinished dessert to one side, she realized that beneath his contained manner he was equally unsettled. The knowledge was oddly comforting.

'Perhaps tomorrow you would write requesting an appointment?'

'I will if you wish. But might it not be better if I wrote this afternoon? The post boy leaves The Standard at seven in the morning to catch the horse-van to Falmouth. If it makes the connection with Allen's van which runs daily between Falmouth and Truro, Mr Daniell should receive your letter the day after tomorrow.'

Laughing, he shook his head. 'Miss Trevanion, you are relentless.'

Familiar with mockery and criticism for she had been the butt of both, she heard only admiration. Sharing important private business with him filled her with pride and shimmering pleasure. Hard on its heels came fear. But she fought hard. Releasing her crumpled napkin onto the table she lifted one shoulder.

'It's the secret of my success,' she said lightly. 'Would you care for tea now? Or shall we do the correspondence first?'

'The letters, by all means.'

Aware of his gaze following her, she moved the bowls aside, fetched fresh paper from the dresser cupboard, uncapped her inkwell, checked her pen nibs, and resumed her seat.

'Whenever you are ready, Mr Polgray.' She had offered him help, and would keep her word. But as soon as his hand was better she would distance herself. For Charles Polgray stirred feelings that frightened her. Her life was busy and fulfilling. She had worked hard to achieve what she had now. She was financially independent, answerable to no one.

But in that brief touch she had glimpsed another world; one of emotion and sensuality; where strength, softness, yielding and power were intertwined: a world she did not know and could not control. The thought dried her mouth and made her heart thud painfully. *Trust me* he had said. But she'd done that once before and been betrayed. She had lost her home and everything that represented security. She could not risk it. Not again. *Yet the memory of his hand warm and strong on hers made her ache for more.*

Chapter Ten

That evening Charles sat in a corner of the taproom in The Standard, a glass of cognac on the scarred table in front of him. Not only had Jenefer Trevanion penned six letters one after another as he dictated, she had also made a list for him of the addressees, the date, and a precis of their contents.

The longer he spent in her company, the more she fascinated him. He rubbed his forehead where it ached and the back of his neck where conflict weighed on him like a yoke. His conscience urged him to confide his situation. But what if he had misread her? What if the interest he sensed was merely her attempt to make him – a stranger – feel welcome? Were that so, she might consider his revelation an impertinence, for it assumed a partiality she might not feel. Even worse it would achieve nothing except to cause them both acute embarrassment.

Surely there must be word from the Archdeaconry Court soon? He had made the application months ago, as soon as he had discovered the treachery of people he should have been able to trust. Why burden her with information that would – if justice was done – shortly be irrelevant? A bond dissolved as if it had never existed. *The child would still exist.* Regardless of Eve's lies they both knew it could not be his. Let the man who had fathered it take responsibility.

Yet once he was free, what then? His work had required him to go wherever Kerrow & Polgray's interests dictated. He was often away from Cornwall for weeks at a time. He had been in Mexico almost a year. Until now he had never minded, finding interest in each change of scene and challenge in each new location. But coming here had changed everything.

This wouldn't be an easy project. Indeed he expected it to prove particularly demanding, not least because of the different interests at stake. But he liked the village and the people he had met. He particularly liked the house he had leased and would move into within the week. The main cause of his upheaval was his profound attraction to Jenefer Trevanion.

He had moved to Porthinnis to put distance between himself and the people who had misused him. His sole purpose had been to expand the harbour and increase Kerrow & Polgray's trading profits. Nowhere had women figured in his plans.

Innate honesty forced him to acknowledge that his pride and self-esteem had suffered most. Though fond of Eve he had not loved her. In his family love had never been considered a necessary condition of marriage. Loyalty mattered far more.

Fury stirred as he recalled how he had been used. Telling Jenefer would mean revealing what a fool he had been, how easily he had been duped. Sweat prickled his forehead at the thought and he shifted on the settle, his shirt clinging damply to his back. He must receive word soon. Then it would be over and she need never know.

He took a mouthful of cognac. As the smooth spirit warmed his stomach and loosened muscles knotted by tension, he pictured her fair head bent in concentration as her pen moved swiftly across each sheet of paper.

It was hard to believe they had met only days ago. It was as if he had known her always. Her quiet manner belied a shrewd intelligence, and he relished her dry wit even when it was directed at him. More used to male company, he was astonished at how comfortable he felt with her.

While writing the letters she stopped frequently to ask questions which resulted in a discussion about cranes, winches and building materials. Startled to realize he had talked to her as he would to another man he told her so.

She had arched her brows. 'Is that a compliment?'

Briefly unsure, he had taken refuge in stiffness. 'It was intended as such.'

'Then,' she said lightly, 'that is how I shall take it. Thank you.'

Only with the benefit of hindsight did it occur to him that his remark might have sounded patronizing.

When all the letters had been written and daylight was fading, they parted on her doorstep. The urge to touch her had been almost irresistible. But he had held back. Despite the protectiveness of her neighbours the fact that she lived alone made her vulnerable, and he was wary of doing anything that might be considered an imposition or taking advantage.

Though grateful for her help while his wrist mended his deepening attraction to her was a complication both unexpected and thoroughly unsettling. He drained his glass and signalled to one of the serving girls as she collected tankards and glasses from a nearby table.

Before he could ask her to fetch him another brandy there was a commotion near the door. A group of fishermen moved aside as a newcomer swaggered in. Having captured attention with his entrance he paused, surveying the taproom. His blue coat with brass buttons, fawn waistcoat over a blue-striped shirt, knotted black kerchief and grubby white duck trousers suggested a uniform of sorts. Seeing the pistol jammed into his broad leather belt from which a sword also hung, Charles guessed the man's profession even as the girl's in-drawn breath hissed between her teeth.

'Preventive officer?' he murmured.

She gave a quick nod. Anger brought patches of colour to her sallow cheeks and thinned her mouth. 'Jake Pendarvis. Captain of the Customs cutter, *Speedwell*.'

'All right, my 'andsomes?' Pendarvis roared, gazing around.

The broad smile on his red face did not reach his eyes. As he made his way to the bar counter, men moved aside. Some turned their backs.

'Not local, is he?' Charles asked softly.

The girl shook her head. 'He told me he come from Penzance, but someone else said he live over Brague. I wouldn't trust 'n to tell me the time of day.'

Charles guessed the girl had been taken in by the captain's brash charm and now bitterly regretted it. 'What's he doing here?'

She eyed him in weary surprise. 'What d'you think? He've come for his sweetener. I'll be back d'rectly.' Balancing the heavy tray she moved quickly between the tables. Watching from behind the counter, the landlord drew off a tankard of ale then poured a glass of cognac and pushed both along the counter towards Pendarvis. Then he lifted the hinged counter top so the girl could pass behind him.

Propped on one elbow Pendarvis leaned across the counter and spoke to her. She ignored him and the landlord, stone-faced, stepped between them. Pendarvis laughed. He drank the beer in one long draught then lifted the cognac. As he did so, the landlord reached beneath the counter and slapped a leather draw-string purse on the dark varnished wood.

Pendarvis tucked it inside his waistcoat and, after draining the glass, set it down with a sharp crack. Then pushing himself away from the counter he bellowed, 'Good night, one and all. Here's to fair winds and a rich harvest.' Men watched in silence as he raised a hand in farewell then disappeared into the passage.

A few moments later a voice said, ''Tis all right. He've gone.' Someone spat into the fire and the buzz of conversation resumed. Charles mused on what he had witnessed. Uncaring of the villagers' obvious dislike, the preventive officer took pleasure in their fear. He knew they had no choice. Either they paid him off, or risked confiscation of their smuggled cargoes: a harvest gathered in darkness.

*

On Sunday morning Jenefer woke in the grey light of dawn after a night filled with dreams of Charles Polgray. Still tired, knowing she would not sleep again, she pushed back the covers and got up. Putting on the chemise gown of faded apricot dotted muslin she wore to do her morning chores, she threw a shawl around her shoulders, and walked through silent streets down to the harbour.

There wasn't a breath of wind. All the fishing boats were moored by the bow to the back quay, for no fisherman ever put to sea on a Sunday. Within the arms of the small harbour the water resembled rumpled black satin. The harbour faced south. To the west above the dark expanse of sea several diamond-bright stars still glittered against a backdrop of midnight blue. But to the east behind the village, a pale green and turquoise sky heralded the approaching sunrise.

The air was cool against her face and smelled of seaweed, tar, and old fish, especially near the boats. At the rear of the quays, the sturdy wooden doors of stone buildings where fishermen stored nets, oars, spare sails and spars, were closed and locked.

Hugging her shawl closer to ward off the morning chill, she walked slowly across the worn stones. She loved the silence and solitude of Sunday mornings. At this hour on a weekday the quay would already be busy as boats that had stayed out overnight unloaded their catch.

Men arrived with horses and panniers to buy the fish then carry it inland to re-sell it. Housewives hurried down with plates. Mabel Couch, a local jowster, would pack her pockets with salt and a cone-shaped basket with fish. Then heaving the basket onto her back supported by a strap across her forehead, she would set off to neighbouring villages and farms. Mabel was sixty years old and often walked fifteen miles a day to sell her fish.

Jenefer considered she worked hard. But compared to Mabel's, her life was easy. She paused to look over the waste ground where Charles Polgray planned to build the new road. The dawn light revealed gorse and brambles and patches of nettles surrounded by a litter of broken spars, old tar brushes, bits of wood, ripped nets, rusted ironwork and scraps of sail canvas dumped and forgotten.

Clearing the land would take days. Then the rubbish would need to be disposed of. The best way would be to burn as much as possible in the old quarry on the moor and drop the rest down an abandoned mineshaft. She felt a tremor of excitement. The whole village would benefit from the harbour expansion, either through employment or increased trade.

She turned again to the sea, trying to picture the alterations. With added protection for the harbour and more space for ships to moor alongside, limestone shipped from Plymouth could be landed here instead of at Penzance. Moved by wheelbarrow from ship to kiln to be burned then powdered, it would be available to sweeten the acid Cornish soil far more quickly and at a considerably lower cost than at present.

Cargoes of barley and oats bound for buyers in Guernsey could be shipped directly from Porthinnis, instead of first having to be carried by cart to Falmouth or Penzance.

As far as trade was concerned, Charles Polgray's plans could not be faulted. But his arrival had added greatly to her confusion.

The sky lightened to primrose then pale pink and sunrise painted streaks of high cloud with rose and gold. The scent of burning wood made her glance round and she saw grey-blue smoke rising from a cottage chimney. It was time to return home before she was seen.

Because she looked after their money, the villagers felt entitled to take a proprietary interest in her. She knew it was well intentioned. Lizzie had told her everyone wished to see her as happy as her sister. But her heart had been frozen, paralysed, by the actions of her father and her fiancé.

She had hoped that without anything to fuel it, interest in her private life might wane. Instead it had increased. A few weeks ago Lizzie had rushed in with news that two of Hannah's customers had nearly come to blows in the shop over whether Mr Ince intended to propose marriage to Miss Trevanion, and whether she should accept.

After a moment of angry frustration, Jenefer had flung up her hands in defeat and started to laugh. What else could she do?

Back in her cottage she completed her morning chores then carried hot water upstairs. Her hair brushed and swept up into a coil high on her crown, she put on a clean shift and stockings, her stays, and a pale yellow muslin gown. Over this she wore a long-sleeved short jacket of emerald velvet fastened with gold buttons and a matching hat made by Louise Laity.

Walking up the path through the churchyard, she nodded politely to Mr Penkivell, the notary, who was accompanied by his wife and two daughters. They lacked the courage to cut her. But their acknowledgement was minimal: registering their disapproval. She wondered which upset them most: her way of life or her friendship with fishermen's wives and shopkeepers. Noticing that the girls had adopted the same tight-lipped expression as their mother, Jenefer felt sorry for them.

Once inside she passed the font and turned into the main aisle towards the Trevanion family pew. On the far side, Branoc and Roz Casvellan sat with their little daughter between them. She looked for Devlin and Tamara but was not surprised at their absence. With Tamara's confinement due shortly, no doubt Devlin had decided against a long and uncomfortable drive across the moor.

The cool air was fragrant with the scent of beeswax candles. Arrangements of cream roses and greenery cascaded from twin pedestals on either side of the altar.

Kneeling, Jenefer closed her eyes and was instantly swamped with memories of the meal she had shared with Charles. She recalled their banter, his animated description of the new lifting equipment he planned for the quay and, all too briefly, his hand covering hers.

Unable to concentrate, she offered up a silent prayer for forgiveness and sat back on the hard pew. Looking towards the altar she told herself romantic daydreams were forgivable at eighteen, but a woman of five-and-twenty ought to know better. It didn't help.

Beams of sunlight angled down through stained glass windows. One fell on the slight balding figure of Mr Ashworth seated at the organ. He played with much affectation but too little pace. Recognizing the tune, she longed to go and tell him to play it as it should be played, a celebration not a dirge.

She had trained herself not to dwell on the past. She and Betsy had escaped the fire alive and unhurt and for that she was profoundly grateful. But if she could have saved just one piece of furniture it would have been her mother's spinet. She pictured the one at Kegwyn, where Charles would soon be living.

The heavy door latch clattered. Behind her whispers rustled like dry leaves in autumn. She heard brisk footfalls and resisted the urge to look round. Then her heart leaped into her throat as the man who had occupied almost every waking thought since their introduction, stepped into the pew beside her.

She noticed immediately he had discarded the sling but still wore a supporting bandage on his right hand. Placing his hat to his left, which brought him closer, he bent one knee and bowed his head. After a swift sideways glance, Jenefer stared straight ahead. Acutely aware of the heat in her cheeks she was grateful for the gloom.

As he sat back his right arm brushed hers making every nerve tingle. Inclining his head towards hers he whispered, 'I hope you don't object? It would not do for me to cause offence by occupying a pew customarily used by another family.'

'No, indeed,' she whispered back. Where a family sat reflected their status and was jealously guarded. Yet by joining her in the Trevanion pew he was offering the congregation opportunity to speculate. As he must be aware of that, she could only assume he considered it beneath his notice.

The vestry door opened. Mr Ashworth played a chord and the

congregation rose. Led by the cross the choir processed slowly up to their stalls. William brought up the rear, carrying his Prayer Book and the notes for his sermon. Over his black cassock he wore a gleaming white surplice so stiff with starch that it crackled as he walked.

Jenefer lowered her eyes, fighting the urge to laugh. But it wasn't William and his starched surplice she was seeing.

Charles Polgray's coat of dark-blue superfine fitted his broad shoulders snugly. Cream pantaloons were tucked into polished black calf-length boots. His thick hair appeared to have been raked with an impatient hand, but his linen was spotless and his jaw freshly shaved. As he moved she caught his scent: clean, warm, and indisputably male. Her throat dry, she opened her hymn-book.

William had taken for his text a line from St Matthew: *The harvest is plentiful but the labourers few.* While he explored the different layers of meaning, Jenefer gazed blindly ahead aware in every nerve of the man beside her.

Eventually the service ended. Leaving the pew first, Charles stepped aside so she might precede him. On her way to the door she nodded at people she knew, amused as their gazes slid past to the tall man behind her.

William stood outside the porch, bidding farewell to each member of his congregation. As he turned from an elderly couple his eyes brightened and his cheeks grew pink as he greeted her. 'Good morning, Miss Trevanion.'

'Good morning, Mr Ince.' She turned towards Charles. 'Mr Polgray, may I introduce Mr William Ince, our parish curate. He also runs a school for the village children.'

Charles inclined his head. 'A school is a brave undertaking, Mr Ince. There are those who believe educating the poor to be a threat to the natural order. I wish you success with your venture.'

'You are most kind, sir. I am fortunate to be blessed with an excellent assistant in Miss Trevanion.'

'She is a person of remarkable qualities,' Charles agreed.

'Do you stay long in the village?' William enquired, his gaze moving uncertainly between them.

'I hope so. Good day, Mr Ince.'

As Charles's palm cupped her elbow Jenefer felt a quaking in the pit of her stomach. They passed through the lych gate and out onto the road.

'Jenefer!' Roz settled her daughter on her arm. 'And Mr Polgray. Is it not a lovely day?'

'Indeed it is, ma'am.' Charles bowed then turned to Jenefer. 'I'll be but a moment.' He strode towards Casvellan who was unhitching two beautiful thoroughbreds from a rail in the shade of an oak tree.

As Roz nuzzled her daughter's neck and Enor hunched tiny shoulders, gurgling with laughter, Jenefer experienced a painful stab of envy.

'My husband tells me you are assisting Mr Polgray with some business,' Roz said softly. 'Does all go well for the two of you?'

'Oh, Roz.' Jenefer pressed one gloved hand to her cheek. 'Don't be anxious,' she added quickly as concern puckered Roz's forehead. 'I'm fine. Really.' She released a shaky breath. 'It's just— He is— I didn't expect—' She shook her head.

'Ah.' Roz's gentle smile held a world of understanding. 'Would you like me to make up a herbal draught? Something soothing?'

A wry smile tugged at the corners of Jenefer's mouth. 'Oh Lord. Do I sound deranged? I do, don't I?'

'Not at all. But I think perhaps you are in need of a good night's sleep.'

'It would help.' Jenefer felt her eyes prickle and grow hot. This wasn't like her. She had always been the person others leaned on. She swallowed hard. 'Are your parents well? And your brother?'

Roz glowed with happiness. 'They are all very well. You would not recognize Tom, he has grown so much this year.'

'And the harvest?'

'Almost finished.'

'How many have you been cooking for this year?'

Roz thought for a moment. 'About forty. Thank heavens I have Mary to look after Enor. Mrs Reskeen does the midday roast and has called in three of her relatives to help with the vegetables. I make bread, heavy cakes and saffron buns for five o'clock tea.'

'You must be exhausted,' Jenefer sympathized.

Roz shook her head. 'I worked far harder at The Three Mackerel.' She glanced towards her husband, adoration softening her gaze. 'Doing whatever helps him is my privilege and pleasure. I am truly blessed.'

'No more than you deserve,' Jenefer said with sincerity. Would she ever be that fortunate? Experience that depth of love? Her gaze sought Charles Polgray.

'About the harvest dinner,' Roz said, 'I know how busy you are—'

'I would not miss it for the world. Just send word of the date and what you want me to bring.'

Swinging himself into the saddle, Casvellan walked his horse forward and leaned down to take his daughter. 'Good day to you, Miss Trevanion.' He settled Enor in front of him, one arm holding her close.

'And to you, Mr Casvellan.'

Roz climbed the mounting block, settled herself on the side-saddle, then with a smile and a wave followed her husband as Charles returned to Jenefer's side.

'May I escort you home, Miss Trevanion?' Reaching into his pocket he withdrew a small drawstring purse of soft leather that clinked. 'First I must give this to Mr Ince. It's a donation for the school,' he said before she could ask.

'But you could have—'

He shook his head. 'Not in front of an audience.'

'Don't you want anyone to know?'

'Do you do your giving in public?'

She thought of how she had pressed Eddy Barnicoat not to tell Cora who had paid for her father's funeral. 'No,' she admitted as they retraced their steps to the church.

'Nor will I. Our agreement is a private matter: your time in exchange for my contribution to village charities.' With so much happening it had slipped her mind. But he had not forgotten. 'Though it appears my need of you is greater than either of us anticipated.'

Their eyes met and she saw in his gaze recognition of a meaning that went far beyond the inconvenience of his sprained wrist.

'Excuse me.' As he walked briskly towards the porch, she followed more slowly, her heart beating fast as joy shimmered inside her. She had *not* imagined his interest.

William emerged from the porch wearing his customary black coat and breeches.

Charles offered him the purse. 'A small contribution towards your school.' Taking it, William glanced from the purse to its donor. He opened his mouth to speak but Charles raised a hand. 'With my compliments.' He made a brief bow then returned to Jenefer.

'Thank you,' William called.

Taking her arm Charles guided her down the path.

'I fear I may prove too expensive for you, Mr Polgray,' Jenefer said, her tongue firmly in her cheek.

'Miss Trevanion,' he said drily, 'you are . . . priceless.'

'Perhaps you wish to renegotiate?'

His dark brows climbed. 'And forfeit my opportunity to support Porthinnis's many worthy causes? Perish the thought. We made a bargain, did we not?'

Jenefer nodded. 'We did.'

'Do you wish to withdraw?'

His expression gave nothing away. But as she looked into his eyes and felt the irresistible attraction, there was only one possible answer. 'No. No, I don't.'

Chapter Eleven

After an uneventful run to Guernsey, spirits and tobacco, silk and lace wrapped in oilcloth, and wooden crates containing glassware and pretty china tea sets packed in straw had been swiftly unloaded then carried to isolated barns and ivy-shrouded sheds.

While Jenefer worked by candlelight at her kitchen table compiling accounts, men moved, silent as shadows, along quiet lanes and through dark alleys collecting and delivering.

She had more than enough work to fill each day. But for the first time since setting up her business maintaining concentration had become a struggle: one she was losing. All too often her thoughts strayed to Charles Polgray. She found herself replaying their conversations, reliving the hours spent in his company.

It was five long days since he had escorted her home after church. She woke each morning wondering if *today* he might call on her to ask for help with additional correspondence, or perhaps to ask her to recommend masons or labourers.

She tried to shake herself out of her preoccupation with him. Her life had been busy and fulfilling before he came. Why should it be any less so now? Yet it was.

His arrival had shone light into dark corners of her life she had been too busy to notice or had tried to ignore. Only too aware of loneliness, she hadn't known what to do about it. Accepting William's offer of marriage, if he ever plucked up sufficient courage to propose, would have helped win back the good opinion of Porthinnis's well-to-do. Yet she had managed very well without it. And it was certainly not a good enough reason for marrying.

Anyway, she knew now that she could not marry William. There was nothing *wrong* with him. Indeed he was a good man who would make an excellent husband, but not for her. When he took her arm or offered his hand, she felt nothing.

Meeting Charles Polgray's gaze – his eyes were the colour of stormy seas – made her quake inside. When he reached across the table and covered her hand with his, her heart had clenched like a fist, stopping her breath in her throat while her blood sang and every nerve quivered in response to the sensation of his skin on hers. Having experienced that, she could not – would not – settle for less.

So she worked on accounts at her kitchen table and waited for him to call. In the village on necessary errands she hoped to see him. She wanted him to need her. She wanted to be involved in the harbour expansion because the whole village would benefit, but also because it was his project. He had conceived it and would turn his vision into reality.

As she walked briskly down the main street these hopes warred with a small warning voice that would not be ignored. *When work on the harbour is complete he will leave.* He has taken a house. *For comfort and privacy. But he's only renting. His stay here is temporary.* Then she must make the most of each moment.

She knocked on Louise Laity's door.

'Miss Trevanion,' Louise beamed. 'Come in, come in.'

'Thank you, but I won't stay.'

'Won't take me but a minute to put the kettle on.' Louise opened the lower door wider. 'I'm just refilling my trays. I got some beautiful silks, braids and ribbons, and a bolt of lace so fine he's like cobwebs. Handsome, 'tis.'

'I'm so pleased. Your customers will be too. I just called to let you know that two of the outstanding accounts have been settled.'

'They have?' Louise's smile widened further. 'That was quick. They letters you wrote certainly done the job. Much obliged to you, Miss, I'm sure.'

With Louise's gratitude ringing in her ears Jenefer continued down the road, bidding people good day, enquiring after sick relatives, and agreeing with hopes that the weather would remain fine until the last of the harvest was in.

'I'm just putting up your groceries now,' Hannah Tresidder greeted her as she entered the shop. 'I s'pose you heard Mr Polgray have moved into Kegwyn?'

Jenefer's heart gave a little kick at the sound of his name. 'Oh?' she replied carefully. Hannah would be dreadfully disappointed if she said she already knew.

'I'd have thought you'd know: you and he being connected through your father.' She didn't wait for a reply, bustling about behind the counter. 'He've taken on Cora Eustace as cook-housekeeper. Couldn't have come at a better time for Cora, dear of her. With her father's being the last life on the lease of that cottage, she'd have been out on the street come end of the month. Rose said she seen Eddy Barnicoat taking Cora's few bits of furniture up there on his cart.' She shook tea scooped from a wooden chest onto brass scales. 'In here this morning she was. Cora, not Rose. Looking ten years younger she is.'

As Hannah paused for breath, Jenefer rested her basket on the counter. 'I'm so glad for her. She's had such a sad time.'

Pouring the tea into a twist of paper, Hannah set it down beside Jenefer's basket. 'Too true. Anyhow, I asked her how mister was settling in. She said he seemed to like it. But she wouldn't let on who else he got working up there. Said it wasn't her place to say.' Hannah clicked her tongue. ''Tisn't no great secret, surely? Oh well, I'll find out soon enough.'

'I'm sure you will, Hannah,' Jenefer agreed with a smile. There was no malice in Hannah. She simply liked to know.

'I did hear her niece have started as housemaid,' Hannah went on. 'You remember Ellen Collins's girl, Ruth? Quiet little thing she is, and a hard worker. Not that she had much choice, what with three younger brothers and Ellen dripping on and forever taking to her bed.'

Checking the list she took a bundle of beeswax candles from a shelf and set them on the counter. 'If you want to know what I think, 'tis a good job Ruth's out of it. She'll like working for Cora. Get on well they do. I always thought 'twas a pity Cora never had children. Want cheese, do you?' As Jenefer blinked, caught out by the sudden change of subject, Hannah pointed to the big wheel of cheddar at one end of the counter with a narrow triangle cut out of it. 'Fresh in, he is. Mrs Avers do dearly love a bit of strong cheddar. Only 'tisn't on your list.'

'Oh. Isn't it? Give me four ounces, please.'

Cutting the cheese onto a piece of waxed paper then laying it on the scales and adjusting the weights, Hannah continued. 'I reck'n Harry Tozer is doing the garden. I see 'n going down through the street each morning. Carrying a fork yesterday he was. And one of they curved hook things this morning. So it look like he've got some brave job on. And word is one of Mr Casvellan's grooms have come down to be mister's valet. You'd think he'd have hired someone from the village.'

Jenefer bit back a smile. Knowing how swiftly village gossip spread, thanks mainly to Hannah, she understood very well why Charles Polgray had preferred to consult Branoc Casvellan regarding a valet. Perhaps he had made the enquiry on Sunday while she was talking to Roz. Strange, though, that he hadn't brought his own man from home.

It occurred to her that, in spite of the time they had spent in each other's company, she had no idea where his home was. Presumably he had staff there. Hiring local staff for Kegwyn suggested he wished to maintain both properties. *Didn't I warn you?* her inner voice demanded. *As soon as the work is finished he'll leave.* She pressed one hand to the sudden void in the pit of her stomach

'That's your list done. Anything else? Miss? Feeling all right are you?'

Recoiling from an inevitability she didn't want – couldn't bear – to contemplate, Jenefer gave Hannah her attention. 'I'm fine.' She made herself smile. 'Just trying to think of too many things at once. That's all for now, thank you. How's Percy?'

Hannah rolled her eyes. 'His chest is bad again. Had me up half the night with his coughing. Tried everything, I have. Butter, sugar and vinegar; honey and lemon juice in hot water. Bessie Richards said if I put sliced onions with layers of brown sugar and left the basin by the fire overnight it would make a syrup. Well, I done like she said and in the morning I gave Percy a couple of spoonfuls. But he couldn't stomach it. Mind you, his breath would have stripped paint.' She heaved a sigh. 'Last time he was took bad, Mrs Casvellan sent me a bottle of mixture with linseed, coltsfoot and liquorice in it. Worked wonders for 'n it did. And he liked the taste. But 'tis all gone and she haven't been in for weeks.'

'She's been really busy,' Jenefer said. 'You know what it's like at harvest time with all the extra workers to feed. When I see her would you like me to ask for another bottle?'

'Would you? I'd be some grateful,' Hannah said. 'If Percy isn't no better tonight I'm going to try a poultice. And if that don't work, he's going out in the shed.'

Jenefer laughed. 'Oh Hannah, I do sympathize. Though that's not much help.' Picking up her basket, knowing Hannah would add the cost of the groceries to her account, she turned to the door as it opened and two women entered.

As she started up the street she heard her name called. Recognizing William's voice, she fought reluctance as she stopped and waited for him to reach her.

'Good afternoon, William.'

He bowed. 'Miss Trevanion.' A blush flooded his face and turned the tips of his ears red. 'Jenefer. This is a happy surprise, and most opportune. May I escort you home?'

She sighed inwardly, and smiled. 'Thank you.'

'Allow me to take your basket. It looks much too heavy.'

Once more she reminded herself that his insistence on treating her as if she were fragile and helpless – when he must know she was neither – was well meant, and she forfeited nothing by accepting his offer. 'How kind.' She handed it to him.

As he felt the weight the shock on his face made her catch the inside of her lower lip between her teeth. She averted her head, laughter trembling in her chest.

'Miss Trevanion, Jenefer—?' He paused to clear his throat.

Exasperation replaced amusement as she turned on him. 'William, it really isn't necessary for you to address me with such formality. It is several months since I invited you to use my first name as a token of our friendship.'

'And I did – do – appreciate it. It's just' – his voice was low and intense as his complexion reddened – 'I cannot – nor should I – forget the peculiarity of your circumstances. You and I in our different ways have to be particularly careful regarding public perception. You must know I have always been deeply appreciative of your help regarding the school, and of your friendship. You cannot be in any doubt about my regard for you. And it is that regard, that fondness' – his gaze slid away and his face was now crimson, his upper lip beaded with perspiration

– 'which urges me to what you consider an unnecessary formality. But I must lead by example. And I would rather be thought stuffy and old-fashioned than offer you public insult by appearing over-familiar.'

Yet again Jenefer was torn between affection and sympathy for him and impatience at his pedantry. 'You are indeed most considerate, William. But—'

'Forgive me,' he cut in urgently. 'I know this is not the ideal time. But I have not seen you since last Sunday.'

'I've been particularly busy this week. No doubt you have too,' she said, stopping as they reached the alley leading to her cottage.

'Exactly. So now that I have your undivided attention,' – he gave a sweet, shy smile – 'I must take advantage.'

Sudden foreboding tightened Jenefer's stomach. 'William, I really don't think this is the time or place—'

He glanced round. 'There is no one to overhear.'

'Even so. . . .'

'I have no wish to make you uncomfortable, Miss— Jenefer, but I would be failing in my duty – '

Relief weakened her legs. Whatever he wished to say, it would not be a proposal of marriage. That she could have imagined William capable of such a spontaneous act was an indication of her turmoil. Since meeting Charles Polgray her emotions had grown more volatile with each passing day.

'Then by all means, William, do your duty and say what is in your mind.' Seeing the uncertainty in his expression she regretted the edge to her voice. The fact that she was tired was not a good enough excuse. He looked past her into the alley and she wondered if it was to ensure no one was coming, or because he wanted to accompany her to her door. He would not offer. He knew, as she did, that were her neighbours to see this particular attention they would inevitably assume the beginning of a deeper connection.

Charles Polgray had dined with her. Then they had worked alone in her kitchen until twilight.

William cleared his throat, regaining her attention. 'As a minister it is my duty to welcome Mr Polgray to Porthinnis. His contributions to village causes have been particularly welcome. First his donation to the school, then another yesterday to one of the overseers, Mr Hocking, to be used for the benefit of the village's poor and sick. Such generosity from a stranger is rare indeed.'

Jenefer had to look away, fearing he might wonder at the intensity of her pleasure. Let down by her father and the man he had arranged for her to marry, a man living a double life of which she had known nothing, she had become wary of trusting. But Charles Polgray was a man of his word.

'However,' William's tone snagged her attention, forcing her to concentrate. 'As someone with your best interests at heart I must question the wisdom of your . . . connection with this man who is, after all, a newcomer of whom we know nothing.'

Fighting anger that surprised her with its heat, Jenefer opened her mouth to point out how much benefit the village would gain from the harbour expansion. Just in time she remembered her promise to Charles not to speak of the project until he had the finance in place.

'What is it you wish to know, William? Mr Polgray inherited Pednbrose as my late father's heir. Knowing the speed at which news spreads in the village, I would be astonished if you were not already aware of that.'

William's cheeks coloured once more. 'Well, yes, I had heard. But that does not explain why he is still here. Or indeed why he has moved into Mr Trembath's property.'

Jenefer shrugged. 'Perhaps he intends to rebuild Pednbrose. You question the time I spend with Mr Polgray. As the school is closed during harvest, I have no pupils to teach. That aside, I should not need to remind you that I am answerable to no one but myself. Who I choose to see or spend my time with is no one else's business.'

'Please don't be angry with me. I have your best interests at heart.'

'Indeed?' Anger spiked as she eyed him. 'You are happy to accept Mr Polgray's donations. Yet you question his motives. I find such cynicism unbecoming.'

'And I fear,' he whispered fiercely, as emotion flamed his face and whitened his lips, 'you have been seduced by his wealth.'

Jenefer had reached the end of her patience. 'You insult me, sir,' she snapped, furious and indignant. 'I have no interest in anyone else's money. I am, as you well know, perfectly capable of supporting myself. Indeed I am proud to do so.' Taking her basket from his hand, she dropped a brief and very stiff curtsy. 'Good afternoon.'

As she turned away she glimpsed his face, now ashen and wretchedly miserable.

*

Charles laid down the pen and massaged his bandaged hand. He shouldn't be writing. Checking off the tasks completed, listing everything that still needed to be done, then rewriting the list in order of priority had seemed a sensible idea when he began. But as additional points occurred and needed inclusion, the end result was concern at the scale of the task he had undertaken and a renewed ache in his wrist.

Why had he not sent a note to Jenefer asking her to come? He always worked alone. He preferred doing whatever was necessary in the manner he considered best. He had no wish to be beholden to anyone. The time she had spent helping him must have delayed her own work.

All were legitimate reasons, but they weren't the real one. His desire to see her was a constant distracting ache. She was unlike any woman he had ever met. This strength of attraction to someone he had known for such a short time was deeply unnerving.

He had made one disastrous mistake: was he on the brink of making another?

By nature a solitary man, content in his own company, this physical attraction, the shock effect of her touch, his hunger to be near her, to hear her opinions, challenge her, make her laugh, had taken him completely by surprise.

She was *different*: hardly remarkable given her experiences in recent years. The ways in which she had risen above misfortune fascinated him. Yet he sensed in her a reserve, an indefinable sadness that made him want to comfort and protect. What right had he even to think of her in such terms? He pressed fingertips against a knot of tension in his forehead created by frustration, impatience and too little sleep.

The curate's interest was plain to see. He was a good man with laudable ambitions for his congregation. But Ince was not her equal and would not make her happy.

And you would? his conscience demanded. *You, who lie by omission every moment you spend in her company?* I gave my word. I cannot break it. *You are afraid.* Yes. I am. I cannot speak, but am condemned by my silence. I hardly know her, yet to lose her would be unbearable.

At the sound of the doorknocker he looked up. Perhaps it was the postman bringing replies to his letters. He recalled the meal they had shared after inspecting this house, their conversation, then her writing to his dictation until failing light and respect for her position demanded he leave. In the five days since, not an hour passed that he didn't think of her, wonder where she was and what she was doing.

He rubbed the back of his neck, glancing up at the sound of a tap on the door. It opened and the little maid bobbed a curtsy. Neat in her blue gown and white apron, her small face beneath its frilled cap was pink and serious.

'If you please, sir, Mr Vincent to see you.'

Shifting his chair back from the bureau where papers covered the baize-covered writing surface, Charles rose to his feet, adjusting his coat. 'Show him in, Ruth. And kindly tell Mrs Eustace we have a guest for dinner.'

'Yessir.' Bobbing another curtsy, Ruth scuttled out.

'Steven, my dear fellow, I am so pleased to see you.' Charles grasped his friend's outstretched hand and shook it firmly.

'And I you. What's this?' Steven eyed the bandage.

'A stupid accident. An owl spooked my horse and we parted company. It's just a sprain, but still damned inconvenient. Anyway, what brings you here? You know I'm always delighted to see you.'

'I have news. On two matters, actually.' Resting the leather satchel the back of a sofa, Steven unbuckled the flap. 'By the way, the house is delightfully situated. You have an excellent view of the harbour and village. How did you learn of it?'

'From Miss Trevanion's neighbour.' Just speaking her name made his blood quicken. 'She had heard I was looking for a property to rent and wondered if this might suit. I obtained the key, came up to inspect it, took advice regarding staff, and closed with the person acting as agent, all within two hours.'

Steven laughed. 'That was certainly decisive.'

'When something feels right . . .' Charles gave a brief shrug. 'It is, as you say, a delightful property and perfect for my needs. What news?'

Extracting an envelope sealed with red wax, Steven passed it across before seating himself on a sofa upholstered in green and cream striped brocade. 'If this is what I think it is, I knew you would want to see it as quickly as possible.' He laid the battered leather satchel on the floor by his feet.

Charles broke the seal and unfolded the sheet inside, frowning as he read. 'It's from Archdeaconry Court in Bodmin.'

'I guessed as much,' Steven said.

'I am requested to attend a hearing.'

'You will remember I warned of this possibility,' Steven reminded. 'As marriage is a status conferred by the church, only an ecclesiastical court can grant an annulment. When is the hearing?'

Charles paused by the window, re-reading the letter. 'Mid-November.' He blew a sigh of frustration. 'The timing is most inconvenient. Construction of the mole and the new arm will be underway by then. I should be here.' He turned, brandishing the letter. 'Why am I summoned? I'm petitioning for a declaration of Nullity on the grounds of concealment and fraud.' Bitterness burned like acid in his gut. 'Eve married me knowing she was already pregnant by another man. Is that not clear enough?' A thought struck him and he swung round in horror. 'You don't think— Surely she does not intend to contest?'

'Were that the case I'm sure the letter would have mentioned it. In any event, to forestall such an occurrence I asked for an additional copy of the statement you obtained from your wife's—'

'Don't call her that!' Charles snapped. 'She has no right to my name, or married status.'

'I beg your pardon,' Steven said quietly.

Seeing sympathy in his gaze, Charles flung himself into a chair still clutching the letter. 'No, it is I who should apologize. It's just—' *I have not seen Jenefer Trevanion for almost a week. That is as it should be. She has her business to run and I have mine. She is free. I am not. Yet with each passing day I miss her more.* He swallowed. 'There is a great deal to do here.' He studied the letter once more.

'Why must I travel to Bodmin when the court already has all the facts? I assume the copy you refer to is the doctor's statement declaring her pregnancy to pre-date our marriage by three months?'

Steven nodded. 'I hope this second copy won't be needed. But it's as well to be prepared. The doctor's statement will convince her parents that contesting would be futile, and should such an attempt become public, the result would be a scandal. Neither they, nor Eve, will want that.'

'Of course. Forgive me. I'm not— It has been a difficult week.'

'Nothing major, I hope?'

Charles shook his head. 'No, no. Just this.' he raised his bandaged hand. 'And waiting for replies to various enquiries. I thought you might be the postman bringing confirmation of an appointment with Ralph Daniell at the Cornish Bank in Truro. Steven, about the hearing: why have I been summoned?'

'So you can make your statement under oath to the court in person.'

'And that will be the end of it? I'll be free?'

'It may be a few days before you receive the decree. But essentially, yes. All being well that will be the end of it.'

Charles suppressed a deep shudder of relief. It could not come soon enough.

Steven shuffled papers. 'Now to my other news. It's about the mine. All is well,' he added quickly. 'The lode is yielding high quality copper and the price is continuing to rise. But two tributers came to see me yesterday. In case I didn't understand how the work was organized, they took care to explain that Polgray miners work in pares of between two and six men with each pare bidding for a pitch every two months on a profit-sharing system in lieu of wages.'

A brief smile quivered on Charles's mouth. 'Go on.'

'In your absence, on pay-days Edward Barton has been handing one man a cheque, drawn on his bank, for the money due to the whole pare. When they asked how they were to obtain change so the money could be shared out, he told them to go to The Bell inn where his son would cash the cheque for them. But not only did John Barton charge them commission for cashing the cheque, he also made it clear that if they wished this favour to continue they must buy a round of drinks.'

Charles was still, his anger ice-cold. 'How long has this been going on?'

'Four months.'

'Too long. Thank you for bringing it to my attention, Steven.'

'Would you like me to—?'

Charles shook his head. 'No. I will write to Edward Barton myself.

If he fails to pay each man in cash from the next accounting date, I will transfer all K & P's business to another bank. What was he thinking of? It's sharp practice, Steven, and totally unacceptable.' He put the matter aside. 'You'll stay for dinner?'

'I should be delighted.'

Charles enjoyed showing Steven over the house. Then, carrying a cut glass tumbler of fine whisky, they walked out through the French doors into the garden. Harry Tozer raised a forefinger to his cap as they passed, then returned to weeding an overgrown flowerbed. They walked through the gate onto the coast path and looked out over rocky coves to the sea.

'Injuring your wrist must have been dreadfully inconvenient,' Steven said. 'Especially now when there is so much paperwork.'

'It would have been,' Charles agreed. 'But for Miss Trevanion. Did I tell you Casvellan recommended her to me? He holds her in very high esteem.'

'I believe you mentioned it.'

Charles knew he should stop. But the opportunity to speak of her to the one person who knew the entire sordid story of his marriage, a man he knew he could trust, was impossible to resist. 'She is a most unusual person. In truth, I have never known anyone like her. Were you to meet her you would see for yourself.'

Steven was silent for a moment, gazing into his glass. Then he looked up, meeting Charles's gaze. 'Do I sense something warmer than mere gratitude?'

With a helpless shrug, Charles gulped a mouthful of whisky, glad of the spirit's burn in his throat and the smoky warmth curling in his stomach. 'In law and the eyes of the church, ' he said bitterly, 'I am still a married man. I have no right – for her sake I must not—'

He broke off, shaking his head. 'I'm damned if I tell her and damned if I don't.'

'Isn't it all a bit sudden?'

Charles's smile held little humour. 'It certainly took me by surprise. I wasn't expecting— Dammit!' The words burst from him with rare ferocity. 'If only—'

'Stop,' Steven interrupted. 'Regrets are pointless. Look to the future. In just a few short weeks you'll be free. Between now and then, as soon as the rest of the finance is in place, you'll be so busy the hearing will be upon you before you know it.'

Charles raised his glass in salute. 'You're a good friend, Steven.'

Draining their glasses they returned to the house.

Chapter Twelve

'All right, bird? 'Tis after one,' Lizzie said, entering with Jenefer's dinner on a tray. 'I done veal cutlets with green beans and carrots, and damson tart for afters.'

Jenefer dropped her pen and leaned back, flexing her shoulders and spine. 'It sounds lovely, and smells delicious.' Quickly closing and stacking ledgers, she gathered letters and invoices into a neat pile and set them aside. Then rising from the table she fetched cutlery and a napkin from the dresser as Lizzie set the plate and dish on the table then started towards the door.

'Lizzie? You're very quiet. Is anything wrong?'

'Just me being daft. Sam have took Will fishing. What worries me is they got to go so far out to catch anything. What if they're caught by one of they navy boats? 'Tisn't just that. This weather is bound to break soon. We always get storms in late October.'

'But if the storms are bad then none of the fishermen will be going out.'

''Xackly. Then Sam'll be home fretting because there's no money coming in.' Tucking the tray under her arm she flapped her free hand. 'Don't take no notice. I just got one on me today. You have your dinner. I'll see you d'rectly.'

Sitting down and unfolding her napkin, Jenefer wished she could tell Lizzie of Charles's plans, and the well paid work which – if they wanted it – would be available for Sam and Will. But she could not break her promise.

Yet she needed to know what was happening. If Charles were too busy to come to her, she would go to him. She had the perfect excuse: the two jars of quince jelly. With so much happening recently it had slipped her mind. But he had kept his promise to donate to village charities, now she must keep hers.

*

The front door opened. Neat in a blue and white check gown covered by a clean white apron, her hair tucked up into a mob cap, Ruth bobbed a curtsy, her anxious frown softening into a smile of welcome. 'Aft'noon, Miss Trevanion.'

'Good afternoon, Ruth. Is Mr Polgray at home?'

'He is, miss. If you'll step inside, I'll go and tell'n you're here.'

Leaning towards her Jenefer whispered, 'How very smart you look. Are you enjoying your new job?'

'Love it I do, miss. I ain't never been happier. And Aunt Cora – Mrs Eustace' she corrected herself quickly, 'is learning me to cook proper.'

'She is *teaching* you,' Jenefer correctly gently, 'you are learning.'

Ruth nodded, her eyes shining. 'I am too. I wish I could've come to the school. Only Mother needed me home. But coming here to work' – she heaved a sigh of pure happiness – ''tis like a dream come true.'

Making a mental note to ask Hannah about Ellen Collins's health, Jenefer said, 'No one would ever guess you have only recently taken up your position. Mrs Eustace must be very pleased with you.'

Before Ruth could respond, the sitting room door opened and Charles appeared. 'I thought I heard something.'

Blushing furiously, Ruth stammered, 'Miss Trevanion have come, sir.'

'So I see.' His tone was dry. 'Bring a tray of tea, will you?'

'Yessir,' Ruth bobbed, then scuttled back to the kitchen.

'Miss Trevanion,' Charles bowed, formality mocked by his smile.

'Mr Polgray,' Jenefer curtsied, gripping the handle of her basket in both hands as her heart skipped beneath her green velvet jacket.

'Please, come in.' He stood back, gesturing.

As she walked past, her shoulder almost brushing his chest, every nerve in her body was acutely aware of him. Her heart fluttered like a trapped bird and she swallowed, then moistened dry lips.

The room looked familiar but felt different. All the shutters were fastened back and light streamed in through the long windows. Jenefer imagined Cora and Ruth cleaning them with vinegar-soaked scrim cloths. Apple logs burning in the grate filled the air with fragrant warmth.

The last time she'd been here the furniture had been shrouded with Holland covers. Now she saw a pretty striped sofa and two high-backed armchairs. Between them a low dark-wood table had been polished to a shine.

An open walnut bureau stood against the wall, its writing surface piled with papers. Her gaze moved on past a glass-fronted bookcase and several small tables and tapestry-covered stools to rest for a moment on the spinet.

Hearing the door close she turned to face him, aware of heat climbing her throat to burn her cheeks. 'I brought—' she began.

'I'm so—' he said at the same time. They both stopped.

'Please,' he gestured. 'You first.'

She lifted her basket. 'I've brought the quince jelly. It's so long since – I just – I didn't want you to think I'd forgotten.'

'I was beginning to wonder.'

At the gleam of laughter in his gaze she relaxed. Nothing had changed. 'A promise is a promise.' Seating herself on the sofa she put the basket down by her feet and began to remove her gloves. 'How is your wrist? I see you have removed the bandage.'

He nodded. 'Much better. Though it aches like the devil when I try to write.'

'Why are you surprised? It's not yet a week since you sustained the injury. Anyway, you had only to ask; I would have – '

'It seemed unfair to burden you further with my work when you already have your own.'

Jenefer tucked her gloves into her basket. 'It's not a burden. Actually, I consider it a privilege.' She paused for an instant. 'How else will I find out what progress has been made?'

'Why, Miss Trevanion, are you chiding me for not keeping you informed?'

She tilted her head. 'How could you think me capable of such impertinence? But now that you mention it. . . .' She smiled.

'I have been trying to contain my impatience – unsuccessfully, I might add – while waiting for replies to the letters we wrote last week.

An hour ago the postman brought three, so your visit is well timed.'
As he crossed to the bureau there was a tentative knock and the door
opened.

Frowning with concentration Ruth carried in a tray containing a
pretty set of bone china decorated with flowers. Setting it on the low
table between the sofa and armchairs she hurried to the door.

'I'll be back d'reckly, sir. I just got to fetch t'other one.'

As Ruth disappeared, Jenefer caught Charles's eye. 'Other one?' she
mouthed.

'You'll see,' he muttered, returning to his chair with a handful of
papers as Ruth came in with a second tray containing a plate of shortbread, another of buttered scones, a glass dish of raspberry jam and a
fruit cake with two slices already cut.

'Thank you, Ruth,' As the girl gazed at him in mingled awe and
anxiety, Jenefer saw his quick kind smile. 'Please thank Mrs Eustace.
I'll ring the bell if I need anything else.'

Blushing deep rose, Ruth bobbed like a cork.

As the door closed behind her, Charles met Jenefer's gaze. 'I am
grateful for your recommendation. Apart from Mrs Eustace's determination to fatten me up, she is proving excellent in all respects. Her
niece has a lot to learn but appears very willing. But you know this
already.'

'I'm still happy to hear it from you.' She smiled. 'Cora is causing
Hannah Tresidder considerable frustration by refusing to relay any
information whatever concerning your staff and arrangements.'

Something changed in his eyes: a moment of frozen stillness. Then
he matched her smile, arching one dark brow.

'And what is Mrs Tresidder's interest?'

Dismissing her impression as simple surprise, Jenefer laughed. 'Are
you serious? Nothing happens in this village without Hannah hearing
of it. She has remarkably acute hearing, and people chat in the shop
while waiting to be served. You are a stranger recently arrived in our
midst. Now you have taken a house. Of course there is curiosity.'

He nodded. 'I hope soon to satisfy at least part of it.' Glancing up
from the papers he held he indicated the teapot. 'Would you be so
kind? My wrist – I'm too likely to drop something.'

'Of course.' As she leaned forward and placed the silver strainer over one of the cups she could see the fine tremor in her hand. She did not look up and he made no comment. She poured tea into the cup nearest him, adding the merest dash of milk and no sugar. Moving the cup and saucer within his reach she glanced up, met his gaze, and realized what she had done.

'Exactly as I like it,' he murmured.

'One of the benefits of a good memory,' she said lightly, then bent her head, hoping the brim of her hat hid her face as she poured her own. The cup rattled against her teeth, but the hot tea soothed her dry throat and calmed her nerves.

He offered the plate of shortbread. 'Please, you must have some-thing.' As Jenefer began to shake her head he added, 'You will not wish to hurt Mrs Eustace's feelings.'

Jenefer gave a gasp of laughter. 'That's blackmail.'

He nodded. 'It's desperation.'

Enjoying his teasing and recognizing the kindness beneath it, she took a piece of shortbread. 'You mentioned replies?'

'This one is from John Macadam,' he said, lifting a buttered scone. 'It concerns construction of the new road and is very detailed. I'm sure you don't—'

'I most certainly do.' Jenefer replaced her cup on its saucer. 'What does he suggest?' Her cheeks grew warm and she held her breath as he looked into her eyes.

'You really are the most. . . .' he began softly, then caught himself, cleared his throat and dropped his gaze to the paper in his hand. 'He advises firming the subsoil and shaping it to the finished camber, digging side ditches to drain the road bed, then applying a layer one foot thick of small broken granite between two and two and a half inches in diameter.'

Jenefer waited, then asked, 'Is that all?'

'What do you mean?'

'Well, does he not specify some kind of binding material?'

Charles shook his head, swallowing a mouthful of scone. 'None is necessary. Apparently dust created by the wheels of wagons grinding the stones together will fill all the gaps.'

She finished her shortbread and sipped her tea as he read letters from Mrs Crago at Talvan Quarry in Penryn confirming a supply of dressed granite blocks for the quay extension, and several tons of cheaper moorstone for the mole.

'This one' – he lifted the third letter – 'is from Penryn ship-broker Thomas Trenerry, quoting for shipments of two-inch granite stones at a very fair price.'

'Which will you build first?' Jenefer asked. 'Hopefully harvest will be finished within a few days, before the weather changes.'

'How do you know it's going to change? Are you a witch?'

Laughing, she shook her head. 'Late October always brings rain and gales. And once the weather breaks it will probably remain unsettled.'

'Then the sooner we can get the mole constructed the greater the protection for the quay. The problem is, I also need the new road as soon as possible so I can transfer our cargo business here from Hayle. I doubt the village will be able to supply enough labour.'

'Then why not ask the miners?'

'Miners?' he repeated blankly.

Jenefer nodded. 'They lost their jobs when the copper market collapsed. At least twenty have been coming in from outlying villages to help with the harvest, though being skilled men they loathe farm labour. I know some mines are pumping out in preparation for re-opening. But that will take time. Meanwhile these men still have to feed their families. I imagine many of them would be only too glad of any work you could offer.'

He studied her through narrowed eyes, his expression unreadable.

Unused to such scrutiny, and acutely self-conscious, she felt her skin grow hot. 'Is something wrong, Mr Polgray?'

He shook his head slowly. 'I was just wondering how I managed before I met you.'

Pleasure arrowed through her leaving a shimmering wake of pride. But just in case he had been teasing she nodded. 'It must have been difficult.' Seeing his mouth quiver as he tried to suppress a smile kindled a warm glow inside her.

'You have no idea,' he murmured.

Leaning down she lifted the two jars of quince jelly from her basket and placed them on the table, then rose to her feet.

Immediately he stood, a slight frown between his brows. 'Must you go?'

'I think it best,' she said quietly. 'I have been here over an hour.' Never had time sped by so swiftly.

'What has that to do – '

'Come now, Mr Polgray. Don't be obtuse. You cannot imagine my arrival here went unobserved?'

'I beg your pardon. Of course I understand. It's just—' Raking his hair, he gazed towards the window for a moment then turned to her. 'I shall walk you home.'

'It's kind of you to offer, but quite unnecessary.'

'Kindness, Miss Trevanion, has nothing to do with it. You say you must go, but there is another matter I need to discuss with you. And no, it won't wait. We can talk on the way. Excuse me. I will fetch my hat and gloves.'

Leaving the house, they passed Harry Tozer trimming back the overgrown hedge with a pair of shears. As they passed he paused, politely touched the brim of his cap, and immediately resumed his work. He didn't smirk or wink or betray the slightest interest, and for that Jenefer could have hugged him.

They walked side by side down the road towards the harbour. Though they did not touch, Jenefer was very aware of him beside her, deliberately slowing his stride to her pace.

'Miss Trevanion.' He cleared his throat. 'The letter I did not have time to read to you is from Mr Daniell.'

Jenefer looked at him quickly. 'Mr Ralph Daniell, the banker?'

He nodded. 'I have an appointment with him the day after tomorrow. And it occurred to me – that is, I was wondering if you might care to ride with me to Truro. You might enjoy the opportunity to do some shopping, or indeed,' he added quickly, 'pay a business call or two. Then we could have a late dinner and tell each other of our respective successes.'

She gazed at him, stunned by his invitation and wanting more than anything to accept. Then hot colour flooded her face as she wondered about his motive and hated herself for doubting him.

'You must be aware that the distance makes it impossible for us to return the same day.'

'Of course. But you may be assured of a comfortable private room at The Red Lion. I usually stay at The Bull, opposite the Coinagehall, as its popularity with mine owners and ship captains enables me to catch up with all the news. I would call for you after breakfast for our ride back to Helston.'

Weak with relief, Jenefer glanced up at him. 'I really appreciate you asking me, and I'm grateful for your consideration—'

'But,' he said, forestalling her. His expression had hardened, becoming withdrawn and aloof. Far from being intimidated, she smiled inwardly, knowing him better now.

'I would have liked nothing better than to accompany you,' she said, speaking from her heart. 'And were it only a matter of pleasing myself, I would happily set my work aside for two days. But harvest is almost finished and I promised to help Roz with the harvest dinner. Tamara – Mrs Varcoe – is soon to be confined so Roz will be short-handed. There is another reason: one I think you must recognize. My absence occurring at the same time as yours is sure to be noticed. Mrs Avers, Mrs Penkivell and others in their circle make frequent trips to Truro. Mrs Penkivell is not among my admirers and would enjoy nothing better than to spin a scandal out of seeing us together. The most important thing right now is the harbour expansion. That is the reason you are going to Truro. Gossip and scandal, no matter how unfounded, might cause problems. That is the last thing you need.'

He looked down at her. 'I should never have— It was selfish and thoughtless of me.'

'Sshh.' Jenefer touched his arm lightly. 'I can't go. But I'm not sorry you asked me.'

Reaching her cottage he remained on the threshold while she dropped her basket on the table and crouched to open the fire door on the range. Taking a spill from the pewter vase on the hearth she pushed it through the bars, shielded the flame with her cupped hand, and lit the candle left in readiness in the centre of the table. Then she returned to the open door where he waited.

'Thank you for escorting me home.'

'It was my pleasure. Perhaps, on my return from Truro. . . . He stopped and turned his head away, gazing across the cobbled yard to the stone wall and the gardens beyond.

As the silence stretched she took a breath. 'I know how important this meeting is so I'd very much appreciate hearing the outcome.

When you get back, if you have time, perhaps you might call? I'm usually here.' She shrugged. 'Most often found behind a stack of ledgers.' *Why didn't he say something?* Her skin prickled the way it did before a thunderstorm.

He turned back to her, his features taut. She waited. Suddenly the conflict that gripped him melted away.

'You may depend upon it.'

She nodded. 'Goodbye, then.'

He gazed at her for a moment then caught her right hand and raised it to his lips. Releasing it, he made a brief bow and strode briskly away, his boots loud and firm on the cobbles.

Closing the door, Jenefer leaned against the wood, cradling her right hand against her breast, still feeling the soft warmth of his mouth on her knuckles.

Her head told her she had done the right thing by declining. But her heart wished she were going with him. It was unlikely there would be another opportunity. If his meeting with the financier was successful, and for his sake and that of the village she hoped it was, then work would begin in earnest. His wrist was mending. Soon he would no longer need her help. She would miss—

A rapping on the door made her jump. 'You home, bird? George Laity come round earlier hoping to see you about some nets.'

With a sigh and a smile, Jenefer turned and lifted the latch. 'Yes, Lizzie, I'm home.'

Chapter Thirteen

Charles followed the black-clad clerk, mentally preparing himself for some tough negotiating. He had spent the previous evening reviewing projections of costs and income. Even by conservative estimates the expansion was a sound investment. Knowing this steadied him as the clerk knocked then opened a panelled door. 'Mr Polgray, sir.' He withdrew quietly, closing the door behind him.

Charles saw panelled walls, walnut armchairs, a Turkish carpet, and a tall cabinet with glass-fronted bookshelves. It was a comfortable well-appointed room equally conducive to business discussions or solitary thought.

A stocky man in his early forties whose brown hair was streaked with silver at the temples, Ralph Daniell rose from his chair behind a kneehole desk of burr walnut inlaid with dark green leather. His blue coat fitted perfectly and a diamond pin sparkled in the snowy folds of his neckcloth.

'Good morning to you, Mr Polgray.' His handshake was firm, his smile welcoming. 'Another lovely day. And fine weather is always good for business.'

'Indeed,' Charles agreed, glimpsing in Daniell's gaze the shrewd businessman behind the hearty façade.

'Please.' Daniell indicated a chair angled a short distance from his desk. As Charles sat, resting the leather satchel containing all his paperwork against the chair leg, Daniell resumed his own seat. Leaning back he supported his elbows on the arms of his chair and steepled his fingers. 'What can I do for you, Mr Polgray?'

Charles had outlined the expansion plan in his letter when requesting the meeting. He knew Daniell would have made enquiries before agreeing to see him, just as he had considered other possibilities before deciding to approach The Cornish Bank. The question appeared superfluous. But Charles had expected it.

Daniell would listen to the presentation then balance his impressions against his own assessment of the project and ability of the man behind it to bring it to fruition. In Daniell's place he would do exactly the same.

'As I wrote in my letter,' Charles spoke quietly and with confidence, 'I intend building port facilities and expanding Porthinnis harbour to handle exports of copper and imports of coal. My intention is also to increase two-way trade in general cargo. Our own company Kerrow & Polgray has already provided a proportion of the necessary capital. But I need more. What I am seeking from you is an unsecured loan of fifteen thousand pounds.'

'Over what period?'

'Three years.'

Daniell pursed his lips. 'The copper market is only just coming out of a major depression.'

Charles nodded, crossing his legs and resting his folded hands on his thigh. 'During which Kerrow & Polgray's copper and silver mines continued operating. Those that shut down and were allowed to fill with water will require weeks, perhaps months, of pumping out before work can resume. Meanwhile our mine is producing copper and the price of Cornish ore is climbing steadily.'

'True. However, my understanding is that Kerrow & Polgray is still burdened with the annual engine dues.' He raised a hand before Charles could speak. 'I'm aware they were halved during the worst of the depression to keep as many mines as possible in work. But with the price for copper ore rising, understandably Boulton & Watt are anxious to recoup the money they are owed. This means an increase in dues.'

Charles knew Ralph Daniell and his partners had invested heavily in Boulton & Watt's steam engines. They would have pressed hard for the increase.

'Under those circumstances,' Daniell continued, 'you must see that an unsecured loan is simply not possible.'

It had been worth a try. But, as he had never expected agreement,

Charles was not disappointed. Now the real bargaining would begin.

'So,' Daniell said, regarding him steadily, 'what security can you offer?'

'I have obtained a twenty-year renewable lease on the harbour. I'm willing to assign it to you.'

Daniell's brief gesture was dismissive. 'It will be of no value if the venture fails. I'm sure you understand my need to protect the bank's money.'

'And I want to build a thriving business. Despite the repayment of engine dues there is substantial money to be made in copper mining and smelting if the company is efficient. Kerrow & Polgray have an excellent reputation in that regard, as you will no doubt have learned.'

Daniell tipped his head, acknowledging the point.

'The expansion of Porthinnis harbour,' Charles continued, 'will provide long-term employment for a large portion of the local community. Naturally, they will be made aware of your assistance and interest in the venture.'

A smile flickered across Daniell's mouth. 'That would be greatly appreciated. But we are not philanthropists, Mr Polgray. You are asking us to take a considerable risk. That being the case, you must give us something in return.'

As Daniell paused, appearing to think, Charles knew what was coming. He knew because had their positions been reversed he would have made the same demand. He wished there might have been an alternative. But there wasn't.

'I understand you inherited an estate above the harbour,' Daniell said. 'Pednbrose? After receiving your letter I took the liberty of having the property valued and the sum mentioned was twelve thousand. So my proposal is this: I will lend you eight at nine per cent in return for which you assign the deeds of the estate to us. These will be restored to you when the loan is paid off in full.'

'In that case,' Charles said calmly, 'eight thousand is not enough. I want the full fifteen. You can have the deeds to the estate, plus the lease on the harbour.'

Daniell shook his head. 'The lease is no use to me. I'll take the deeds to the estate and increase my offer to ten, provided repayment is made in two years.'

'No, I can get ten thousand in two years anywhere with these.' Charles opened his leather satchel and withdrew a bundle of folded papers tied with thin red ribbon. Knowing Daniell would demand security against any loan he had collected them from Steven on his way here. 'My estate is worth twelve thousand and that's what I want. But I will accept two years.'

'I would have to put that to the board, and they would not accept it.'

Charles recognized the tactic and knew how to deal with it. 'I beg your pardon.' He was cool. 'I assumed you spoke for your board and were empowered to make the decision. If that is not the case, perhaps you would arrange for me to talk to those who can decide?'

The banker sat forward, resting his fingertips on the edge of the desk and looking slightly flushed. After shaking his head slowly he smiled and stood up. 'Twelve thousand in two years.' He offered his hand.

Charles paused as if considering the offer. But having done his research he knew this was the best deal he would get. He gave a decisive nod. 'You drive a hard bargain, Mr Daniell. But I accept your terms.' Rising from his chair he took the banker's hand.

'Then we have an agreement, Mr Polgray.'

Charles replaced the deeds in his satchel.

Daniell rubbed his hands together. 'I will have my lawyer prepare a document confirming the terms of our agreement. As a businessman yourself you will be aware that should you default on repayment my bank may sell the property to reclaim our money then give you the balance. The legalities will take several days to set up. So I suggest we meet here at the same time next week to sign the agreement, if that suits you?'

'Certainly.'

'A pleasure doing business with you, Mr Polgray,' Daniell said, escorting him to the door.

After a final handshake Charles left the banker's office with a spring in his step. He enjoyed the cut and thrust of negotiating. Obtaining only £12,000 instead of the full £15,000 meant he was short, though not disastrously so. But now he was sure of the funding it was essential to get the work underway as soon as possible. He needed to get income flowing and start paying off the loan.

He strode swiftly towards The Bull where Cyrus Keat waited. Meeting him the previous evening and learning he had been employed as clerk of works on a recently completed harbour expansion in north Cornwall, Charles's impression of the man had been favourable. After Keat left, agreeing to return the following midday, discreet enquiries of the landlord who knew far more about his customers than they realized, had confirmed Charles's own impression. Now the money had been agreed, he planned to offer Keat the post of clerk of works to start in two days' time. Then after a drink and something to eat he would leave for Porthinnis.

His position with Kerrow & Polgray had required him to travel to wherever he was needed. Enjoying the challenge and changes of scene, he had never minded what some might have considered loneliness. Indeed he preferred to rely solely on himself. He knew this to be a legacy from his motherless childhood. His father's response to the loss of his wife had been to send his son off to boarding school so he might concentrate on the business.

Having effectively lost both parents, Charles suffered a wretched few months before finding salvation in his studies. High marks won his father's approval and, eventually, the offer of a position in the company.

After startling both partners by stating the conditions of his accept-ance, he had carved a niche for himself that proved invaluable to K&P while allowing him to retain the freedom to do the job as he saw fit.

He had spent twenty years comfortable with his own company. His short-lived marriage and the complex process of annulling it had made solitude even more appealing. So he was shaken by the strength of his desire to share the morning's events with Jenefer Trevanion.

*

'Are you sure you can manage?' Jenefer asked Tamara as they followed the path to Trescowe's rear entrance. Each carried a large rice pudding baked golden brown with sugar and nutmeg.

'Of course I can. Don't fuss, Jenna,' Tamara chided, her smile wry. 'I get enough of that from my mother.'

'She seems very solicitous.' Jenefer saw temper flash in Tamara's eyes.

'That is not concern for me; she simply wants to prove her influence is greater than that of my husband. Which it isn't and never will be.' She blew a gusty sigh. 'Mama has never really forgiven me for marrying Devlin.'

'But she appeared delighted,' Jenefer said.

Tamara grinned. 'That was relief. After all, I was carrying Devlin's son. Imagine the scandal. Certainly she is thrilled with his position as Mr Casvellan's bailiff. Devlin is polite to her for my sake, but he will not tolerate her attempts to interfere.'

'Will she still be there when you get home?'

Tamara pulled a face. 'Probably, unless Devlin gets back before I do. I hope he does for she will leave at once. My condition forbids me going to the dance, but I'd have hated to miss the harvest dinner as well.'

'I know. But—'

The sound of tramping feet and laughter reached them on the breeze. 'You go on,' Tamara urged. 'Warn Roz.'

'They're on their way,' Jenefer shouted above the clatter as she entered the big kitchen.

'Did you persuade Tamara to stay at home?' Roz's face was flushed from the heat of the cooking range.

Jenefer set the pudding down on a table crowded with brimming platters and bowls. 'Her mother is there, and nagging her to death.'

'Then we must find her something to do sitting down.'

As Tamara waddled in Roz hurried to her, took the pudding and passed it to Jenefer who found a space on the table.

'Tamara, may I ask a favour? Would you mind watching the children? Make sure they have enough to eat and drink, and the smaller ones aren't bullied or left out?'

'You want me to sit in comfort while the rest of you rush about, fetching and carrying?'

Roz's blush deepened and Jenefer rolled her eyes heavenward.

Tamara laughed. 'Of course I will.'

'We just want to take of you.' Roz patted her arm gently. 'That's my godchild you are carrying.'

'True,' Jenefer agreed. 'But there's a far more important reason.' Seeing Tamara's bafflement, she pulled a face. 'We're terrified of Devlin.'

'They're here,' Margaret called above the racket of voices and booted feet as the harvest labourers entered the yard. Jenefer heard the squeak of the pump handle followed by splashing water.

Tucking a stray curl into her cap, Roz went out to greet them.

During the next hour Jenefer, Roz, Margaret and Sarah hurried between hearth and table. As reserve evaporated, voices grew louder and laughter more uproarious.

Needing escape, Jenefer carried a trayload of dirty plates to the scullery. Fastening an old Hessian towser over the white cotton apron Roz had supplied, she filled the sink with hot water from the copper, added lye soap, and began washing the plates and cutlery.

'Here, miss, you shouldn't be doing that!' Margaret gasped, horrified.

'Yes, I should. You'll need them for the puddings. Besides, while it's lovely to hear everyone enjoying themselves, I'm not used to so much noise.'

'Making some racket, aren't they?' Clicking her tongue, Margaret smiled. 'Be even noisier at the dance.'

'Will you be going?'

'Wouldn't miss it for the world. Look, why don't you let me—'

'I'll tell you what would really help,' Jenefer interrupted with a smile. 'More water to top up the copper.'

'If you're sure. But it don't seem right, you doing this.'

'I worked in the fish cellars, Margaret,' Jenefer reminded her. 'Now I run a business. There are people in the village who consider me quite *im*proper.'

'Well,' Margaret tossed her head. 'More fool them, that's all I can say.' Reaching for the buckets she scurried out to the pump.

Touched, Jenefer plunged her hands back into the hot soapy water. Where was Charles now? Had his meeting been successful? Was he still in Truro, or on his way back? Would he arrive in time for the dance tonight?

Sarah came into the scullery carrying another tray piled high with plates and cutlery. 'God a'mighty, miss! You shouldn't be doing that. Where's Margaret?'

'In the yard fetching water. We've already had that argument and I won.'

Setting the tray down, Sarah snatched up a cloth and began wiping plates. 'Missus need 'em for the puddings.'

'How is Mrs Varcoe coping with the children?'

'Got some way with her, she have,' Sarah said. 'Looked like there might be a bit of trouble with a couple of the bigger boys. But she told them to behave, or they could eat their dinner in the barn. Then she started telling the young ones about the great storm. How it blew roofs and chimneys away and broke down the harbour wall. Hanging on her every word they are, with eyes big as saucers.'

As Margaret clanked in with the buckets, Sarah returned with her tray of clean plates to the kitchen.

*

It was after five and the light was beginning to fade as Jenefer slid down from the cob's back and led him towards the stable in Harry Rollason's yard. The butcher emerged from the back of his shop still swathed in a blood stained apron.

'Just put the bar across, miss. I'll send the boy to unsaddle 'n.'

'That's kind of you, Mr Rollason. I'm running a little late.'

'Dinner all right, was it?'

Slotting the broad wooden plank into place, Jenefer left the stable. 'It was a great success. There was enough food to feed an army, and the workers ate like one. But I daresay by the time they've walked home and got changed then walked down to The Standard and danced for an hour or two they'll be ready to do justice to the harvest supper.'

'Shall us see you there?' he grinned.

'You certainly will. With such a good harvest this year we have plenty to celebrate.' She started towards the gate.

'Here,' he called after her, 'I know what I was going to ask you. How's mister settling in up Kegwyn?'

'Very well, I believe. But it's him you should ask, not me.'

'I'll do that. Be there tonight, will he?'

'I have no idea,' Jenefer said cheerfully. They both knew he was fishing. He would have heard she had accompanied Charles Polgray to view Kegwyn. Now he was curious about the exact nature of their relationship. *She wished she knew.* Giving him a wave, she left the yard and walked down the hill towards home.

Would Charles be at the dance tonight? She really hoped so. She had missed him.

As Jenefer opened her door, Lizzie came out of her cottage, wiping her hands on her apron.

'Go all right, did it, bird?'

'It was like feeding the five thousand, Lizzie. I've never seen so much food vanish in so short a time. But they certainly earned it. Speaking of food, what have you made for tonight?'

'Two squab pies and two apple tarts. Cooling now they are.'

Lizzie's squab pies: layers of bacon, apple, onion and mutton with a little cream added for moisture and richness, all encased in shortcrust pastry, were a welcome addition to every village supper.

'I made a dozen scones this morning,' Jenefer said. 'I'll take butter and two jars of strawberry jam to spread when I get there.'

'You'll do no such thing! 'Tis Susan Mitchell's turn for organizing the supper. You know what she's like.'

'Ah,' Jenefer nodded.

'Get teasy as an adder she would if you tried to help. Just give her the basket and leave her do it. Oh, 'fore I forget,' Lizzie said, 'mister called to see you.'

Jenefer's heart leapt. She tried to speak but no sound emerged. She cleared her throat. 'When?'

'About half an hour ago 't was. He said he was on his way home from Truro.'

That he was already thinking of Kegwyn as *home* made her feel warm inside. 'Did he—?'

'I could see he wanted to ask but didn't like to.' Lizzie nodded. 'So I put 'n out of his misery. I said you was up Trescowe helping with the harvest dinner, but you'd be home before dark. Then seeing he was here I thought I might as well ask 'n.'

'Ask him what?'

'If he's going to the dance.'

'Lizzie!' Jenefer gasped, startled and delighted.

'He said he would if you'd go with 'n. Well, you can't blame the man for not wanting to walk in by hisself. They'll all be gawping at 'n as it is. Anyhow, he said to tell you he'd come by about seven. So you'd better go on in and get yourself changed.'

JANE JACKSON

'Thank you.' Jenefer planted a kiss on her neighbour's cheek.

'Dear life! What's that for?' Lizzie tossed her head pretending impatience, and went back into her cottage.

Closing her door, Jenefer crossed to the range. Stirring the embers into life she added a small shovel of coal from the scuttle then pulled the big black kettle over the flames. Pulling off her hat, she unbuttoned her jacket as she ran up the steep wooden stairs to her bedroom. Her heart beat faster. Charles was taking her to the dance. Flinging her hat and jacket onto the counterpane, she opened her wardrobe. What should she wear?

Chapter Fourteen

Jenefer dabbed a little rose water on her wrists and throat, then fastened around her neck the single strand of pearls that had belonged to her mother. She wished – but stopped the thought before she could complete it. Wishing could not change the past, and time spent looking back was precious time lost. Tonight she was happy. Though *happy* was far too weak and colourless a description for what she felt. Joyful anticipation bubbled inside her like sparkling wine.

Stepping back she examined her reflection. Her gown of rose-pink figured muslin had a wide neckline, short puffed sleeves and a high waist with the fullness of the skirts concentrated at the sides and centre back. Her white silk stockings were held in place by garters above the knee and on her feet she wore white kid slippers, each adorned with two pink silk rosebuds that matched her dress.

After brushing her hair until it shone, she had gathered it into a coil pinned high on her crown. Damping the tendrils in front of her ears she twisted them around her finger into loose curls, grateful for naturally wavy hair that spared her the need for heated tongs or the discomfort of trying to sleep with a headful of rags.

Fetching a long cloak of dark-green wool lined with cream silk from the wardrobe, she took one final look at her image. Rosy colour in her cheeks made pinching them unnecessary, and her eyes had a definite shine. A knock on the door made her start.

Catching her breath as excitement zinged along her nerves, she ran lightly down the stairs. She dropped her cloak over the back of a chair and crossed to the door, pausing for an instant to draw a deep breath before opening it. Charles stood on the threshold. Seeing her he immediately removed his hat.

'Miss Trevanion.' Though his bow was a perfectly judged politeness, his eyes gleamed in the candlelight and the corners of his mouth tilted upward.

She matched his formality, bobbing a demure curtsy while her heart quickened at the contrast between his reserved manner and the warmth in his eyes. 'Good evening, Mr Polgray.' She stepped back. 'Please, come in.'

Bending his head to avoid the low lintel, he straightened up and she felt his gaze like the brush of fingertips as it swept from her hair to her slippers before returning to her face. 'You look . . . beautiful,' he said softly.

Buoyed by delight she felt as if she were floating. 'Thank you.' Closing the door she turned to him. 'Please forgive me, but I must ask for I have found it hard to think of anything else. Was your meeting with Mr Daniell successful?'

In the candlelight she saw surprise and pleasure flare in his eyes. Then he nodded. 'It was. He has agreed to advance most of the fifteen thousand.'

Jenefer clasped her hands together. 'I'm so pleased for you. Though with such a sound investment he could hardly have turned you down.' She paused. 'You said most. What is the shortfall?'

'Three thousand.'

She nodded. 'That's not too bad. I don't suppose you expected to obtain the full amount anyway.'

'How did you—? Of course. No doubt you receive requests for financial investment every day.'

'Not quite that often,' she demurred. 'And certainly not for the sums you are accustomed to.'

'I'm curious, have you ever agreed to advance the full sum asked for?'

'Yes, but only in a few exceptional cases. What was your opinion of Mr Daniell?'

'Shrewd and hard, but not unfair.' Charles held her gaze. 'He requires the deeds to Pednbrose as security.'

Jenefer absorbed the implications. Then shrugging lightly she nodded. 'In his place I'd have done the same. What time period did he stipulate?'

'Two years. His original offer was for eight thousand repayable in three.'

'But that wouldn't have been anything like enough.'

'I know,' he reminded gently.

Jenefer pulled a wry face. 'I beg your pardon. Of course you do.'

'Anyway, after some further negotiating we settled at twelve repayable in two. I return to Truro next week to sign the agreement and give him the deeds to the property. Now the money is finally in place work can begin. My plan is to have it completed and operational in six months. That will leave me the remaining eighteen months to repay the loan. But to achieve that I shall have to improve profitability by—'

'Eight thousand a year,' Jenefer said. 'Then why not tell the villagers of your plans tonight? It's one of the rare occasions when the whole village gets together. Now the harvest is over many have no work. Truly, Charles, tonight would be the ideal opportunity to make your announcement.'

She saw his brows lift and realized that in her excitement she had used his first name. Before she could cover her gaffe he caught her hand between his and raised it to his lips.

'Then tonight it is.' He lowered her hand but did not release it and the warm strength of his fingers curled around hers created a sensation at the base of her throat like softly beating wings. 'I am used to working alone.' His tone was soft and bemused. 'I never ever imagined— But talking to you—' He shook his head. 'Forgive me, I'm rambling.'

'You're not. It's the same for me.' His fingers tightened on hers and her heart lifted.

'You are more familiar with these gatherings than I am,' he said. 'When do you think would be the most suitable time?'

She thought for a moment, thrilled that he should ask. 'When supper is announced. That's when people mingle and chat, and there are bound to be questions.' Awareness of their linked hands, of his nearness, made her quiver inside. 'By then everyone will have become used to your presence. If you wish, I can introduce you to different people so you will be seen as approachable.'

He raised her hand again, his lips grazing her knuckles. 'Jenefer.' He spoke her name softly and for the first time.

Something turned over inside her. 'Yes?'

'You have so many facets,' he murmured. 'When I came to Porthinnis I never imagined— Meeting you at Trescowe. . . .' He shook his head and a crease appeared between his brows. 'I wasn't – I didn't expect—'

'Nor did I.' That his reactions echoed her own touched her deeply.

'Jenefer, we need to talk. But—'

She slanted him a wry look. 'This is not the time?'

Releasing her hand he picked up her cloak and held it open. She turned her back and he set it gently around her shoulders. His hands rested there for a moment and she sensed he was about to speak. But he didn't, moving away instead. He put on his hat then opened the door. Reaching for her basket containing the scones, butter and jam, she blew out the candles.

The sky was clear and filled with stars, the night air cold enough to make her glad of her warm cloak.

As they set off up the cobbled yard he drew her hand through his arm. 'I cannot have you fall. How would I manage? You are quite literally my right hand.'

He heard the smile in her voice. 'You no longer need the bandage?'

'Not tonight.' In truth, his wrist ached like the devil. But he knew the importance of first impressions and had no intention of betraying weakness. 'I want people's attention focused on the benefits of the development, not on me. While I was in Truro I did have one excellent stroke of good fortune.'

'Oh?' He heard the eagerness in her voice, the quick interest.

'I met a man named Cyrus Keat, and have hired him as my clerk of works.'

'Goodness, he must have impressed you.'

'He did, especially as he recently held the same position on a recently-completed harbour expansion in North Cornwall.'

'Really?'

'Really. The letter of commendation from his previous employer was most impressive. But I wanted to be sure. So I made my own enquiries of various acquaintances. Everything I learned convinced me he would be a valuable asset.' He felt the pressure of Jenefer's fingers as she briefly squeezed his arm.

There was a short silence. 'I imagine this means you will no longer need me.'

I will always need you. He bit the words back just in time. He had no right to say them: not yet. But as soon as he was free there was so much he would tell her. How meeting her had changed his life; how much she meant to him; how deeply he had been shaken by the realization that he – previously content with solitude – wanted her by his side, in his heart and in his bed for as long as they lived.

He cleared a sudden thickness from his throat, and looked down at her. 'On the contrary. Mr Keat's job is to manage the practicalities: overseeing the men, ensuring they have the tools and materials they need, keeping a close watch on progress and dealing with any problems that arise. Meanwhile I retain control of planning, quantity estimates, ordering materials, finance and overall supervision.'

'It must have been such a relief to find a man of experience. I'm so pleased for you.'

'Not as pleased as I am,' he said drily. 'However, if you could continue assisting me with correspondence and financial paperwork, I would be truly grateful.' Where her hand rested on his forearm he covered it with his own. 'Can you? Will you?'

The buzz of conversation and laughter grew louder as they passed The Standard's main entrance and walked round to the side. An oil lamp hung over the lintel and the open double doors were fastened back.

She lifted her face. In the lamplight her eyes gleamed and he saw she was smiling. 'I should like that above all things.' Reluctantly he released her arm and allowed her to precede him.

Candles burned in holders all around the walls and Jenefer saw the room was already half full of people.

'George will take your hat,' she told Charles as she removed her cloak and passed it to the young man standing in the doorway to a small anteroom lined with rows of wooden pegs.

'Will I ever get it back?' he murmured in her ear, making her skin prickle. But he handed it over.

'Oh yes,' she nodded. 'George has an excellent memory.' She picked up her basket and they moved towards two long trestle tables.

Three women were busy setting out quantities of food. Platters of cold beef, chicken and mutton were flanked by dishes of chutney and pickles. Herby pies, leek pies, and Lizzie's squab pies had been sliced and arranged on large plates. Alongside plates of buttered bread were apple tarts, plum tarts and squares of *hevva* cake.

'All right, miss?' Jenefer's other neighbour beamed at her from one end of the table where she was spreading jam on halved scones then topping them with a spoonful of thick clotted cream. At the other end a stout middle-aged woman wearing a white kerchief over a maroon gown was busily directing the placing of laden dishes and plates as more women arrived with their contributions.

'Hello, Ernestine.' Jenefer handed over the basket. 'I'm not sure you'll need these.'

Peering into the basket, Ernestine gave a decisive nod. 'Don't you b'lieve it. Go like snow in sunshine this lot will.' She darted a shy glance at Charles.

'I don't think you've met Mr Polgray,' Jenefer said. 'Charles, this is my good friend and neighbour, Miss Rowse.'

'I'm delighted to make your acquaintance, Miss Rowse.'

As Charles bowed, Ernestine's sallow complexion turned bright pink and she bobbed an awkward curtsy. 'I heard you're up Kegwyn living. Like it up there, do you?'

'Very much.'

Ernestine lifted out the scones, butter and jam. 'Don't you worry about your basket,' she said to Jenefer. 'I'll bring 'n home and give 'n to 'e tomorrow.'

'Thank you, Ernestine.'

As she and Charles turned away, Jenefer saw more people thronging through the door. Carrying baskets or plates wrapped in clean cloths, women headed towards the tables.

'It's less crowded over on the other side,' Jenefer said.

'If you say so,' Charles murmured, taking her elbow and guiding her through milling people exchanging greetings, news and gossip. 'We are being watched,' he whispered.

'Naturally,' Jenefer whispered back. 'You cannot have expected otherwise. Just smile and look as if you are delighted to be here.'

'You make it sound so simple,' he murmured, and his warm breath on her cheek made her stomach quake.

She slanted a wry glance at him. 'The more you practise the easier it becomes. I have considerable experience in this matter.'

His fingers tightened momentarily on her arm: a brief gesture that told her he understood. She should have realized he would. The more they talked the more she felt they shared a bond that ran deeper than words. It defied explanation, because there was still so much she did not know and had yet to learn about him. But as he had said, now was not the time. As they reached the far side the musicians played a chord.

Doctor Avers, Mr Penkivell and other gentlemen accompanied by their wives and daughters had gathered in a group. Like Charles, the gentlemen wore black coats, white breeches, white stockings and black shoes with silver buckles. But none of them was as handsome, nor, despite their self-importance and Charles's reserve, did they have a fraction of his presence.

The older ladies were expensively clad in silk and lace of every shade from emerald and crimson to lilac and primrose. Some had covered their hair with matching turbans decorated with spangles and feathers. Others favoured bandeaux of pleated chiffon and jewelled pins. Their daughters wore embroidered or figured muslin with silk flowers entwined in their ringlets. They whispered and twittered, surveying the room from behind fluttering fans.

Many of the village women had given an old gown a fresh look with a bright sash or a pleated kerchief. The younger girls wore coloured ribbons that matched their dresses.

Then Jenefer saw William making his way through the crowd, smiling and exchanging greetings as he passed. He reached the stage. Standing in front of it he raised his hands. Gradually the crowd fell silent.

'Ladies and gentlemen, friends. Welcome. With your permission I should like to begin this evening's celebration with a short prayer.'

Jenefer compressed her lips on a smile. *With your permission*. Had William not entered the church he could surely have entered politics or become a diplomat, for just saying those words made it impossible for anyone to object.

'Let us pray.' He waited a few seconds for complete silence. 'Dear Lord, we thank you for your bountiful blessings; for the harvest now safely gathered in, and for the gift of fellowship we share here tonight.

Amen.' As heads lifted Jenefer saw people nod and exchange approving glances. They appreciated brevity on such occasions.

William spread his arms wide. 'Let the dancing commence. We will begin with' – he glanced over his shoulder and the violinist leaned down and murmured – 'The Barley Mow,' William announced.

As couples moved to take their places Jenefer saw William scanning the crowd. Fearing she might be the person he was looking for, she turned to Charles. 'It will be at least an hour before supper is called, so—'

'Will you do me the honour of dancing with me?'

Delight shivered down her spine but Jenefer hesitated. 'Are you sure? We will be closely observed.'

He nodded. 'We will be anyway. But if I am to win over the villagers it is not enough that I am seen. Nor can I simply stand and watch, for I might be thought to consider myself above the company. I must take part.'

'And that is why you asked me?' Jenefer enquired drily.

'No,' he said softly, his gaze holding hers. 'Everything I said is true. But I asked because . . . because I very much want to dance with you.'

As her heart did a slow sommersault Jenefer felt a blush climb her throat. She could feel her face glowing. *What would people think?* Whatever they wished. Other people's opinions were outside her control.

'What are you thinking?' Charles murmured as they came together in the dance.

'It would take too long to tell you,' she smiled up at him before whirling away.

'Then be brief,' he demanded, as their paths crossed again.

She lifted one shoulder. 'I'm happy.'

A shadow crossed his face and in that instant she thought she glimpsed . . . *anguish? Guilt?* Then his features softened as he smiled. 'No one deserves it more.' The yearning in his gaze made her heart swell, and she swiftly dismissed her earlier impression as a trick of the light.

'Whom should I meet first?' Charles whispered as he escorted her from the floor at the end of the dance.

'Doctor Avers and Mr Penkivell and their families. Then I'll introduce you to Mr Gillis. He owns a boatyard at the top of the beach. He's a lovely man. Unfortunately, his wife. . . .' As he bent his head to catch her whisper, she breathed in the faint fragrance of soap and warm skin. Her senses swam.

'Gillis? Isn't their daughter—?'

'Married to Devlin Varcoe, Mr Casvellan's bailiff. Tamara and Roz are my closest friends. However, Mrs Gillis is not the easiest of women.'

'I appreciate the warning.'

During the next hour Jenefer made introductions, and when courtesy demanded that Charles dance with wives or daughters, she stood up with the gentlemen. But this required her to politely deflect questions that verged on impertinence. And, as she moved through the figures of the dance, she kept catching sight of William watching her.

It was with a sigh of relief that she heard supper announced. Her face ached with the effort of maintaining a smile while she fought an urge to give Mr Penkivell the set-down he deserved.

Leading her to a chair, Charles disappeared, returning a few minutes later with a plate of food.

'What about you? Aren't you hungry?'

He shook his head. 'I'll fetch you a drink. What would you like?'

Her throat was parched. 'Lemonade, please.'

She watched him cross the room, noticed others watching him then whispering to each other, their curiosity plain. He returned with a glass of lemonade for her and a tankard of ale for himself.

Taking a mouthful of the cool tart liquid that slid like nectar down her throat, Jenefer looked up. 'When will you tell them?'

Lifting his tankard, Charles swallowed deeply then bent to place it beneath her chair. 'Now,' he said, straightening up. Making his way to the dais on which the musicians were playing softly he spoke to the leader. A chord was struck and people turned to look. Charles stood calmly, waiting for silence.

'Good evening, ladies and gentlemen. My name is Polgray. Please forgive my interrupting your supper, but I wanted to take this opportunity to tell you about a project that will benefit the whole village. I intend to expand the harbour and increase the number and size of ships using the quays.'

'What do that mean, expanding the harbour? What are 'e going to do to 'n?' A voice called from the crowd. As some glanced round to see who had spoken, others nodded, glad someone else had asked the question uppermost in all their minds.

'Increasing the length of the western quay by a hundred feet will partially enclose the harbour and provide a safe haven for the fishing boats during rough winter weather.' This time nods were accompanied by murmurs of approval. 'A new road will be constructed across the waste ground at the back of the quay linking the harbour to the main road so that the wagonloads of ore need not pass through the village.'

'You can't put no road down there,' someone objected. ''Tis too steep.'

Arguments broke out. Charles raised his hands again and the protesters were shushed. 'You are quite right. It would not be safe, or indeed possible, to drive a team down such a slope. To overcome that there will be a pulley system anchored at the top. Unhitched from its team, the wagon will be attached to a stout rope on a large drum and lowered down the road. A strong brake will control the speed of descent, and the weight of the full wagon going down would pull an empty wagon back up to the top.'

During the silence while everyone tried to picture this arrangement, Charles continued, 'In addition to the road and the quay extension, I also intend building a free-standing mole fifty yards seaward from harbour entrance. This will absorb the force of storm waves and thus protect the new quay and the harbour.'

'Dear life!' An elderly man spoke up. 'That's some plan all right.'

Another man asked, 'How long is all this going to take?'

'My intention,' Charles said, 'is to have it completed within six months. But if I am to achieve that I shall need stonemasons, carpenters and labourers. There will be work for every man who wants it. After the expansion is complete, increased cargo traffic through the harbour will provide regular work.'

'What cargo is that, then?' Jenefer could see the man who had asked. Though his tone was sceptical, his expression, and those of the men around him, betrayed hope and a wish to be convinced.

Again Charles waited until the excited buzz of conversation died away. 'Kerrow & Polgray, a company founded nearly forty years ago by my father and his cousin, owns a silver mine in Helston, and a highly productive copper mine near Wendron. Until now we have shipped copper ore to our smelter in South Wales from Hayle harbour. This business, plus imports of coal and wood, will be transferred from Hayle to Porthinnis. You will earn fair pay in return for hard work.'

He paused, taking time to look around the room and everyone in it. 'The thought of change is unsettling. Even change for the better. But increased trade will bring greater prosperity to everyone in the village. I will be down at the quay at eight o'clock on Monday morning to sign up any man interested. Thank you for your attention. Enjoy the rest of the evening.'

As the buzz of conversation exploded into a roar, Jenefer watched him come towards her. 'Congratulations,' she whispered, handing him his ale. After two deep swallows he lowered the tankard.

'Have I persuaded them?'

She nodded. 'No doubt of it. How could you not? There may be resistance from a few die-hards who would prefer to see the village fall into dereliction rather than embrace change. But once the work is underway and they can see what you intend, I'm sure even their resistance will crumble.'

A few minutes later the musicians struck up once more. And as dancing resumed people gathered into groups that expanded, broke and reformed to further discuss the plans.

Seeing Dr Avers and Mr Penkivell approaching, clearly intent on a conversation with Charles, Jenefer politely drew back. Mr Penkivell demanded to know if Mr Casvellan was aware of these ambitious plans.

'Of course,' Charles responded coolly. 'We discussed them at length when I first came to the village.'

'What is his opinion?' Dr Avers enquired.

'As he expressed an interest in becoming a shareholder, I must assume he is very much in favour.'

Biting her lip as she struggled to hide a smile, Jenefer turned and came face to face with William.

His normally pale face was flushed. He bowed. 'May I have the pleasure of the next dance?'

Though she would have preferred to remain with Charles she could not in all conscience refuse. With a curtsy she placed her gloved hand in his. As they moved to take their place in the line he lowered his voice so only she could hear.

'Miss – Jenefer, I want you to know that what I am about to say is motivated by the very best of intentions.'

Irritation stirred like a creature roused from sleep. But she made herself smile as she glanced sideways at him. 'Goodness, William, that sounds ominous. Perhaps you might prefer to think again?'

'Believe me, I have thought most carefully, and can see no alternative but to question the wisdom of your deepening involvement with Mr Polgray.'

As the figure separated them, rage flooded her body with heat. Rejoining the set, his grip on her hand was limp and tentative as they stepped forward then back. Tempted to give him a set-down for his presumption in questioning her behaviour, she contained it behind clenched teeth.

'Were you not listening to what he said, William?' she enquired. 'And if you were, surely you must see how much this project will benefit the village?' Knowing he would interpret her anger as proof that he was right and she was wrong she swallowed it down and drew a slow deliberate breath.

'Now the harvest is finished, men are in desperate need of the work Mr Polgray can offer. I am astonished at your failure to recognize this.' The dance ended. William opened his mouth. But Jenefer was in no mood to hear more. 'Please excuse me.' With the briefest of curtsies she turned from him and saw Charles on the far side of the room. As his gaze met hers the crowd and the noise faded away, and there was only him.

Bending his head as she reached his side he murmured, 'I missed you.'

She forced a smile and knew instantly that he had seen through it.

'You are tired. Come, I will walk you home.'

'Thank you, but you had far better stay here and— '

Cupping her elbow he guided her towards the door. 'It was less an offer than a statement of intent. As for talking to people, I shall have plenty of opportunity during the months ahead. But tonight they will be happier talking to each other.'

He was right. Beaming, George handed over Jenefer's cloak, waiting until Charles had placed it about her shoulders before proffering his hat. A coin changed hands and George's smile widened as he raised a gnarled hand to his forehead.

'Thank 'ee kindly, sir. 'Night, Miss Trevanion.'

After the heat generated by the press of bodies and scores of candles flickering in their holders around the walls, the night air was sharp, cool, and fresh. As she took a deep breath and waited for her eyes to adjust, Charles drew her hand through his arm. She felt hard muscle beneath the fine cloth of his black coat. They set off down the road. She glanced skyward and saw stars playing hide-and-seek behind ragged clouds.

They walked through the alley, down the cobbled yard and stopped at her door. With everyone at the dance all the cottages were in darkness. Somewhere in the trees at the top end of the gardens an owl hooted mournfully. Reluctantly she withdrew her arm from his. As she did so he caught her hand.

She felt the pressure of his thumb on her knuckles. He was standing so close she could feel his breath feathering her cheek. She wanted – she wanted this evening not to end. He talked to her as no other man ever had. His touch aroused delicious sensations, and stirred emotions that were new and intoxicating.

Painful memories loomed at the back of her mind, warning her to be wary. But this powerful attraction, this depth of feeling, demanded she leave such fears in the past where they belonged.

She raised her face but it was too dark to see his expression. It was late. He had escorted her home, now propriety demanded they part. But they had spent the entire evening in company. He had told her so little of what had transpired in Truro and she wanted so much to hear more.

'W-would you—?' she began, about to offer him a cup of tea, when his head came down and his lips brushed hers, once, then again, the touch silk-soft. Her breath stopped and she stood utterly still. He made a sound deep in his throat, as if he were in pain. But before she could speak, his mouth covered hers once more. His lips were warm and exquisitely gentle, his kiss cherishing and so achingly tender that her eyes stung and tears clogged her throat. The world tilted and she gripped his arm to stop herself from falling.

He raised his head and her lips felt bereft. 'Oh God, Jenefer.' His voice sounded hoarse and strained. 'I—'

She covered his mouth with her fingertips. 'If you are about to apologize, I wish you will not.' Her voice was unsteady. 'I should be sad to think you regretted—'

'I don't. I should, but I don't.' Grasping her forearms he stepped back, deliberately putting space between them. 'Go in now.' Leaning past her he opened the door. 'Please. Go inside. When I hear you bolt it I will know you are safe.'

As he strode down the deserted street, the sounds of revelry drifting faintly on the air, he could still taste the sweetness of her lips. He should not have kissed her. But he had wanted to ever since meeting her in the walled garden.

The more time he spent with her, the more he realized how rare she was, how special. They had known each other only a few short weeks, yet there was an affinity, an understanding between them that did not need words. It was there in the depths of her gaze, in her smile. He had never imagined such a thing possible between a man and woman. Aware of her losses, her suffering, he felt a powerful need to protect her. *Yet he was the greatest threat to her happiness.*

Chapter Fifteen

Waking early, Charles had summoned his valet. Shaved, washed and dressed, he was anxious to start the day. But knowing it would be both long and demanding, he made a hearty breakfast of cold roast beef and buttered bread followed by two cups of strong coffee.

He stepped out into a grey chilly morning. The long balmy days of summer were now a fading memory. As he walked briskly down to the harbour the sky was just beginning to lighten above a dark and restless sea. Falling leaves were tossed and swirled by the breeze. More crunched beneath his boots.

He reached one end of the back quay just as Cyrus Keat approached from the other.

''Morning, sir.' Keat touched the brim of his hat.

'Good morning, Mr Keat. I appreciate your promptness. When did you arrive in the village? Yesterday?'

Keat shook his head. 'Don't travel on a Sunday, sir. I come down on Saturday and stopped overnight at the Three Mackerel. I asked about lodgings and the landlord directed me to Mrs Passmore backlong.' He jerked a thumb over his shoulder towards the road. 'Very pleasant woman.'

'I hope you'll be comfortable there.'

'Sure I shall be, sir.'

'When we talked at The Bull, I gave you an idea of what the project entailed. Would a written list of jobs be useful to you?'

'I'll take one if you want, sir, but I don't need it.' He tapped his temple. ''Tis all here.'

'As you wish. However, since we spoke there has been a development concerning the cement.'

'Parker's can't supply? Don't fret, sir, I haven't got the second sight,' Keat said straight-faced. 'I already heard they got the contract to supply the docks at Bristol and Southampton.'

'So I was informed in their letter. As a result they can only supply a quarter of what we need. Nor can they deliver for three weeks.'

Keat shrugged philosophically. 'Better'n nothing, I s'pose. Where you going to get the rest? From Morton's?'

'I've ordered five hundredweight, to try. Have you used it?'

Keat shook his head. 'No. But 'tis plain as day they're hoping to take some of Parker's trade, and they'll have to be good to do that.'

Charles nodded. 'If it proves satisfactory I'll double our order.'

'So, what d'you want done first?' Keat asked, as they walked to the edge of the quay and looked out past the harbour entrance.

'As soon as we have working parties organized and one gang clearing the waste ground, I want the leading marks put in place to indicate the position of the mole. If we begin construction at the end nearest Pednbrose headland,' – Charles pointed – 'the poles can be sited on the seaward side of the property. Those for the quay extension can be sited on the south-west side.'

Keat nodded. 'I'll get both sets in place today. I took the liberty of arranging hire of a horse and cart for two days to carry away all the rubbish.' He nodded towards the waste ground.

'Hired from where?'

'Hammill's farm. Mrs Passmore is a cousin to Mrs Hammill. I sent the boy from next door round with a note promising payment at the end of the two days.'

'I applaud your foresight, Mr Keat.'

''Tis what you're paying me for.'

Hearing voices and the tramp of boots, Charles looked round and saw men streaming onto the quay from all directions. But it was Jenefer Trevanion who caught and held his attention. Walking ahead of the men, she looked neat and elegant in a short dark-green jacket over a gown of pale primrose, and a simple but fetching hat. Then he noticed her shoes. Instead of fashionable kid slippers coloured to match her gown, she wore neat, practical brown lace-up boots. He found this almost unbearably touching.

As she drew closer the colour in her cheeks, stemming perhaps from her walk or the chilly air, deepened from pale pink to rose. But she met his gaze directly as she dropped a curtsy.

'Good morning, Mr Polgray.'

Charles bowed. 'Good morning, Miss Trevanion. Permit me to introduce Mr Keat, my clerk of works.' As Jenefer inclined her head in polite acknowledgement, Charles turned to Keat, noting the crease between his brows. He did not blame the man for wondering what this lovely young woman was doing on the quay at daybreak. In his clerk's place he too would have been curious, and irritated at the apparent distraction.

'Recently, Mr Keat, I hurt my wrist in a fall.' Adjusting his right cuff, feeling the bandage beneath, Charles tried to ignore the nagging ache. Controlling his spirited horse during the long ride to Truro and back had aggravated the injury. Though it was frustrating, it also provided a legitimate reason to seek Jenefer's continued help.

'Since then Miss Trevanion has managed all correspondence and administration relating to the project. As a bookkeeper for many local businesses and acquainted with everyone in the village, her understanding of finance and her local knowledge have proved to be of immense value.' Pleasantly stated it was nonetheless a clear warning.

Keat nodded again, his gaze flicking briefly between them, and Charles knew he had made his point.

'Mr Keat,' Jenefer smiled, 'I understand from Mr Polgray that you are a man of considerable experience. Naturally you will have your preferred way of doing things, but if I can be of help you have only to ask.'

He studied her for a moment. 'Who's the best carpenter in the village?'

'Eddy Barnicoat, if you can get him,' she replied promptly. 'His workshop is just down the street from Tresidder's shop. He is well liked in the village. But more important from your point of view, he has a reputation for good work, fairly priced and completed on time.'

'Much obliged.' Keat touched his cap again, and this time Charles glimpsed respect.

Glancing into Jenefer's basket, he saw a new ledger and several pencils. Catching her eye he silently arched one brow.

'It occurred to me – you will need a list of names. For the wages book?'

'Of course.' He should have known she would come prepared. Again his heart gave a peculiar stutter. Why could he not have met her a year ago? Before he fell into the trap so artfully laid for him by Eve and her mother? 'No ink-pot and pens?'

She met his gentle irony with a droll look. 'No desk or writing slope. It will take but a few minutes to ink the names in later.'

He held her gaze for a moment. Long enough, he hoped, for her to read his gratitude and so much more he was not free to say. As her lashes fluttered down he turned to face the gathered men, waiting until they fell silent.

'Good morning. Let me introduce Mr Keat. As clerk of works he will oversee all practical aspects of the project, and will be on site at all times. Though we shall need tradesmen, much of the work is straight-forward labour.'

From her vantage point Jenefer was able to see the expectancy, feel the hope.

'The first task for the road gang' – Charles gestured towards the site – 'is to get rid of all the rubbish and debris. Mr Keat has already hired a horse and cart to carry it away for disposal. Next, the furze, heather and bracken must be cut down and burned. After the width of the roadbed has been measured and marked, the turf will be stripped and drainage ditches dug on either side. The spoil from the ditches is to be piled in the middle then tamped, shaped and rolled to a camber. A hundred and fifty tons of two-inch granite stones have been ordered and will be arriving by sea. These will be evenly spread to a depth of nine inches.'

He turned to Jenefer. 'Where will it be most convenient for you to take the names?'

She had already thought about this and indicated a small stone building on the corner between the eastern and back quays. 'The fishermen's hut.' Though closed, the wooden double doors were never locked. Inside there was a table and several chairs where the old fish-ermen gathered to smoke their pipes, share a tot of spirits and chat. They usually wandered down around mid-morning. She would be finished long before then.

'Miss Trevanion will be in the fishermen's hut. Give her your name for the wages book, then tell Mr Keat your trade if you have one. He will organize the working parties. I want the road ready for use in seven weeks, and the new quay completed in twelve.'

Jolted by his words, Jenefer made her way through the crowd. Charles's voice followed.

'I won't tolerate bullying, and any man not pulling his weight will be instantly dismissed. If you have a grievance tell Mr Keat. If he cannot resolve it I will be informed. Any questions?'

'What about after, when the road's done?' someone asked.

'There will still be work on the new quay and the mole. And when they are completed the increase in cargo traffic will provide jobs for all those who want them. Are there any miners here? Men familiar with timber-work?' Half-a-dozen hands went up. 'As soon as Miss Trevanion has taken your names, meet me at the end of the quay.' He turned to his aide. 'They are all yours, Mr Keat.'

It was his straightforward manner, Jenefer realized as she took out the ledger and opened it on the stained and rickety table, which made him so valuable to K&P. That surely was the reason he, and no one else, was dispatched to solve problems and settle disputes. But with the project completed he would move on to wherever the company needed him. She wouldn't think about that. Work had only just started. At the dance he had said completion would take six months. But now he was talking about half that. It was hardly any time at all.

'Quiet!' Keat roared, silencing the buzz of conversation. 'How many of you own an axe, saw, billhook, shovel or wheelbarrow?' A forest of hands went up. 'Bring them back with you after dinner.'

Jenefer scribbled names, addresses and trades as fast as she could. Her writing deteriorated and her hand cramped. But she pressed on, anxious not to delay the work or keep the clerk waiting. As the last man hurried away she closed the ledger and flexed her aching fingers.

Rubbish collected from the waste ground was fast forming a growing pile. A large high-sided farm cart drawn by a sturdy brown horse with fringed plate-sized hoofs clattered onto the quay. She recognized the driver as one of the Hammills' grandsons. As Cyrus Keat went to speak to the lad, Jenefer looked for Charles. Seeing him on the western quay gesturing as he explained something to the group of miners, she returned the ledger to her basket and left the harbour. He knew where to find her.

Late that afternoon, Jenefer walked down to Hannah's shop to collect the money for the next free-trade cargo. Though there was no one else in the shop Hannah leaned over the counter and she pushed the purse across, and lowered her voice. 'Now you know I aren't one to pry.'

Swallowing a rising bubble of laughter, Jenefer fastened her teeth on the soft flesh inside her lower lip. There wasn't a man or woman living in the village more curious about other people's lives. But because they knew Hannah wasn't malicious, few minded. Indeed, if it was necessary to circulate news or enlist help for a village function, people simply told Hannah. She made it her mission to inform everyone who entered the shop.

'But?' Jenefer teased gently, arching her brows.

'But 'tis all over the village that you been helping mister, writing letters for 'n and suchlike, because of his bad hand.'

'Is it?'

Hannah nodded. 'And who better? If it wasn't for you taking on our accounts when Percy was so bad with his chest, well, I don't know what I'd have done, and that's God's truth.'

Reaching across the counter Jenefer patted Hannah's arm. 'You were my first client. Do you remember? I had no money and asked you to pay me in groceries?'

Hannah clapped her hands to her cheeks. 'I aren't likely to forget. I feel awful about that.'

'There's no need. I was delighted. As for my helping Mr Polgray being all over the village, I can't say I'm surprised. But surely people have more important things to— '

'More important than hoping for a love match? 'Tis plain as day the two of you are well-suited.'

As she felt telltale warmth in her cheeks, Jenefer knew denial would only make her look coy and simpering. It would also be a waste of breath. They *were* well suited. She was as certain of that as she was of her own name. Yet regarding his intentions she was as much in the dark as everyone else. Deflecting twin darts of hurt and anxiety, she forced a smile. 'Why, Hannah. You're quite a romantic at heart.'

'Nothing wrong with that.' Hannah's face softened. 'I remember when Percy used to come courting me. He even wrote me a poem once. Four lines it was and they rhymed lovely. I've still got 'n in a drawer upstairs. The paper have broke all along the folds. But it don't matter.' She patted the crisp white kerchief swathing her from throat to waist. 'Every word is writ on my heart.'

'Oh, Hannah.' Jenefer was surprised and touched.

Hannah clicked her tongue. 'Dear life! Hark at me going on. You didn't come in for that.'

Sensing her embarrassment Jenefer quickly changed the subject. 'How is Percy's cough?'

'Nearly gone. Good job too. I couldn't have took much more of it. But that there mixture Mrs Casvellan sent down for 'n worked a treat. He been feeling so much better he walked down to the harbour this morning to see what's going on.' Hannah rolled her eyes. 'Him and half the village. Still who can blame 'em? I reck'n mister is the best thing to happen to this village in years. Once that new quay is finished and there's more ships coming and going, life will be better for everyone.'

'I hope so, Hannah.'

''Course it will. You just wait and see.'

Walking home, Jenefer hoped the rest of the village shared Hannah's feelings. As for the rumours, had Charles heard them? Very much his own man and valuing his privacy he would not enjoy being the subject of gossip. Yet he must be aware that the two of them working together made it inevitable. She knew he was not indifferent to her. So why did he not say something?

She chided herself for her self-absorption. This was his first solo venture: a heavy responsibility and hugely important to him. There would be time enough to talk of more personal matters. *When?* Once the work was finished, what then? He would leave.

All her concerns about marriage and her fear of losing her independence flooded back to mock her. How ironic that just as those fears had begun to fade and her feelings for Charles Polgray were growing deeper and stronger every day, with his time here limited, the chance of anything permanent between them seemed ever more unlikely. Was that why he had not declared himself, or made promises he would be unable to keep?

If that were so, the sensible *ladylike* course of action would be for her to withdraw. With Mr Keat overseeing the work, Charles would have more time to concentrate on planning and finance.

Establishing distance between them might help her retrieve some dignity. But when they were together dignity mattered not at all. When he touched her, kissed her, when his gaze pierced her very soul, the sensations he ignited and the yearning that gripped her were profound and passionate. They were not remotely ladylike.

By midmorning the following day, having added up the same column and arrived at three different totals, she conceded defeat and threw down her pencil. Leaving papers and ledgers spread over the table, she put on her hat and coat, closed her door, and walked down to the quay.

Gorse and heather crackled on two bonfires. Higher up the slope men sawed and chopped. Others dragged the brush down to piles waiting to be fed into leaping flames fanned by a fitful breeze. Even from yards away Jenefer could feel the heat and smell the sweet-scented smoke.

Then she saw Charles, magnificent in a dark blue coat, buff panta-loons and polished black boots. A black beaver hat covered his thick hair. Watching him she felt something leap inside her. He stood near the quay edge talking to his clerk. As she hesitated, unwilling to inter-rupt, Cyrus Keat spotted her and politely touched the brim of his hat. Charles turned. Recognizing her he smiled, and she felt herself open like a flower to the sun. With a final word to Keat, he came towards her.

'I hope I'm not intruding,' she said quickly.

'Never.' Deep and soft, his voice sent tingles along her spine. Shadowed by the brim of his hat his eyes gleamed as they gazed into hers. 'I am happy to see you,' he said softly. 'I wondered if you might come down today.'

Swallowing the questions she dare not ask, she moistened her lips. 'I am glad I did. Such progress in so short a time is remarkable.' She turned her head, unable to hold his gaze, afraid of what he might see. She pointed to two tall white posts on the sloping ground below Pednbrose. 'Are those the leading marks you spoke of?'

He nodded. 'If you would care to walk with me I can show you their purpose.'

She looked at him, a quick shy glance, and smiled. 'I'd like that.'

A brig carrying a cargo of limestone was moored to the seaward side of the quay. A derrick raised a fresh load from the hold, swung slowly across, and lowered it onto the quay where a relay of men filled wooden barrows and pushed them to the kiln.

'I intended to build the extension using massive granite blocks so it would look the same as the original,' Charles said as they reached the end. 'But that would have required a cofferdam to keep out the water while foundations were laid.'

'Would have?' Jenefer looked up at him. 'You're not going to do that now?'

He shook his head. 'The financial shortfall means I can't afford it. So I'm taking the quick and dirty option.'

'I beg your pardon?' Jenefer said, startled.

'Forgive me. It means getting the quay built as quickly as possible.'

'But . . .' she hesitated.

'Go on.'

'I don't want to offend—'

'You won't.'

'It's just, well, it sounds a lot more. . . .'

'Risky?'

'I was going to say *temporary*.'

A brief smile touched his mouth. Then he nodded. 'There is a chance it won't last more than a few years. But the sooner I can pay off the loan, the sooner I will begin accumulating profit. And that will allow me to make a proper job of rebuilding it later.'

'So how long will it last?'

'It depends how severe the winter storms are and how successful the mole proves to be. I would hope for several years.'

'But if you can't use stone, how will you build it?'

'With wood. A thirty-foot-long oak pile placed every two yards. On my way back from Truro I stopped off at Trelowarren and ordered forty-eight of them.'

'When will they arrive? And how? The cost of transport—'

'Will be negligible.' He grinned. 'Thrown into the water at Gweek and towed round, they should be here any day. It was the quickest and cheapest way.'

Jenefer found herself smiling back at him. 'Of course! What an excellent idea.'

'I'm having another derrick erected here at the end of the quay to unload stone. As soon as each ship leaves, the stone will be dropped around the piles and cemented in place to hold them firm. Then the piles will be braced with cross members and a deck laid over the top. As the quay lengthens, the shiploads of stone can be unloaded onto the new deck.'

Jenefer nodded, seeing it clearly. Then her pulse quickened as he cupped her elbow, led her to the outer corner of the quay and pointed across the water. 'How many poles do you see?'

Acutely aware of his palm, the gentle pressure of his fingers, and her shoulder brushing his chest, she tried to concentrate. 'One.'

Without a word, he led her across the quay to the inner wall. 'And now?'

'Oh.' She looked up at him. 'Two.'

He nodded. 'The poles are a line-of-sight guide to ensure the outer row of piles remains perfectly straight.' He turned her gently to face him. 'Will you come to dinner next week? I know how busy you are,' he added before she could respond. 'But I do so appreciate everything you have done.'

'That's why you've invited me? Out of gratitude?' Driven by a complex tangle of emotions the question spilled out before she could stop it. One hand flew to her mouth. Then she clasped both tightly in front of her, shaken and mortified by her lack of control. 'I beg your pardon. That was unforgivable. I—' She caught her breath, falling abruptly silent as he laid his forefinger lightly on her mouth.

'Don't.' His voice was rough, strained. 'I want no apology. Just say you'll come. Please.'

How could she refuse? She nodded, and answered with the truth. 'I'd love to.'

'Thank you.' His smile was brief. As it faded she was suddenly aware of the lines of strain bracketing his mouth and shadows of weariness like sooty thumbprints beneath his eyes. A wave of sympathy enveloped her. And with it, shame at her selfishness. He had allowed her a glimpse into his world, but what did she really know of the demands and responsibilities he carried?

'Wednesday? Three o'clock?' He must have seen her hesitation for he hurried on, 'I wish it might be sooner, but I leave for Truro on Monday and have a lot to do before then. I'm meeting Mr Daniell on Tuesday to sign the agreement, hand over the deeds, and collect his draft for the money. I will ride back first thing Wednesday morning.'

She nodded. 'I shall look forward to it.' She had arranged to ride over to see Tamara on Wednesday morning. But she would leave a little early to allow herself plenty of time to wash and change.

By unspoken agreement they turned and began retracing their steps as Keat hurried towards them.

'Jenefer?'

'Yes, Charles?'

'We both know how much I owe you. But that is not why I invited you.' His bow was brief and formal but the look in his eyes made her quiver. 'Until Wednesday.' He left her and walked swiftly to meet his clerk.

Watching him go Jenefer touched her mouth where his finger had rested and wondered how she would survive the next five days.

*

Apart from attending church on Sunday morning, she worked. There was plenty of her own to catch up on. Then to her surprise and delight, Charles called on her just after nine on Monday morning with a list of letters to be written. He stayed less then ten minutes. But just seeing him lightened her heart and her mood and filled her with energy.

Over the next three days she completed all the paperwork. Then, because she hadn't had time before, and had to do something to burn off her surplus energy, she cleaned her cottage from top to bottom. On Tuesday afternoon she was ironing the washing Lizzie had done for her when someone passed the window. She looked up as her neighbour tapped on the open door.

'I finished the shawl.'

'Come in, Ernestine.' Jenefer set the flat iron down on the slab. 'I've been looking forward to – ohhh!' she gasped softly as Ernestine shook out the lacy shawl. It was as light as gossamer, as fine as cobweb. 'It's beautiful.'

''Tidn' bad,' Ernestine allowed. 'By time I'd finished, he was a bit grubby, so he've been washed. I put a drop of rose water in the rinsing water then dried 'n flat. Lovely and soft he is.'

Jenefer gathered the shawl and held it to her cheek. 'It's like thistle-down. Thank heaven I asked you to make it. If I'd tried it would have ended up looking like a dishrag, which would have been a shocking waste of yarn. I'm useless at anything like this. Betsy is the creative one.'

'Your sister is a fine needlewoman, dear of her,' Ernestine allowed. 'But there isn't no one in this village can do what you do. So don't you go running yourself down.' Pink and flustered, she stopped. 'Begging your pardon, miss.'

'Why, thank you, Ernestine.' Laying the shawl on the table Jenefer went to the dresser drawer for her purse.

'No hurry like that, Miss,' Ernestine said, backing towards the door.

'Indeed there is,' Jenefer said firmly, pressing several silver coins into Ernestine's gnarled hand then folding her fingers over them. 'Not another word,' she warned as the old woman looked up wide-eyed and opened her mouth to protest at the amount. Ernestine's reluctance to charge full price for her work was a long-standing bone of contention between them. 'You have done a superb job and I'm truly grateful.'

'Well, if you're sure.' Clutching the money to her ample bosom, Ernestine went to the door.

'Do you know what you've done?' Jenefer said. 'You have created another heirloom. Just like the one you knitted for Jon, this beautiful shawl will be treasured. When Mrs Varcoe's new baby no longer needs it, it will be put away and passed on when both children have children of their own.'

'Well! My dear soul. You really think so?'

'I'm sure of it.'

'Well!' Ernestine said again. Shaking her head as a slow smile spread across her face, she bustled away up the yard.

Closing the bottom half of the door, Jenefer picked up the shawl again. Five feet square, it weighed almost nothing. Carefully folding it in tissue from the dresser drawer, she tied the package with a gold ribbon and set it aside. Then she finished the ironing.

That night she lay in bed and listened to the rain, the first for weeks, pattering against the window and gurgling down the gutter into the big wooden butt. At least it would lay the dust.

She pictured Charles. How handsome he had looked in his blue coat. She recalled his blunt forthright manner as he talked to the men. Then his smile: a smile he kept just for her. It changed him; softening the stern cast of his features, making him more approachable, less aloof. It made her feel special. She hoped he had achieved everything he wanted from his meeting with Mr Daniell.

He would leave Truro early tomorrow morning. And tomorrow afternoon she would see him again. She felt she had dealt with his absence sensibly. Her days had been full and busy with no time to waste on daydreaming. But last thing at night, when there were no more tasks demanding her attention, she missed him. She missed him more than she had expected to. And, missing him, she realized how lonely she had been.

Like a phoenix she had risen from the ashes of tragedy and loss, and rebuilt her life. She was busy and successful with a thriving business. She had truly believed it was enough. Meeting Charles Polgray had shown her that it wasn't. She wanted more. She wanted his love. She could hardly wait for tomorrow. Turning onto her side she closed her eyes. And slept.

Chapter Sixteen

Leaving the butcher's horse in the care of the manservant who also doubled as groom and valet, Jenefer lifted the carefully wrapped shawl from the saddle-bag and walked quickly towards the farmhouse.

As she knocked and waited, she guessed the time to be just after noon. She would stay for an hour and, after hearing Tamara's news, perhaps share – what? Her pride and delight in assisting with a project of such importance to the village?

Tamara knew that. She would ask about Charles: searching questions to which Jenefer had no answers. Torn between hope and doubt, she was also torn between wanting to confide her wretched confusion and, rather than appear a pathetic fool, staying silent. She *knew* her feelings for him were reciprocated. But unless – until – he *told* her what was in his heart, she could only lurch between doubt and faith, trust and fear.

She loved being with him; loved all she was learning. Yet the effects of that same proximity kept her wakeful long into the night. Where was he now? In just a few hours she would see him again. They would have so much to catch up on.

An hour with Tamara, then half an hour to ride back and returning her mount to Mr Rollason, would still leave her more than enough time to get ready. She wanted to look her best. Dinner with Charles at Kegwyn: happy anticipation fountained inside her.

About to knock again, surprised that no one had yet answered, she heard running feet. The front door flew open.

Jenefer's smile froze at the panic on Molly's face.

'Oh, miss. I'm some glad you've come. Mrs Bosanko's mother took poorly yesterday so she've gone to Helston to see her. Mr Varcoe has gone off with Mr Casvellan. And Missus is having pains and I got Jon to look after so I don't – '

'Molly, calm down.' As her stomach clenched, Jenefer kept her voice level as she pushed the maid back gently. Stepping inside she closed the door. 'Where is Mrs Varcoe?'

'In the morning room. She was—'

'And where is Jon?'

'Upstairs. I'd just put 'n down for his nap when— '

'Yes,' Jenefer interrupted before the young maid's panic exploded again. 'Go and put the kettle on.'

The maid clapped both hands to her flushed cheeks. 'Oh my dear lord. I should've thought— '

'Molly,' Jenefer interrupted firmly, 'this isn't helping. Come now. Pull yourself together. Getting into a state will not help Jon or his mother. Now go and do as I've asked. The kettle?' she reminded in the face of Molly's wild-eyed bewilderment. 'Does Jon usually have something to eat when he wakes up?'

'Yes, miss.' Molly nodded. 'A slice of bread and butter with a bit of cheese, some fruit and a glass of milk.'

'Then as soon as you've brought a tea tray to the morning room, go back to the kitchen and get it ready.'

'Yes, miss.' Clearly relieved to have handed over responsibility, Molly dropped a quick curtsy and hurried away to the kitchen.

Jenefer's heart thumped hard against her ribs as she approached the morning room. Calming the maid had been easy enough. And practice had made her expert at hiding her own fears. The baby wasn't due for two weeks. Perhaps Tamara was simply experiencing what Betsy had called practice contractions. *Please let it be a false alarm.* Untying her bonnet she pulled it off, tucking it beneath her arm as she tapped lightly then opened the door.

Tamara stood at a side table supporting herself with stiff arms, head drooping, her shoulders hunched.

The knot in Jenefer's stomach tightened. She was out of her depth here. She had no experience of childbirth, and no idea of what to do or how best to help. She quickly crossed to Tamara's side. As she placed a gentle arm around her shoulders, Tamara gradually relaxed then glanced up. To Jenefer's astonishment, though her face was glistening with perspiration, a smile curved her mouth and her gaze was warm.

'I'm so glad you've come.'

Dropping her bonnet and the tissue-wrapped package onto a small sofa, Jenefer took her friend's hand. 'Molly says you've been having pains.'

Tamara nodded. 'I've been having them for the past two days. But they were no worse than cramp and sometimes an hour or more would pass between one and the next, so I thought little of it. The same thing happened when I was expecting Jon and went on for two weeks.' She started to sit down then shook her head. 'I'm more comfortable on my feet. I'd like to walk a little.'

'Then we'll walk.' Jenefer drew Tamara's hand through her arm and they slowly crossed to the window. Bright light streamed through the window, then faded as fast-moving clouds driven by a gusty wind hid the sun. 'Does Devlin know? Sorry, that was a foolish question,' she said, as Tamara shot her a dry look.

'If I had told him he would have wanted to stay with me. But this meeting he and Casvellan have gone to is really important. I would have felt stupid – and guilty – if he had missed the meeting on my account, all for a false alarm.'

'Is it, do you think? A false alarm?'

'I—' Tamara stopped suddenly, sucked in a sharp breath, and curled forward, sliding her free hand beneath the mound of her belly to support it.

Jenefer bit the inside of her lip, ruthlessly suppressing panic she could not afford. Tamara needed her. *What should she do?* Used to taking action and dealing with situations, hating her helplessness, she held Tamara whose fingers tightened on her arm. Features taut, eyes closed, Tamara groaned as the pain climbed and peaked.

Jenefer knew the instant it began to subside. Tamara slowly relaxed, released a shuddering breath, and straightened up. 'No,' she whispered. 'I think the baby's coming.' She looked at Jenefer, her mouth trembling. 'I wish—'

'Would you like me to send someone for your mother?'

Tamara flinched. 'God, no! Can you not picture it? She would sweep in and start giving orders. I am more comfortable on my feet, but she would have me flat on my back with the curtains drawn. This is my baby and I want—'

The door opened and Molly nudged it wider with her hip as she carried in the tea tray. 'Mrs Varcoe, Master Jon have just woke up. What d'you want me to—?'

Pressing Tamara's hand in reassurance, Jenefer spoke up. 'Molly, give Jon what you have prepared for him, then put on his coat and hat and walk him round to Trescowe. Ask Mrs Casvellan to come as soon as possible. If it's convenient for Jon to stay and play with Enor, you come back with her for you'll be needed here.'

Molly looked aghast. 'But I can't - I've never—'

'In the kitchen, Molly. That's where you'll be needed during Mrs Bosanko's absence, to supply whatever Mrs Casvellan may need, and prepare dinner. I'm sure you can do that.'

Visibly relieved and with dawning pride, Molly nodded. 'Yes, miss. 'Course I can. You leave it to me.'

As the door closed, Tamara released Jenefer's arm. 'Do you mind pouring the tea yourself?'

'Not at all. Will you have some?'

Tamara shook her head. 'I've lost all taste for it.'

'What about a cold drink? Some lemonade perhaps?'

'Maybe later.'

Jenefer gazed at her feeling helpless and inept. 'Is there anything I can get you? Anything at all that would help?'

Tamara's face crumpled for an instant. She made a valiant effort to smile but her mouth quivered. 'Only Devlin. But he's not here and cannot be reached.'

Leaving the tray, Jenefer crossed quickly and hugged her friend, careful to avoid her huge belly. 'Oh, Tamara. I'd find him and fetch him if I could.'

With a sound that was half laugh, half sob, Tamara wiped her eyes with the heel of her hand. 'Perhaps it's just as well. If he were here he would drive us all to distraction with his fretting.'

Gently rocking Tamara, offering what comfort she could, Jenefer pictured the Devlin she knew: a man who inspired loyalty in his friends and hatred in his enemies. He had risked his life on a mission to France to rescue her fiancé whose whole life was a lie: who had conspired with her father and betrayed her trust. While saving his best friend, now Betsy's husband, from the wild waves, he had almost drowned. He would have, had not Tamara, heedless of her own safety, waded thigh-deep into the crashing surf and dragged him out.

The image of them both soaked to the skin, oblivious of the crowd, holding each other as if they would never let go, while rescuers struggled to save the rest of the boat's crew and Mrs Gillis shrieked in hysterics, was indelibly etched on Jenefer's memory.

The past three years had only deepened their love. Yet Jenefer was astonished that Tamara should want her husband with her at such a time. It was unheard of. Childbirth was the most intimate of women's experiences. And yet to love a man so much, and know you mattered to him more than anything else, what must that be like? Suddenly she recalled the intensity of Charles's expression the night he had kissed her. *But if that look had meant what she hoped it did, why had he remained silent?*

The gentle pressure of Tamara pushing her away brought her back to the present.

'Drink your tea, Jenna. Go on,' she urged, with an impish grin. 'I am sure you need it after arriving here to such a to-do.' Fine curls had escaped the coil pinned high on her crown. Wet and dark, they were plastered to her forehead, temples and the nape of her neck. Frowning in discomfort she untied the kerchief draped about her shoulders and flung it aside, then pulled at the sleeves and bodice of the spotted peach muslin clinging damply to her skin.

With a hand that was not quite steady, Jenefer poured tea into a cup. The pot rattled as she set it down. She added a dash of milk.

'How—?' she began, then shook her head.

'How what?' Tamara looked round as she continued her slow progress around the room, cradling her belly with one hand while she rested the other on a chair back for support.

'No, it was a stupid question.'

'Ask me anyway. I'll tell you if I can.'

'How do you bear the pain?'

Tamara shrugged. 'I have no choice.'

Jenefer made an apologetic face. 'I told you it was a stupid question.'

Tamara touched her arm as she passed. 'You didn't let me finish. I have no choice while it's happening. But if I am as fortunate this time as I was with Jon, it will only last for a few hours. It's not like being ill. I'm bringing a new life into the world: our child, Devlin's and mine. Through Jon and this new baby, some part of us will go on. They are our stake in the future.' She grinned over her shoulder. 'Hark at me.'

'Actually, it's a rather beautiful thought.'

'Then you must remind me of it when I am inflicting yet another bruise on your poor arm. Though I should warn you now, if you do I will probably bite your head off.'

'I shall try to make allowances. But only because you are my particular friend.'

Tamara's eyes filled. 'I'm truly glad you are here.' Impatiently she dashed the tears away. 'Take no notice. I am not unhappy. It is just—' words failed her and she shrugged. 'What's in the parcel?'

'A gift for your new son or daughter.'

'Oh, Jenna. How kind. Thank you.'

'You haven't seen it yet.'

'It's from you, so I shall love it.' Tamara moved slowly round the sofa.

'Let me—'

'Drink your tea. And sit down. You need not remain standing. I promise I am not about to fall over. And I am perfectly able to open my own gifts.' Laying the parcel on the side table she pulled the bow loose, carefully unfolded the tissue then lifted out the shawl. 'Oh!' Closing her eyes she held it to her face. Jenefer was appalled to see huge tears tremble on her lashes, then spill down her cheeks.

'Tamara—?'

'It's so beautiful. So fine. I can't— ' Her chin dropped and she reached out. 'Jen – please— '

Swiftly setting her cup down, Jenefer tossed the shawl onto the sofa, put her arm around Tamara and took her hand, ready this time for the vice-like grip.

As the pain subsided, Jenefer heard footsteps in the hallway and turned as the door opened and Roz walked in with Molly close behind.

Swallowing relief that left her decidedly shaky, Jenefer smiled. 'Roz, you have no idea how happy I am to see you.'

Setting her basket on a table, Roz began removing her hat and coat, turning to the maid as she did so. 'All right, Molly, off you go. Kettle first. Then take two sheets and a blanket to Mrs Varcoe's bedroom. The oldest ones you can find.'

'Yes, Mrs Casvellan.' With a quick bob, Molly scuttled out.

Tossing her coat over the back of a chair and dropping her hat on top, Roz came to Tamara and took both her hands, her tone warm and gentle. 'How often are the pains coming?'

'I'm not sure— '

'About every fifteen minutes,' Jenefer said.

Roz nodded and Jenefer was amazed at her calm. Then she realized: having borne a child herself, Roz was familiar with everything it entailed.

'Shall we go upstairs now?'

'I'm so uncomfortable, Roz.'

'Might a sponge down with cool water and a clean nightgown help?'

'Oh yes,' Tamara's response was heartfelt. 'But I don't want to lie down.'

'Then you need not,' Roz said calmly. 'Until you tell me you are ready.' She took one arm, Jenefer the other, and they supported Tamara up the stairs.

As they entered the master bedroom, Jenefer's gaze flew to the big oak bed where Tamara and Devlin lay each night. Heat flashed over her skin and, pierced by an arrow of longing, she averted her eyes.

Tamara's grip tightened. 'Roz—' she gasped. Then shaking them both off she grasped the footboard and braced herself on outstretched arms, bowing her head as the contraction strengthened.

'Jen, light the fire, will you?' Roz gently rubbed Tamara's lower back.

Molly brought a pitcher of steaming water. After a quick glance at her mistress that combined sympathy and fear, she looked away. 'I'll fetch the sheets now.'

'Bring up my basket first, will you?' Roz said. 'Then fill a clean teapot with boiling water and bring it up with a cup and spoon.' As Molly rushed out again, Roz explained. 'An infusion of raspberry leaves and golden seal will help with the contractions.'

Jenefer shrugged helplessly. 'I've never – I'm completely out of my depth.'

'So would we be if we tried to do your job,' Roz said. 'But I'm so glad you're here. I'd be hard-pressed to manage alone, and Molly would be more hindrance than help.'

'Neither use nor ornament, according to Mrs Bosanko,' Tamara said; her voice tight, her eyes still closed. 'But she has endless patience with Jon and he adores her.'

'Just tell me what to do,' Jenefer begged.

'Stop worrying,' Roz said. 'Tamara is fine. Everything is just as it should be.'

'That's all very well for you to say,' Tamara grumbled as she slowly straightened up.

'So you're back with us again. Arms up.' Lifting Tamara's gown over her head, Roz passed it to Jenefer who was about to lay it over the back of a chair when Molly ran in with the basket, grabbed the sweat-damp gown and dashed out again.

Roz handed Jenefer a clean white apron and quickly tied another around her own waist. Then while Roz sponged Tamara down and gently patted her dry, Jenefer prepared the bed with a square of tarpaulin covered by a folded blanket and an old sheet.

As the afternoon wore on, Tamara's contractions grew more frequent. Clad in a fresh cotton nightgown she prowled the room, occasionally sipping the herbal infusion, and supporting herself on anything within reach when the pains came.

Jenefer fetched in the crib, and hung small sheets and blankets, a tiny shirt and several muslin squares on an airer in front of the fire. Molly emptied the slop bucket, brought in a second pail, more hot water and fresh towels. Then Roz sent her to find scissors and silk yarn.

When Tamara could no longer walk, Roz helped her onto the bed, bathing her flushed face with a cool wet cloth while she groaned.

Wrenched by Tamara's suffering, Jenefer moved about the room. She added more coal to the fire. Thick clouds obscured the sun and darkened the room. Jenefer lit every candle she could find, hating her own helplessness.

'Patience,' Roz mumured, pressing her shoulder gently as she passed.

'How does she bear it?'

'Because she has no choice. Yes, it's hard. But it has a purpose. As soon as she sees her baby all this will be forgotten.'

Though she would not argue the point, Jenefer could not imagine how anyone could ever forget such agony.

Suddenly Tamara raised her knees and curled forward. 'Roz, I need – I have to—' Her whole body shuddered as she grunted with effort.

'If you're ready to push, it won't be long now. You're doing so well,' Roz encouraged, as Tamara slumped back, her eyes closed as she heaved in air. Her face was drawn with exhaustion and plum-coloured shadows had formed beneath her eyes. Seeing her tongue snake across her dry lips, Jenefer trickled a little lemonade into her mouth and was rewarded with a weary smile. Then Tamara tensed for another push, her lips drawn back as she strained.

From her position near the foot of the bed, Roz glanced up. 'I can see the head.'

Pins and needles tingled in Jenefer's arms and legs. Her heartbeat was fast and loud in her ears. Then pain knifed through her chest. Realizing she had been holding her breath in sympathy she released it and the unpleasant tingling faded.

'Wait, Tamara,' Roz urged, her hands busy. 'All right. Push now. Your baby is nearly here. One more.'

After a mighty effort, Tamara fell back against the pillows. Jenefer heard a quivering kitten-like cry.

'Well, look at you,' Roz crooned, laughing in delight as she lifted a small slippery pink body and laid it on Tamara's deflated stomach. 'You have a beautiful daughter.'

Jenefer marvelled at the little face, screwed up as if in angry complaint. Tiny arms waved. Little legs kicked erratically. Her vision blurred then tears slid down her cheeks as she watched Tamara reverently stroke her baby's dark head.

'Ohhh!' Tamara breathed. 'Aren't you just perfect?'

The mewing cries stopped with a hiccup. The baby's eyes opened and a frown creased her downy forehead.

Jenefer swallowed the huge lump in her throat. 'She knows your voice.'

'Of course she does,' Tamara said softly. 'I have been talking to her for months. Welcome, Zoe Varcoe. I am so happy to see you.' She raised her head. 'Thank you, Roz, with all my heart.' Then she looked up at Jenefer. Drawn and damp from her exertions, she was radiant.

In that moment Jenefer understood. This perfect little being, this new life, made all the pain and effort worthwhile. 'And you, Jenna.'

'I'm so glad I was here. To be part of this – it is such a privilege. You were so brave.' For the first time she understood what was meant by *labour*.

Roz quickly tied two lengths of silk yarn around the silver-blue cord then cut it, then gently wrapped the baby in a length of warm muslin. 'Jenefer, would you like to hold her? We're not quite finished.'

Jenefer looked at Tamara. 'May I?'

As Tamara nodded and winced in the grip of an after-pain, Roz placed the bundled baby in Jenefer's arms and began to gently massage Tamara's flaccid belly.

Cradling the warm weight, awed by the miracle she had witnessed, Jenefer swallowed more tears and crossed to the window. Raindrops streaked the glass and she was astonished to see how dark it was. *Charles.* She caught her breath, thoughts racing. He would be waiting, wondering where she was, *if she had forgotten*. No, he would not think that. Surely he must know that only something of great importance would have prevented her from keeping their appointment?

She heard voices, Molly's protesting and a man's raised in anger, then the sound of booted feet. She turned in time to see the door flung open. Devlin burst in, his coat wet and dark across the shoulders, his face a mask of fear. Roz quickly drew a sheet over Tamara's lower body.

Without a glance at either woman, Devlin crossed to his wife. Dropping to one knee beside the bed, he clasped Tamara's hand, kissed it then held it to his cheek.

'Are you all right?' His voice was hoarse.

'I'm very well,' she touched his face.

'Why didn't you tell me? I would never have gone.'

'Better for you that you did.' Tamara's smile softened into tender adoration. 'Would you like to meet your new daughter?'

'What? My—?' Looking round Devlin rose to his feet in one lithe movement. He glanced from Roz to Jenefer then his gaze fell on the bundle she held. They both stepped forward and she placed the baby in his arms. Her throat stiffened at the expression of awe on his harsh features, and she gulped back fresh tears.

Roz caught her eye and they quietly left the room and met Molly on the landing.

'A tray of tea and toast for Mrs Varcoe, please Molly. The proud parents wish for a few private moments with their baby daughter.'

'A little girl! That's 'andsome, that is. A little sister for Master Jon, dear of 'n.' Molly beamed. 'Mrs Bosanko will be spitting feathers for missing it.' She hurried down the stairs.

'Roz,' Jenefer touched her friend's arm. 'I would not have missed this for the world. But I must go.'

'Judging by Devlin's appearance, it's pouring outside. Come back to Trescowe and spend the night with us. You are more than welcome.'

'That's so kind of you, but I really must get home. I was supposed to be having dinner with Charles' – she glanced at the grandfather clock in the hall – 'two hours ago.'

'And he will be wondering where you are and why you did not keep the appointment,' Roz said. 'Then of course you must go home. But you cannot cross the moor alone in the dark.'

As Jenefer opened her mouth, ready to protest that she knew the moor like the back of her hand, Roz raised her hand.

'I know you could find your way home blindfolded, but my husband would never forgive me, nor would Tamara. Nor, I imagine, would Mr Polgray. Devlin's man can escort you. Go on down and tell him to saddle both horses. Tamara told me you were visiting her today. She was supposed to ask you to call at Trescowe afterwards so I could give you another bottle of liquorice mixture for Percy Tresidder and a pot of arnica ointment for Mr Polgray's wrist. They are in my basket, so you can take them with you.'

Chapter Seventeen

Devlin's manservant waited while Jenefer dismounted. Grasping the bridle, the lad hunched his shoulders against the rain falling on his bare head.

'Please give Mr Rollason my apologies,' Jenefer said, as she took a bottle and a small pot from the saddle-bag. 'I did not intend being out so late.'

'No trouble, miss,' the boy said. 'Mister didn't need 'n.' Turning away he clicked his tongue, urging the cob into the stable.

Jenefer returned to the gate. 'You go on back now,' she told the manservant. 'My cottage is only a few yards down the road. And thank you. I was glad of your company.'

'No trouble, miss.' With a nod, he wheeled his mount and trotted away towards the moor.

As she closed the door, Jenefer's shoulders sagged as a wave of tiredness rolled over her and with it disappointment. She had meant every word when she told Roz she would not have missed being present for the birth of Tamara's daughter. It had been an amazing, awe-inspiring experience. But it was not the afternoon she had looked forward to so much. Indeed, being present at the birth, then witnessing Devlin's arrival; his blindness to all but his wife; had made her even more aware of longings that, since meeting Charles, she could no longer suppress or ignore.

Wearily, she set the bottle of mixture and pot of ointment on the table, lit the lamp and drew the curtain across the kitchen window. Untying the ribbons holding her bonnet in place, she shook it, dropped it on the table, then unbuttoned her coat. The fire in the range had gone out. But after riddling the ashes and laying furze logs on the kindling, she quickly got it going again.

Leaving the fire door open to warm the room, she shrugged out of her coat and hung it over the back of a chair, then refilled the black kettle and pulled it over the flames. Her stomach rumbled: another reminder of the meal she had missed.

A sudden knock on the door made her start. She went to open it, expecting to see Lizzie. Instead Charles stood on the threshold. Rain had darkened the shoulder capes on his greatcoat and dripped from the brim of his hat as he took it off.

Jenefer's heart gave a great leap and she pulled the door wider. 'Come in! I didn't expect—'

'Where were you?' His features were pale and set.

'I'm so sorry. I would have let you know had it been possible, but—'

'I was under the impression we had an appointment.'

His bitter anger had the effect of a slap, shattering her pleasure at seeing him. Vivid memories of her father's belligerent demands filled her head. William too, since they became friends, had become ever more manipulative. Rage roared through her like a gale, leaving her shaking.

'You forget yourself, Mr Polgray. How dare you speak so to me? I am not your employee. You have allowed me neither time to answer nor opportunity to explain.' A huge lump blocked her throat and her eyes burned. She would *not* weep.

Shock blanked his features for an instant then horror drained his face of colour.

'Oh God.' He raked a hand through his hair. 'I— that was unforgivable. I-I had been looking forward so much to seeing you again. But you didn't come. I waited an hour. I was sure that were you unwell you would have sent a note to inform me. So I came here. Mrs Clemmow told me you had intended visiting Mrs Varcoe and planned to be back by two. But when I spoke to her it was after four and had started raining again.' He turned the brim of his hat round and round.

'I imagined you lying injured on the moor. I wanted to ride up there and start looking. But Mrs Clemmow said it was more likely that because of the heavy rain Mrs Varcoe had persuaded you to stay there for the night, and if I went tramping about on the moor all I'd gain was a soaking and a chill. She advised me to go back to Kegwyn.

So I did. But I couldn't settle. Not until – I needed to know—' The avalanche of words finally halted.

Seeing the anguish in his eyes Jenefer felt the dregs of her rage dissolve. *He had been worried about her. His disappointment matched her own.* She realized that in the five days since she had last seen him he had lost weight. His features appeared sharper, and strain had deepened the crease between his brows and the lines bracketing his mouth.

He dipped his head in a formal bow. 'Now I have seen that you are safe I will leave you in peace. Please accept my sincere apologies.'

'Don't go,' she blurted. 'I should like to explain – I was just about to make some supper.' She made a wry face. 'I missed the dinner I was so looking forward to. Indeed, I have not eaten since this morning. You are most welcome to join me.'

His slow smile kindled sweet warmth in her belly. 'I should like that. Mrs Eustace had prepared an excellent meal. But without you there to share it I had little appetite.'

Pleasure shimmered through her. Lifting her wet coat from the back of the chair she hung it on a wooden peg by the door. 'Let me take yours.'

'I'll do it.' Shedding his coat, he hung it and his hat on the peg next to hers.

'It will be poor fare in comparison,' she warned over her shoulder, opening the larder door. 'Bread and cheese with pickled walnuts, and apple tart to follow.'

A smile lit his tired face. 'A feast in your company.'

'I really am sorry I could not let you know,' Jenefer said, returning to the table with dishes of butter and cheese. 'Do sit down.' He folded his length into the wooden armchair near the range and crossed one booted leg over the other. 'Fortunately Roz – Mrs Casvellen – was at home and came as soon as Molly had given her my message.' She set down a board containing half a wheaten loaf then fetched the pickles.

'I'm sure that would give me great comfort,' Charles said. 'If I knew what you were talking about.'

Turning from the dresser holding two plates, Jenefer looked at him blankly. 'Didn't I—? What an idiot. It was such – I was so—' She stopped and took a deep breath. 'What Lizzie told you was correct. I did ride out to visit Mrs Varcoe this morning. My intention was to keep her company for an hour then come home so I would have plenty of time—' She stopped and set the plates down on opposite sides of the table. There was no need to tell him of her wish to take special care over her appearance. Instinctively she raised a hand to her hair. The front was wet, the rest untidy. *She had so much wanted to look her best.* With an inward sigh she continued.

'But when I arrived I found Tamara – Mrs Varcoe – in some distress. Her confinement, not due for two weeks, had started early. The housekeeper was away due to family illness, and the only other person in the house was Molly, the maid who looks after Mrs Varcoe's young son. I sent her across to Trescowe with a message for Mrs Casvellan to come as soon as possible. Thank heaven she was at home. She was marvellous, and knew exactly what to do.'

'Knowing *you* as I do, I'm sure you were of great help to her, and to Mrs Varcoe.'

'At first I was terrified.' It didn't occur to her to pretend otherwise, not to him. They had shared so much these past weeks. As the attraction between them had strengthened, so the barriers she had erected around her heart had begun to crumble and fall. Necessity had brought them together: his need, her knowledge.

Working together had forged a bond neither had expected, a friendship that had blossomed and deepened, forcing her to recognize what she was missing. Living alone had afforded her protection from further hurt. But even before Charles arrived in Porthinnis she could no longer deny the void at the centre of her life that no amount of work could fill. Why else would she have contemplated marriage to William?

'You, terrified? I cannot believe it.'

'You would have, had you seen me. Fortunately with so much to do I had little time to think of myself. By the time the baby arrived Tamara was so exhausted I truly feared for her. But the instant she saw her daughter it was as if all memory of her effort and suffering were erased. I have never seen such – radiant joy. Then her husband returned.' Vividly recalling his fear and Tamara's tenderness made her throat swell. She swallowed hard.

'There was nothing more I could do, so I came away. Roz wanted me to spend the night at Trescowe. But I was anxious to come home. I had no expectation of seeing you tonight. But please believe that I intended seeking you out in the morning in order to explain.'

Leaning forward, Charles rested his elbows on his knees as he rubbed his face, then looked up at her. 'I would not have thought it possible to feel more ashamed of myself. But I do.'

'It was just one of those things. I'm sorry you were worried. Had there been time or opportunity I would have sent word.' She reached into the drawer for knives and spoons. 'Now we have both apologized I should like to hear how you got on in Truro.'

He held her chair then seated himself opposite. While they ate he told her about his meeting with Ralph Daniell.

'So the money is safely in your bank?'

'It will be tomorrow morning. I left the banker's draft with my attorney to deposit on my behalf. I was anxious to return to Porthinnis.' His gaze held hers across the table.

Powerfully drawn to him and made shy by a need new to her, she glanced away, wondering if he could see the betraying heat in her cheeks, and if so, if he guessed the cause. She rose to gather their empty plates and serve the apple pie. 'You must be delighted with progress at the harbour. According to Hannah, Mr Keat is a marvel. No detail escapes his notice and already he has the men's respect.'

They talked on, and as the clock struck nine she offered him a cup of tea. About to reply he was interrupted by a rap on the door.

As Jenefer hesitated, he rose from his chair and crossed to stand where he would not be seen when she opened the door.

'You will not want my presence here at this hour to be spread abroad,' he said softly, his gaze holding hers. 'It is no one else's business.'

'It's probably Lizzie, just making sure I'm all right, and wondering why I was so late home.'

Leaving the bottom half of the door bolted, Jenefer opened the top half, and jerked back. 'Captain Pendarvis!'

His eyes glittered in the lamplight as he steadied himself with a hand against the doorjamb and winked at her. 'And a very good evening to you, Miss Trevanion. Can I come in a minute?'

'Certainly not. I'm astonished you would even ask. Mr Lawry at The Standard has your money.'

'I didn't come for that.' He was impatient. 'I've been hearing talk.

Talk about you, and I don't like it.'

Jenefer's anger flared bright and hot as a flame. But her tone was crushing. 'You are impertinent, sir. I am not responsible for what others say. Nor are you obliged to listen. If that was your reason for calling at this unsociable hour you should have spared yourself the trouble.'

He swayed forward, clutching at the wall for support, his breath pungent with brandy fumes. 'You shouldn't be living in some old poky cottage, not when you could have a fine great house and—'

'Captain Pendarvis, I beg you will say no more.' Furious, she was also acutely aware of Charles listening. *What must he be thinking?* 'My arrangements are none of your business. And your concern is misplaced. I am very happy here.'

'You don't mean that. You're just making the best of it. Come on, maid,' he wheedled. 'Let me come in. I got money. You know that better'n anyone— '

'You are offensive, sir.' Jenefer started to close the door, but Pendarvis's hand shot out to hold it open.

'No, I didn't mean it like that—'

'Goodnight, Captain Pendarvis,' Jenefer said firmly. In the shadows beside her she sensed Charles stiffen. He was about to come to her aid, which would only make matters worse. Pendarvis had been drinking and was in the mood for a fight. She had no doubt Charles would win. But it was she who would suffer when Pendarvis took revenge for her rejection by spreading it about that she and Charles had been alone in her cottage after dark. Closing the door she shot the top bolt across, then pressed her palms to her hot cheeks.

'Does Pendarvis make a habit of bothering you?'

She shook her head. 'Tonight was the first time and I sincerely hope it will be the last.' Hugging herself she rubbed her upper arms. 'I have never sought his interest and certainly do not desire it.'

'Then may I ask what is your connection with him?'

'He's master of a customs cutter.'

'That I know. He came into The Standard one night while I was staying there. I saw Tom Lawry give him—' He paused. 'Of course: it was a bribe.'

She gave a weary nod. 'He is paid to ensure that every third or fourth run his cutter is patrolling some distant part of the coast.'

'What happens at the other times?'

'Occasionally Will Prowse manages to slip by without being seen. But if he and the captain meet at sea, Will hands over part of the cargo. In return, he is permitted to bring back the rest unhindered. Captain Pendarvis returns to Penzance with proof that he's doing his job. Though I suspect that only a fraction of the confiscated cargo actually ends up in the bonded store.' She darted him a quick smile. 'I offered you tea.'

He caught her hand, held it between both of his. 'Not tonight. It is time I went. You have had a long and tiring day.'

'I'm so glad you came, and that you stayed.'

As she reached for the latch he raised her hand to his lips. Her breath caught as he drew her gently towards him. She knew if she pulled back he would let her go. But she didn't want that.

His free hand stroked lightly down her face, then slid to the nape of her neck.

As her heart quickened she wondered if he could hear it. Cupping her face, he bent his head, whispered her name, then his lips brushed hers once, again, then claimed hers in a kiss as soft as a sigh.

Resting her hands against his waistcoat, she was awed to feel his heart pounding against her palm, as hard and fast as her own.

His arms went round her, drawing her closer still and she went to him willingly, surrendering herself to the wondrous sensations kindled by his mouth on hers. The kiss deepened. Tenderness gave way to passion, need, *hunger*. He offered she took, he demanded she gave, and lost herself in him. When he raised his head he was breathing hard, and she clung to him, momentarily bereft, her legs weak and trembling.

'Jenefer, I – there is so much I have to tell you. But— '

'It's late, and now is not the time?' She smiled up at him shakily, expecting a wry smile in return at the way events seemed to conspire against them. But his expression remained serious, his gaze dark, intense. She sensed a battle raging within him.

'Charles? What is it?'

Another knock came. Jenefer tensed and Charles cursed under his breath.

'You all right, bird?' Lizzie's voice came through the door.

As Charles stepped back out of sight, Jenefer lifted the latch and opened the top half.

'I'm fine, Lizzie.'

'Only Sam thought he heard—'

'It was Captain Pendarvis. I sent him round to Tom Lawry.'

'Mister come looking for you earlier. Some worried he was.'

'I'll see him tomorrow. Tamara gave birth to a baby girl late this afternoon. Roz Casvellan and I were with her. That's why I was late back.'

'Well, bless her dear heart. All right is she? And the babby?'

'They're both very well. But I'm exhausted.'

'You get up over stairs and go bed. I'll see you in the morning.'

'Thanks, Lizzie. Goodnight.'

''Night, my bird.'

Jenefer closed the door and kept her head close to it, listening. 'She's pushed the bolt across.'

'I should go.' Charles's voice was strained.

Seeking comfort and reassurance, needing to touch him, she echoed his gesture and laid her hand along his face. The roughness of stubble against her palm made something swoop inside her. 'Thank you for coming, for worrying about me, and for staying.'

With a groan, he kissed her once more. It was hard, fierce, and her hunger matched his. Tearing himself away, he seized his greatcoat from the peg and snatched up his hat and gloves as she quietly unbolted the door.

'You are everything to me,' he whispered harshly. 'Everything. Don't ever doubt it.'

He walked fast, oblivious to his surroundings. He had arrived in Porthinnis intent on his plans for the harbour: needing the project to be successful to prove to himself that the disaster of his private life was an isolated mistake; that in all else his judgement was sound.

Then he had met Jenefer Trevanion. That first lightning bolt of attraction had deepened into something he never expected and for which he was unprepared. He had fallen headlong in love with her. And loving her he hated knowing he was the cause of her confusion, the fear she tried so hard to hide that his refusal to declare himself implied some fault in her.

He owed her the truth, and regardless of his promise to Samson Kerrow, he must tell her soon. The longer he delayed the greater the risk of her hearing it from someone else. Had he told her the truth of his situation when they first met. . . . But his promise forbade it. Nor had he known then the impact she would have on his life, *on his heart.* Would she forgive him? *She must.* He could not bear to lose her.

*

On Saturday morning Jenefer called into the shop on her way down to the harbour.

'What happened last night?' Hannah demanded quietly as she closed the door behind a departing customer.

Jenefer set her basket on the counter. 'I've no idea, Hannah. I haven't been down to the harbour yet.'

'Nothing to do with the harbour. Jake Pendarvis was waiting for Will Prowse and took half the cargo.'

'*What?*' Shock tingled unpleasantly through Jenefer's limbs.

'I know. Jack Mitchell told me that when they come back into harbour, Will's brother had to carry him home. Far as I can make out, Pendarvis told Will to think hisself lucky he'd got off with a just few bruises. Next time he'd be arrested. And if he was brought up before Sir Edward Pengarrick he'd be sentenced to transportation and his boat sawn into three pieces.'

'I don't understand—'

'Didn't you pay Pendarvis?'

'Of course I did. I took the money round to Tom Lawry as usual last Monday.'

'So what's he at?'

'I have no idea.' Even as she spoke Jenefer remembered Pendarvis's visit to her cottage, and her rebuff. Surely he wouldn't jeopardize an arrangement that had suited him very well just because she turned him down? There had to be another reason. Yet she couldn't think of one. What on earth would have persuaded him that she would welcome his attentions? The very thought made her shudder.

'I suppose the news is on its way around the village.'

'The few who've come in the shop are angry at losing stuff they've paid for. But because all the men have got work, I reck'n people won't feel it so bad about it as they might have done. Still, one thing's for certain, we can't never trust Pendarvis again. And Will Prowse can't go smuggling no more.' Hannah snorted. 'Can you see 'n doing an honest day's work? He won't like that.'

'He would like gaol and transportation even less,' Jenefer pointed out.

'What are us going to do? How shall us get our free trade goods?'

Jenefer thought. 'You might be able to buy from the Brague men. Obviously their prices will be higher. But our people will still be better off as they won't have to pay the bribe, or face the loss of one in every three or four cargoes.'

'We won't have to worry about Pendarvis stopping the Brague boats,' Hannah said with a knowing look. 'Not with Sir Edward Pengarrick putting up the money for their cargoes.'

*

Draining his coffee cup, Charles rose from the table and left the dining room. As soon as the afternoon post had arrived he would return to the harbour. As he crossed the hall pounding hoofs skidded to a halt on the gravel outside. Waving the approaching manservant away, he opened the front door as the rider ran up the steps already reaching for the knocker.

'Steven!'

'Thank God you're here.' The lawyer removed his hat and wiped his perspiring forehead with a crumpled handkerchief. 'Where can we talk?'

'Follow me.' Charles led the way into the sitting room and closed the door. 'My dear fellow—'

'I have bad news. Barton's bank has failed.'

Charles felt the blood drain from his face. For an instant the world went black and he gripped the back of an armchair to steady himself. 'How much have we lost?'

'Only the money from K&P that you paid into the new company account.'

'But – the draft from Ralph Daniell—'

'Is safe.'

As relief coursed through him, Charles tugged a bell rope. 'Ale or brandy?'

'Ale, if you please. I'm parched.'

'Take off your coat and have a seat.' The door opened. 'A jug of ale, if you please, John. See that Mr Vincent's horse is given water, then pack me an overnight bag.' The servant left, closing the door quietly. Tossing his greatcoat over a chair, Steven sank onto a sofa. 'Tell me what you know,' Charles said.

'In truth, I didn't *know* anything until this morning when my clerk ran in to tell me there was a notice on Barton's door announcing the bank was closed. I'd been hearing the odd rumour about his son—'

'What kind of rumour?'

'That he had bought into a flooded copper mine anticipating a resurgence in the market. It was a shrewd move, especially as the Anglesea copper trade has collapsed and the Cornish market is rising. By all accounts the mine contains high-grade ore. But the cost of pumping out and restoring the machinery was higher than expected. He needed more money.'

'So who better to ask than his father who owns a bank?' Charles said bitterly.

Steven nodded, falling silent as the manservant entered carrying a tray.

'Thank you, John,' Charles said.

Placing the tray on a side table, the servant bowed. 'Your bag is packed, sir. I'll saddle your horse at once.' He closed the door quietly.

Charles poured ale and took it to his friend.

'Anyway,' Steven continued. 'I made a few discreet enquiries, and discovered that several of Barton's customers were complaining about what they perceived as unnecessary delays in being able to withdraw money from their accounts. There could have been a simple explanation. But something didn't feel right. So I decided not to deposit the draft until I found out more.'

'I'm grateful for your caution.'

Steven raised the tankard in salute. 'Your very good health.' He downed half.

'Give me a moment to tell my housekeeper,' Charles said, 'and I'll return with you to Helston. My first task is to open a new account for the Porthinnis Harbour Company with another bank and deposit

Daniell's draft. I need to have money available to settle accounts and pay wages.'

'Charles, the loss of this money means—'

'I know,' Charles broke in grimly. 'There won't be enough to complete the project.'

'What will you do?'

'What I must. I'll have to ask Samson for additional funds.'

Chapter Eighteen

As she walked up the road towards Kegwyn, Jenefer felt her pulse quicken in anticipation of seeing Charles. Pausing at the gate she looked back at the harbour. The sea was pewter-grey, the sun a white disc sinking in a pearly sky. Far to the west a low line of cloud bubbled like boiling milk.

Gangs were unloading cargo, barrowing stone to be tipped onto the growing piles ready to be spread as soon as the roadbed was ready. More men laboured on the quay extension: erecting the next pair of piles, sawing planks and cross members for the corresponding section of deck. She could see a small boat tied to one of the piles, tipping concrete. Out beyond the harbour entrance a brig was anchored a short distance from the headland beneath Pednbrose and men were heaving huge lumps of granite overboard to form the base of the mole.

Without warning, and for no reason she could think of, unease slithered down her spine. She brushed it aside. Everything was going according to plan. She breathed deeply as pride and pleasure expanded inside her. Charles was responsible for all this: for bringing work and a prosperous future to the village. Mr Keat too was proving invaluable.

As she crossed the gravel she noticed some deep gouges and wondered what Harry had been dragging across it. Climbing the steps she tapped three times with the knocker.

Cora Eustace opened the door. 'Afternoon, Miss Trevanion. I'm afraid mister isn't here. A gentleman arrived here just after two. In some rush he was: skidded his horse all across the gravel. Harry was afeared the poor thing was going nose over tail. Anyway, John come into the kitchen saying he had to fetch a jug of ale then saddle mister's horse.'

'John?' Jenefer had not recommended anyone of that name.

'John Noall, mister's own valet. Now he've come, Abel Caddy have gone back to Trescowe. Anyhow, couldn't have been no more'n twenty minutes later, mister and this gentleman rode off in some great rush. Mister had an overnight bag with 'n and I had no chance to ask when he'd be home again. But just before he went he did say that if you come by I was to ask you very kindly to pay the wages and he'd see you when he got back. Want to leave that, do you?' She nodded at the folder of letters Jenefer was holding. 'I'll put 'n on the bureau, and he'll see it the minute he go in.'

'Thank you, Cora.' She handed over the folder and bade the house-keeper good afternoon. As she retraced her steps, Jenefer wondered what could have taken him away in such a hurry. It had to be a matter of great urgency.

As the doubts caused by his reticence crowded back, she fought them hard. If the passion in his kisses were not enough to convince her of what he felt, she had only to remember his parting words while standing in her kitchen: *You are everything to me. Everything.*

Her heart still skipped a beat every time she recalled the sound of his voice and the look in his eyes. Why then would he not commit himself? They had come so far since their initial wariness. She recalled the way he had pressed her into helping him find a house; his interest in her business; their discussions about the project; and underlying it all, deep, powerful, undeniable attraction.

But in truth she knew little about him. He had spoken briefly of his childhood and of his work abroad. But courtesy would not allow her to press when he steered conversation away from personal matters. She knew she was valuable to him regarding the harbour project and he had always been generous in his gratitude. He had kissed her with a sweetness that had brought tears to her eyes, and a passion that had stirred her to the depths of her soul, leaving her weak, breathless, and aching for more. *Trust me*, he'd said. She would, she must.

*

As the clerk withdrew and the two men bowed politely, Charles was relieved to have found Samson in his office and was thus spared having to call on him at home. He had no quarrel with Susan. But he was glad to avoid any risk of meeting Eve or her mother.

'It's a pleasure to see you, Charles. Take a seat.' Samson lowered himself into a high-backed chair behind his desk. 'Have you heard the news about Barton's?' He shook his head. 'A bad business, very bad.'

Placing his hat and gloves on a side table, Charles sat, crossing one leg over the other. The moment his gaze had met Samson's he had noted a barely suppressed excitement that warned of trouble. He waited, apparently relaxed. But behind the façade he was wary.

'Mind you,' Samson continued as if sharing a confidence, 'I began having doubts about Edward Barton weeks ago. The man looked ill.'

Charles recalled Barton's pallor when he had visited the banker's office to set up the new company account.

'I knew his son had bought into a copper mine,' Samson went on. 'A good move, considering the price of Cornish ore has doubled in recent months. But then I started hearing rumours about spiralling costs and no money to meet them. Next thing I learn is that Edward Barton has put money into the venture. But I happen to know he lost much of his personal fortune in the copper crash. So where, I asked myself, had he obtained funds to invest? I had a bad feeling. What if Barton was propping up his son's venture using clients' money? Of course, I could have been wrong. But I wasn't willing to take that chance. So I closed Kerrow & Polgray's account and transferred our business to the Helston branch of Praed's Cornish Bank. Just in time as it turned out.'

Charles brushed dust from his thigh as he fought to control his fury. Samson had willingly, *deliberately*, forfeited K&P's investment in the Porthinnis Harbour Company. When he spoke his voice was flat calm. 'It didn't occur to you to warn me?'

'My dear fellow.' Samson spread his hands. 'How could I? You weren't at home, so how was I to know where you were?'

'You could have informed my attorney. You know his address well enough.' Charles took a calming breath. There was nothing to be gained by pursuing it. 'No matter. Your decision was indeed shrewd and timely. The fact that K&P has not suffered financially from Barton's collapse is excellent news. I was less fortunate as the funds K&P invested in the Porthinnis Harbour expansion were lost.'

'And you have come here to beg for more.'

Charles resented Samson's phrasing and his manner, but knowing it was deliberate he refused to bite and merely nodded.

'I have opened a new company account at Praed's with a banker's draft for eight thousand from Ralph Daniell. But that won't be enough. Work has begun on a new road, the quay extension and the mole, and we are making good progress. But to complete the project, the funds lost to Barton's must be replaced.'

'Of course I'll help you,' Samson said. 'On one condition.' Sitting back in his chair he regarded Charles over his steepled fingers. 'You must install a manager at Porthinnis and return home.'

Home? What home? It cost Charles every ounce of will power he possessed to remain seated. Cold rage made him tremble inside, but his voice was rock steady, his tone scathing. 'Have you no shame? Such a demand is disgraceful. It is emotional blackmail. The bank's failure and resulting loss of company money are entirely a business matter. They have no connection to my personal life.'

A dull flush stained Samson's cheeks, but his gaze did not falter. 'Your continued absence is causing gossip, and soon that *will* reflect on the company. Eve is restless and unhappy. Her mother is terrified the truth will come out. If it does, the scandal will dash any hope for Susan's future prospects.'

'I am not responsible for Eve's situation, nor answerable for her behaviour. Both are a direct result of indulgence by you and her mother. Nor will I delegate responsibility for a project of such importance and financial benefit both to the company and the village.'

Samson's mouth thinned and he raised his chin. 'That is my condition.'

Charles rose to his feet. 'To hell with you. Tomorrow I ride to Bodmin to appear at the Archdeaconry Court. My marriage to your daughter *will* be annulled. As far as the harbour expansion is concerned, I withdraw my request. I shall raise the necessary funds myself.'

*

Jenefer pushed her dinner plate aside and turned the page of the *Sherborne Mercury and General Advertiser*. She scanned the latest news of the war reprinted from the *London Gazette*, then her gaze skipped over announcements of a Turnpike Trustees meeting, an advertisement for remarkable cures for cancers, and another for the sale of a brewery and malthouse.

Conscious of the work still awaiting her attention, and hearing the postman's voice as he greeted Ernestine, she was about to close the newspaper when her gaze was caught by the heading BARTON'S BANK.

The notice was small, a few lines only, announcing the bank's failure. Horror gripped her as she read on: an investigation had begun and Barton's clients were advised to contact solicitors whose address was given below. Barton's was the bank in which Charles had placed the funds for the harbour development.

'Letter for you, Miss Trevanion,' the postman called through the open door.

'One moment.' Fetching her purse she paid him, and her heart lurched as she recognized Charles's writing. Hastily she broke the seal and unfolded the sheet.

> *Forgive my scrawl but I write in haste to inform you of the failure of Barton's Bank. Let me reassure you that though some funds were lost, the main part, namely the draft from Ralph Daniell, is safely deposited with Praed's. Though inconvenient, the loss will not jeopardize the project. However, dealing with the repercussions will keep me away a while longer. I apologize for the burden my absence will place on you. But I have the utmost confidence in your ability to liaise with Mr Keat and keep the work moving forward. I will tell you everything on my return.*
> *Ever yours, Charles.*

Closing her eyes, Jenefer pressed the letter to her heart, thrilled by his trust and belief in her. After reading it again she refolded it and tucked it into the dresser drawer, then put on her coat and bonnet and hurried down to the harbour to inform Mr Keat that Charles would be away a little longer, and to ask if he had everything he needed.

*

The archdeacon, his black garb a stark contrast to his white wig and florid complexion, sat in an ornately carved high-backed chair befitting his status as the bishop's representative in matters of ecclesiastical law. In front of him a table held several leather-bound volumes with gold lettering on their broad spines. Below the dais two clerks sat behind

191

smaller tables containing ledgers, paper and writing materials. Their tables, one on either side of the dais, were angled so they could easily see both the Archdeacon and the petitioner's lectern at which Charles now stood. It was clear their function was to take detailed notes of the hearing and record the archdeacon's decision.

Arriving at the old Franciscan friary that housed not only the Archdeaconry Court which specialized in matters relating to wills, marriage and legitimacy, but also an additional courtroom and a house of corrections, he had waited for almost an hour in a large anteroom thronged with people. Some had sat silently on chairs against the wall and stared at the floor. Others, alone or in family groups listened with anxious expressions to black-suited men he assumed were lawyers. Eventually he had been summoned and guided in by a clerk. After taking his place at the lectern he had waited while the archdeacon scanned some papers. Then he looked up.

'I will hear your petition, Mr Polgray.'

'Sir, I request that my marriage be annulled on the grounds of fraud and deception. When Eve Kerrow married me she was already with child by another man. Her mother colluded with her to ensure I was kept ignorant of the situation. In support of my petition I have submitted to you a letter from Dr Edmonds, the Kerrows' family physician, which states that on the date of his examination, June 14th, the pregnancy was by his estimation at least three months advanced. I have included a certified copy of the entry in church records of the date of my marriage to Eve Kerrow dated 24th May, plus notarized statements from four witnesses that prove I was not in England when the child was conceived.' Charles's hand touched the breast of his coat beneath which he had placed the folded documents. 'I have additional copies should you require them.'

One of the clerks rose from his seat, carried a large black Bible across to Charles and set it in front of him on the lectern.

'Place your right hand on the Holy Bible.' Charles did so. 'Do you solemnly swear that all the information you have given this court is true?'

'I do so swear,' Charles declared, his voice strong and clear.

Remaining beside him, the clerk turned to face the archdeacon while his colleague's pen scratched in the silence.

'You may go, Mr Polgray.' The archdeacon nodded dismissal. 'I shall inform you of my decision in due course.'

About to protest, to demand – plead – he be told now, Charles felt the clerk's hand grip his elbow with strength surprising in one who appeared thin and somewhat frail, and was ushered out of the court.

'Wouldn't have done any good, sir,' the clerk said quietly. 'The archdeacon takes his responsibilities very seriously. Even when all the criteria have been fulfilled and a nullity decree is inevitable he never tells the petitioner so during the hearing.'

'If I were to stay in Bodmin tonight, might I be able to collect the decree tomorrow?'

'With respect, sir, the court generates a vast amount of paperwork. The matters dealt with and the decisions made here reflect on the bishop and the church. Procedures must be followed. All this takes time. And, again with the greatest respect, sir, yours is only one of a long list of petitions to be heard during this session.'

'Of course.' Charles reached inside his coat for money. 'I understand, and am more than happy to recompense you for any inconvenience.' Whatever it cost would be money well spent if it meant he could return to Porthinnis with the annulment in his pocket.

'No, sir.' The clerk put out a hand, forestalling him. 'You *don't* understand. The archdeacon is a most able gentleman, and I consider it a privilege to have clerked for him this past twenty years. But he deals with matters in a particular order. In all the time I have known him that order has remained unchanged. I'm sorry, sir.'

'My apologies. I intended no offence.'

'I take none, sir.' The clerk was too discreet to offer commiserations, but there was sympathy in his gaze.

Charles slapped his hat against his thigh as frustration and disappointment boiled over. 'What was the point of summoning me here? Why make me ride all this way for an appearance that lasted less than five minutes?'

'The archdeacon is a shrewd man, sir,' the clerk said, guiding him along a stone-flagged passage towards a massive oak door that stood open. Outside the sun shone; in the passage the light subdued, the air cold. 'And one of great experience. Your manner and conduct will have told him as much as the papers you submitted. May I suggest you go on home?'

'Please, you must have some idea. How long—?'

'Depending on the weather and the state of the roads, a week at most. It may be less.'

Hiding his devastation, Charles made a brief formal bow. 'I'm obliged to you.' Replacing his hat he left, pulling the brim low over eyes that burned. He had pinned all his hopes on returning to Porthinnis a free man, his marriage dissolved as if it had never existed. Now he faced more waiting. Still weary from the previous day's long ride, the shocking news of Barton's collapse and his unpleasant scene with Samson, he considered staying in Bodmin another night and calling on the clerk again in the morning. But he could not afford the time.

He returned to the inn where he had passed the previous night. He had slept little. Now he must move forward. The hearing was over and with luck he would receive the decree within a week. In the crowded dining room he ate steak pie washed down with ale. Then strapping his bag to the back of the saddle, he mounted his horse for the long ride back. Before he reached Porthinnis, he needed to have thought of a means of raising the additional funds.

*

After several days had passed with no further news, Jenefer wrote a note to Charles asking him to call on her when convenient. Needing a break from paperwork, and wanting a walk and some fresh air, she decided to carry the note up to Kegwyn herself, intending to leave it with Cora. But when the door was opened in response to her knock, Cora's harassed expression broke into a smile.

'Miss Trevanion! Come in, come in. Mister got back not ten minutes since. He was asking if you'd been round. I told 'n about the letters you brung.'

'I won't stay.' Jenefer had to force the words out, so great was her desire to see him. 'If he has just returned he will have much to do—'

'He'll be some mad if—' Cora began.

'Indeed, I will,' Charles said.

As the housekeeper turned, Jenefer saw him approaching down the hall. As he came forward into the light, her heart went out to him. His face was drawn and haggard. His boots were muddy, his fawn breeches and dark green coat were streaked with dust, and his hat had left a red mark across his forehead.

'You look exhausted,' she said softly, the words out before she realized. Catching herself, she offered him the note. 'Really, I won't stay. I simply wanted to leave this for you—'

'A moment, if you please,' he interrupted her and turned to the housekeeper. 'A tray of tea, Mrs Eustace?'

'I'll bring 'n to the sitting room, shall I, sir?'

'Thank you.'

Cora bobbed, smiled at Jenefer then bustled back to the kitchen.

Charles stood aside and gestured for her to enter. 'Humour me,' he said as she hesitated. 'I'm tired and thirsty. I have been hours in the saddle. But now I am home, and you are here, and I want to hear what is in your note from your own lips.' His gaze dipped to her mouth and her lips tingled as if he had kissed them. Her breath stopped in her throat as he raised his eyes to hers. 'Please?'

She stepped inside and he closed the front door, then opened the sitting-room door and stood back for her to pass. Crossing to the spinet he opened the lid and beckoned her over.

'While I make myself presentable, will you play something? This house has been too long without music.' He backed towards the door. 'I will be but a few minutes.' Leaving it ajar, he disappeared, and Jenefer heard him take the stairs two at a time.

She smiled to herself. Her reluctance had been genuine. He did look desperately tired. But his determination that she should stay for a while was balm to her troubled soul. Laying the note on top of the spinet, she drew out the stool and sat down. Resting her fingers lightly on the keyboard, she thought for a moment then began to play a sonata by Thomas Arne. She followed that with two pieces by Purcell, glancing up as Cora carried in a laden tray and set it on a low table.

'Don't you stop,' Cora said. 'Sound lovely, it do.' She went out leaving the door ajar, and returned moments later with a plate of buttered scones and another of squares of hevva cake.

Jenefer was halfway through a Bach minuet when Charles returned. She stopped playing. His hair was damp and neatly brushed and he had changed his clothes for cream pantaloons tucked into glossy hessian boots, a dark blue coat and a fresh neckcloth. He came to stand by the spinet, his hands clasped behind his back as he watched her.

'Please, finish it. You play— '

'Very ill.' She smiled up at him. Her fingers trembled and she struck a wrong note. 'You see?' She closed the lid and stood up. He indicated a sofa by the low table containing the tea tray. She sat, and watched him fold into an armchair, his knees so close to hers that they almost touched. He had washed off the dust and grime of the journey, but not his exhaustion. Barton's collapse must have hit him hard.

He smiled at her. 'Will you pour?'

She did as he asked, aware of him watching, and feeling her throat and face grow warm. When she had placed the saucer in front of him he lifted the cup, raising it slightly in salute, then drank deeply. 'So, tell me what is in your note.'

Jenefer cradled her cup, resting her hands on her lap so their tremor was less noticeable. 'Hannah wanted to know if there was any connection between the failure of Barton's Bank and your absence from the village. It's possible she could have made the connection on her own, but I think it more likely she overheard others discussing the possibility. As the most important thing was – is – to maintain confidence in the harbour expansion, I told her that Ralph Daniell of the Cornish Bank in Truro is a major investor in the scheme. I also reminded her of his golden reputation as a shrewd businessman and his nickname of *guinea-a-minute*. I said that though Barton's collapse was tragic for everyone involved, it would have no impact on Porthinnis or the project.' She raised the cup to her lips, heard it clatter against her teeth, felt the hot liquid soothe her dry throat and warm her tense stomach then lowered the cup once more.

'I hope you don't mind. I realize I took a lot upon myself. But it seemed to me that what mattered most was to maintain confidence. And that meant stopping the rumours and quashing any doubts.'

'*Mind?*' He shook his head. 'I could not have done better myself. In fact, had I been here I would have done exactly the same.'

Pleasure swelled like a bubble inside her. She felt light enough to float. She glanced up at him, saw a muscle jump in his jaw, and set her cup on its saucer.

'Charles, you are exhausted. I want to hear your news. I have looked forward so much to your return. But right now you need—'

'I need you to tell me what is in your note.'

'Very well. It – I – I have a business proposal to put to you.'

He gestured for her to continue.

She moistened her lips with the tip of her tongue. 'I want to make you a loan to replace what you lost at Barton's on the same terms as your agreement with Kerrow & Polgray.' She paused to take a breath, growing hot under his intent gaze. 'From my point of view it's an excellent investment. The project is sound. And I like the idea of my money working for the good of the village.' She jumped as he left his chair and strode to the window, clasping his arms across his body as he stared out.

She stayed where she was. Despite his utter stillness, once again she sensed a violent battle raging inside him. 'I didn't actually write all that. My note merely asked you to call on me whenever it was convenient as I had a business proposal to discuss with you. But as I'm here, I thought—'

He did not move. She wondered if he had even heard her.

'Charles?'

He turned. The light was behind him, his face in shadow.

'I don't know. . . .' His voice cracked.

'How to thank me?' she teased, wanting him to respond in kind. Something was preying on him. *Of course it was. The expansion of Porthinnis harbour was entirely his responsibility and he had just lost a sizeable amount of money earmarked for wages and materials.* 'I neither seek nor desire thanks. As an investment opportunity it speaks for itself. So if you were about to turn me down,' she hurried on, 'please don't. Unless – have you found an alternative source of funds?'

He released a deep sigh. 'Since my attorney arrived with the news I have been exploring alternatives. I applied to K&P for further funds, but the terms demanded were unacceptable. So without your investment the development is at risk.'

She went to him, clutched his arm. 'You can't let that happen,' she said fiercely. 'The village needs it.'

'I need it,' he said quietly, laying his hand over hers. 'And I accept your offer. There are no words to express my gratitude.'

Jenefer laid her fingertips lightly against his mouth. 'Then don't try.

I have no need of it.' Her gaze searched his: saw hunger that matched her own, heat that burned her skin and turned her liquid inside. 'I missed you,' she whispered.

Catching her hand he pressed warm lips to her palm, then held it against his beard-roughened jaw. 'And I you. More than you will ever know.'

Knuckles rapped politely on the door. Kissing her palm once more, Charles released her hand and Jenefer moved away.

'Come,' he called, remaining by the window.

The door opened and Cora entered. 'Beg pardon, sir, but Mr Casvellan's here—'

'No doubt the two of you have much to discuss,' Jenefer said, quickly collecting her bonnet and gloves. 'So I will leave you now.'

'My most grateful thanks, Miss Trevanion.' His eyes offered her more, much more. Then he turned to Cora. 'Please show Mr Casvellan in.'

Jenefer met Casvellan on the threshold and dropped a neat curtsy.

'Good afternoon, Miss Trevanion.' Casvellan bowed, then his mouth curved. 'My wife tells me you were of great assistance at the happy event last week.'

'She flatters me,' Jenefer laughed. 'But it was a wonderful and deeply moving experience. Good day to you both.'

Chapter Nineteen

Casvellan declined Charles's offer of refreshment, but lowered himself onto the sofa where so recently Jenefer had sat. 'I am on my way home and will not detain you long. The reason for my visit is threefold. Firstly, to say how impressed I am, not only with the speed of progress on the various parts of the development, but with the quality of work.'

Charles acknowledged the compliment with a nod. 'I must share the credit with my clerk of works. Cyrus Keat was recently employed on a harbour development in north Cornwall. Familiar with this type of work, he has proved invaluable.'

'My second reason,' Casvellan paused, glancing away for a moment as if ordering his thoughts. When he looked up his gaze was level and penetrating. 'You will appreciate, Mr Polgray, that during my years as a justice I acquired a wide and varied circle of acquaintance. Thus I am sometimes privy to information not generally known.'

Charles's mouth dried, but he held Casvellan's gaze, hoping his features betrayed nothing of the sick dread stirring inside him.

'For example, it has come to my attention that your new company suffered a significant loss when Barton's failed. Yet by some miracle Kerrow & Polgray lost nothing, having most fortuitously transferred all company finance to another bank.'

Charles had to use his tongue to free his upper lip from his front teeth. He adjusted the cuff of his left sleeve. 'That is correct.'

'I assume you applied to Samson Kerrow for further investment?'

'I did. But without success.'

'Surely he did not turn you down? After all, he had escaped intact. And the Porthinnis development is guaranteed to return a profit for its investors.'

'No, he did not turn me down. But he attached a condition to the loan that was unacceptable to me.' *How much did Casvellan know?* Charles moistened his lips. If he wanted Casvellan's trust he had to earn it. Much as he loathed revealing what a fool he had been, honesty was the only course open to him.

'Earlier this year I was the victim of a calculated fraud by people I knew and trusted. It has taken several months to rectify the wrong that was done to me. My appearance yesterday at the Archdeaconry Court in Bodmin will, I hope, finally bring the whole wretched business to an end.'

'Miss Trevanion does not know.' Casvellan's tone made it a statement not a question.

Charles could sit still no longer. He rose and started to walk to the window then realized Casvellan would not be able to see his face. Instead he crossed to the spinet and ran his fingers along the polished wood, vividly recalling Jenefer seated there, her fingers dancing over the keys as she played music that struck answering chords inside him. 'When she and I first met, I considered it a private matter, nor was it relevant then. In addition I felt bound by a promise of silence to protect the Kerrows' younger daughter.'

'And now?'

'Now I must and will tell her. But I wanted the nullity decree in my possession first.' He gestured helplessly. 'As proof of what had occurred, and of my intent.'

'How long—?'

'The clerk said a week at most.'

'Let us hope for less.'

Charles assumed his guest would leave now. But Casvellan didn't move.

'Do you recall our conversation at Trescowe when I broached the possibility of my becoming a shareholder in your company?'

Charles had not forgotten, but nor had he wanted to go cap in hand to the landowner until he had exhausted all other possibilities. He waited, his heart thudding heavily. Had Casvellan changed his mind? 'I remember.'

A faint smile lifted the corners of Casvellan's mouth. 'I am not about to add to your problems, Mr Polgray. I wish to formally confirm my interest. I foresee a great future for the Porthinnis Harbour Company.'

Charles swallowed. 'I am very much obliged to you.'

Casvellan rose and offered his hand. 'You have my sympathy. May I be permitted a word of advice? Choose your moment, but don't delay too long. Better she hears the facts from you, than gossip and lies from others who may not have her best interests at heart.'

As Casvellan rode away, Charles crossed the gravel and walked a little way down the gently sloping grass. The rising wind tugged at his hair and blew cold against his face as dark, rain-filled clouds rolled in from the south-west. The sea had developed a heavy swell and foam-crested waves crashed and splintered on the rocks below, hurling curtains of spray into the air. He tasted salt on his lips and turned his gaze towards the harbour and the partially extended quay.

Might it have been wiser to begin building the mole from the end nearest the quay instead of starting construction at the end nearest Pednbrose? Possibly, but he'd had good reason for not doing so. It would have interfered with the trading brigs and the frequent arrivals and departures of those bringing stone from Penryn.

The extension was sound and strong, the quality of work excellent. Mr Keat had seen to that. He was worrying unnecessarily. He returned to the house, ordered John to prepare a bath, and almost fell asleep in it. While eating the tasty supper Mrs Eustace had prepared, he read and signed letters, then jotted down reminders of tasks for the following day.

Lying in bed he listened to the thunder of the waves and the howling wind. This past week he had lurched from the anxiety caused by Barton's failure, to rage at Samson's blackmail. But Jenefer and Casvellan had given him fresh hope. Jenefer: so unexpected: joy of his heart, beloved. *I missed you.* He slid into the deep dark sleep of exhaustion.

Outside the gale raged, tearing twigs and leaves from creaking branches that bowed to its force. Rain lashed down. Waves laden with shingle smashed into the wooden piles and pounded the stones supporting them. Tiny cracks appeared in the cement, lengthened, grew wider. As it crumbled, a large lump of granite broke free and was sucked away by the swirling currents. Then another. . . .

*

Charles tried to ignore the hammering, clinging to sleep. But it continued, demanding attention. He opened his eyes, realized someone was knocking on his door. 'Yes?' he croaked, pushing himself upright and shoving both hands through his hair.

His valet entered. 'Sorry to disturb you, sir, but Mr Keat is downstairs and wishes to speak to you most urgently.' Opening the closet John took out a long quilted cotton banyan and held it open.

Scrambling out of bed, Charles pulled it on over his nightshirt and shoved his feet into slippers. 'Where?'

'The dining room, sir.'

He was still tying the sash as he ran downstairs. Opening the door, he smelled fresh coffee and saw Keat sitting at the table with a steaming cup in front of him. The clerk started to rise, but Charles waved him down. 'No, stay where you are.' Their eyes met and Charles steeled himself, dread a solid weight in his stomach. At the sideboard he lifted the coffee pot. As he poured a tremor shook his hand and some spilled into the saucer. He carried his cup to the table and pulled out a chair. 'Tell me.'

''Tis the quay extension, sir.' Keat's weathered complexion was pale.

'How bad?'

'Gone. All of it.' Keat gripped his own cup with shaking hands. 'Once the piles went down the decking followed. Whole bleddy lot smashed to kindling.' Keat raised angry eyes. 'Some mess it is down there. I tell 'e, sir, it shouldn't have happened. The wood was solid and the work was good. They miners know what they're doing. You seen it for yourself.'

'I did,' Charles nodded. He swallowed hot coffee, feeling it curl in his stomach and send much needed strength through his body. 'I agree with everything you say. So there is only one possible explanation—'

'Bleddy Morton's cement,' Keat said. He drained his cup and stood up. 'I'd best get back. Men'll be arriving for work.'

Charles drained his own cup. 'I won't be beaten.' He spoke softly, the words a vow and a declaration of intent. He stood up. 'We will rebuild, Mr Keat. It will take a little longer than planned—'

'There'll be some mess to clear away first,' Keat said.

'Then get to it, Mr Keat. The tide is ebbing. Concentrate on salvage. With luck, some of the wood will be reusable. As soon as you know how much you need to replace, inform Miss Trevanion and she will order it. The crumbled cement and stone on the seabed must be dredged out of the way. You will need heavy chains.'

'Leave it to me, Mr Polgray. I'll hire men and boats on a day rate. Be down d'rectly, will you, sir?'

Charles knew what Keat was really asking. The men would need reassurance that despite this setback work would continue, and the picture he had painted for them at the harvest dance, the hopes he had kindled, would still be realized.

'I'll be at the harbour within the hour.'

*

Kept awake for much of the night by the howling wind and rain splattering like gravel against her window, Jenefer rose early. She washed; brushed and pinned up her hair, then put on a long-sleeved, high-necked gown of apple green muslin, fine wool stockings and her brown ankle boots. She carried the slop bucket downstairs and opened the top door to a mellow autumn morning.

The sky was a clear blue, the air crisp and scented with wood smoke and frying bacon. She had just finished her breakfast of buttered bread and hot chocolate when she heard running feet on the cobbles outside. She started to smile, assuming Lizzie's son, Billo, had been sent home by his father to collect whatever had been forgotten before they set off for the day's fishing.

'Miss! Miss!' Billo shouted, hammering on her door.

Hearing the urgency in his tone Jenefer wrenched it open just as Lizzie appeared.

'What is it, Billo?' The boy's face was flushed from his sprint and his chest heaved as he sucked in air.

'Dear life, boy!' Lizzie began, but fell silent at Jenefer's touch on her arm.

'Miss, the quay's gone. Washed away in the gale last night.'

'Oh my dear lord!' Lizzie gasped, one hand flying to her cheek.

'Mr Polgray sent me—'

'Go back and tell him I'm on my way,' Jenefer said. Pausing long enough to put on her short jacket and grab a notebook and sharpened pencil from among the books at one end of the table, she dashed out again. 'Lizzie, will you—?"

'Leave it all to me, bird. You get on.'

She arrived on the back quay breathless, heart racing, and stopped abruptly, appalled at the destruction wrought by the storm. Labourers had gathered at the end of the quay. Two boats were already anchored below amid the wreckage of the extension and men were hauling lengths of decking and broken supports out of the water. Two more had managed to secure ropes around a floating oak pile and were preparing to tow it into the harbour where most of the fishing boats appeared to have survived the storm unscathed.

Jenefer looked for Charles, and spotted him among the miners on the quay. As if sensing her presence he looked up. After a few more words with the men, he started towards her. She met him halfway. 'What can I do?'

The quick flare of gratitude in his eyes told her all he did not have time to say. 'I must ride to Truro.'

'To see Mr Daniell?'

Charles nodded, his expression grim. 'I had eight thousand set aside for the construction. I lost two when Barton's failed, and last night's disaster has cost us another £2000.'

'Will you apply for an additional loan or an extension of the repayment period?' Jenefer asked quietly.

'Both. Though I think it unlikely he'll agree.'

'Surely it's in his interest to be flexible? This is a setback to be sure—'

'It should never have happened.' Charles fought to contain his anger. 'The cement was faulty and I intend to prove it. Which is where I need your help. Get a sample of it from Mr Keat. I've told him to expect you. Then write a letter to Parker's – you sign it on my behalf – asking them to test it against their standard product. While I'm in Truro I'll try to find another supplier.'

Jenefer nodded. 'I'll do my best to catch the morning post. Is there anything else?'

'Not at the moment. Except. . . .' He hesitated.

'Yes?'

'I should warn you it is possible Mr Daniell will demand the sale of Pednbrose.'

Jenefer looked across to the headland. 'That was another time, a different life. Perhaps whoever buys it will rebuild. It would be nice to see a house there instead of a ruin.' She darted a grin at him. 'I shall miss the fruit. But as I helped myself to it for three years even though it was no longer mine I'm hardly in a position to complain.'

'You are . . . amazing.'

'No, I'm not. Bad things happen to people all the time. I could have become bitter and resentful. But what would that have achieved? So I picked myself up and rebuilt my life. When I look at where I am now, at all I have learned, and the friends I have made,' – her face grew warm but she held his gaze – 'I would not change a thing.'

He swayed slightly towards her and she felt an answering pull.

'I think' – she swallowed, pointed – 'Someone is trying to attract your attention.'

Reluctantly he glanced round. 'It's John with my horse. I'm not sure how long I'll be away. But when I get back, will you come to dinner? Doubtless I *should* have asked if I might call on you.' His mouth twisted wryly. 'But we are less likely to be interrupted at Kegwyn. And there is so much I need to tell you.'

She touched his hand lightly. 'Thank you. I should enjoy that very much.'

'I must go.'

'Safe journey, Charles,' she smiled up at him. 'And good luck.'

His expression turned grim. 'I'll need it.'

*

Jenefer was kept busy during the next three days. Each morning she walked down to the harbour, detecting a little more warmth in Cyrus Keat's gruff welcome as items he asked her to order were delivered. The roadbed was nearing completion. Seven of the eight oak piles had been retrieved, as had most of the supports and decking. Meanwhile cargoes continued to arrive.

She updated accounts relating to the harbour and her own clients, noted invoices in the relevant ledgers, worked out the wages and drew the money from her own account to pay them. Each time she stopped,

205

for a meal or at the end of the day, she wondered where Charles was, and what success he was having.

It was just after midday on Friday when she left her cottage. 'I'm just taking some money round to Tom Lawry,' she told Lizzie.

Reaching The Standard she saw a dogcart halted near the front door. The driver, and an older woman smartly dressed in a maroon coat and matching bonnet trimmed with ribbons and curved ostrich feathers, were helping a younger woman dressed in sapphire blue to alight from the cart. Though Jenefer was too far away to hear what was being said, it was clear from their voices that the two women were arguing.

She walked through the back door into warmth and the mouth-watering scent of roasting meat. She peered into the kitchen.

'Hello, Nell. Something smells delicious.'

'Lovely great joint of beef, miss.' A white apron covered Nell Hitchens' faded pink gown. Her frizzy hair was tucked into a frilled cap, and flour dusted her forearms as she rolled out pastry with brisk strokes. 'If you want missus I b'lieve she's in the private parlour making up the fire.' Nell rolled her eyes. 'Annie never come in this morning, so there's just the two of us.'

'I won't disturb her then. Where's Mr Lawry?'

'He should be in the taproom.'

Thanking her, Jenefer started along the passage and almost collided with Esther as she emerged carrying a coal scuttle.

'Hello, my bird,' Esther beamed. 'How you keeping? Busy as ever?'

Jenefer smiled and pulled a face. 'Even busier, but it keeps me out of mischief.' She held up the purse. 'I've brought the week's beer money.'

'Best if you give it to Tom. If you give me a minute to drop this I'll tell 'n you're here.'

'No, Esther, it's all right. I'll take it in myself.' But she was talking to herself as Esther had disappeared into the kitchen. Jenefer turned into the short passage that led to the back of the taproom. As she drew closer she recognized the voice of the woman from the dogcart.

'But the road from Helston is very poor and most uncomfortable, especially for someone in my daughter's delicate condition. Something should be done about it.'

Jenefer heard a sound behind her and looked round as Esther reappeared.

'Anyway,' the woman continued, 'we are come to see my daughter's husband who has business here in the village. His name is Polgray. Would you be so kind as to oblige us with his direction?'

Jenefer's gaze met Esther's. *Her daughter's husband? Delicate condition? Polgray?* Jenefer's hand flew up to cover her mouth. There was a roaring in her ears and the world went black. Her legs gave way and she slid down the wall, her hand still clamped across her mouth, afraid she would be sick, afraid she would scream. Then, after the first shattering, numbing shock came a knife-thrust of pain. She pressed her forearm across her waist and bent forward in agony.

'Oh my dear sweet Lord!' Esther whispered. 'All right, my bird. I'll fetch some brandy. You just stay there. Don't try to move.' She went to the door of the tap and called to her husband in a whisper. 'Tom! *Tom!*'

In the far distance Jenefer heard him excuse himself. Then his voice was nearer.

'What?' There was a pause, then, 'God alive! What happened? What's wrong with her?'

'She was bringing you the beer money. She heard—'

'Aw bleddy hell. What's on with 'n? He never said a word about no wife.'

'Never mind that now.'

'I want hot chocolate, Mama,' a petulant voice demanded. 'And hot water and towels. I need to lie down. I'm so uncomfortable.'

'I knew how it would be. Didn't I warn you?' her mother demanded.

'Tom, fetch me a glass of brandy,' Esther instructed, 'then take them up the front stairs to one of the bedrooms.'

Jenefer wished she could die right here, right now. It would all be over and she wouldn't have to think, or feel, or *remember*. She was aware of an arm around her shoulders. Her hand was gently pulled away and a glass pressed against her lips. She inhaled the pungent fumes of cognac.

'Come on, my bird, drink it down. 'Twill do you good.'

She tried to push it away, tried to shake her head, but her body wouldn't work. 'I don't want—'

'Yes, you do,' Esther was gentle but firm. 'You can't stay here on the floor. Come on, now. Drink it down. Soon as you're feeling stronger

I'll take you home.'

Jenefer pictured her cottage. Home. She wanted to go home. Grasping Esther's hand she tilted the glass and gulped down the brandy.

'Careful, bird,' Esther cried in alarm.

It burned like fire and she nearly choked. But as heat spread through her limbs so too did strength. Jenefer scrambled unsteadily to her feet. Steadying herself against the wall she pressed the purse into Esther's hand. 'Please – give it to Tom. I have to go now.'

In the taproom Tom was suggesting that the young lady must be weary from her journey, and would welcome a rest in comfort and privacy. 'There's a nice quiet bedroom at the top of the stairs. Fire's already laid. Won't take but a moment to light it. My wife will wait on you in just a minute. And I'll send word to Mr Polgray.'

'No point,' Jenefer whispered to Esther as the passage swayed and the floor heaved. She blinked hard. 'He isn't here. He went to Truro.'

'Come in the kitchen and sit for a while,' Esther coaxed.

'No. I—' She choked on a sob, and bit hard on her lower lip. It hurt and the pain steadied her. 'I'm going home.'

'I'll come with you—'

Jenefer gripped Esther's forearm for an instant. 'No.' It was all she could manage. She walked as fast as she could across the yard and down the street. Head down, looking neither left nor right, she turned into the alley. Her breath kept catching. She felt as if something inside her was slowly tearing. As she reached her door Lizzie came out with a bowl of scraps for the chickens. Her welcoming smile dissolved into shocked concern.

'What's wrong, bird?'

Jenefer shook her head, went into her cottage and bolted the door. She pulled off her bonnet and threw her coat over a chair. She sat in the armchair by the range, clasped her arms across her body and rocked. Too much pain: she couldn't bear it. *Trust me.*

She had put Martin's betrayal behind her, refusing to let it blight her life. Learning the truth about his double life had been a terrible shock. But it was her pride and self-esteem that had suffered most, for she had not loved him.

What a fool she had been. It was only too clear now why Charles had never spoken of love. He could hardly have proposed marriage to her when he had a pregnant wife waiting at home. *You are everything to me.* How could he have said that? Treated her so? He had told her how much he valued her. But he didn't. He couldn't have. He had been living a lie, and forced her to do the same. She had loved him. While he – he had made use of her. Made a fool of her. It hurt. It hurt so much.

He had never said he loved her. But his eyes, his lips: they had told her his heart. Was it all just a charade? She could not believe that. Because if she did, it meant he thought her worthless. Why had he not told her he was married? Why had he allowed her to think – to hope? *You are everything to me.*

Memories, thoughts and arguments swirled in a tangle of shock and grief until she felt as if her head would burst. She sat, hugging herself and rocking in agony. Now and then rage, hot and blinding as lightning, pierced her. And she hated him. Not just for his lies, but for being so much less than she had believed. But the rage passed like the storm had passed, leaving her wrecked and broken.

Her eyes burned but no tears fell. Unable to sit still she paced, holding herself together. For three years she had struggled against pre-judice to rebuild her life. She had dealt fairly with people, answering criticism with kindness and patience. She had tried always to be honourable. *And this was the result?* Was it somehow her fault? She had refused to conform, had wanted to remain independent and determine her own path in life. It had made her *different*. Yet she had kept the villagers' respect and even won their affection.

Then he had come. He had sought her out, involved her in his plans and trusted her with privileged information. Why had he done that? Why had he led her to believe – or had she imagined it? Seen what she wanted to see? No, every instinct told her his feelings had been as deeply engaged as her own. But he was married and he had not told her. How could she go on? What was the point?

There was a knock on the door. She shivered and realized the room was cold and the light was fading. The knock was repeated. Then she heard Lizzie's voice.

'Open the door, bird.'

'Go away, Lizzie.'

'I've been up to see Esther.'

There was no escape. By tomorrow the arrival of Charles's wife and her mother would be all round the village. Jenefer opened the door then, suddenly light-headed, stumbled back and sat on the stairs. Lizzie walked in, closed the door and went straight to the range.

'Dear life, 'tis cold in here.' She riddled the ashes, pushed in a few kindling sticks then tipped a shovelful of coal onto the embers and opened the damper. By the time she had lit the lamp and closed the curtains, the fire was roaring and throwing welcome warmth into the room. Only then did she come and kneel in front of Jenefer. 'I'm some awful sorry, bird,' she said softly.

'Oh, Lizzie,' Jenefer whispered. 'What am I going to do?' Leaning forward she rested her forehead on Lizzie's shoulder. As Lizzie's arms went round her, Jenefer's chest heaved. She tried to hold on.

Lizzie stroked her back. 'Let it go, bird. 'Tis only me.'

Jenefer gave a low shuddering cry, and like a dam bursting, all her shock and pain, the shame and grief poured out in wrenching sobs.

Chapter Twenty

Charles rode through the gateway at Kegwyn, relieved to be back. He was tired to his bones. As he reached the house, the front door opened and Cora hurried out waving a piece of paper.

'Tom Lawry sent his boy round with this. He said you must have it the minute you got back.'

Charles reached down and took the note. Written in obvious haste it said simply: *Come at once. Trouble.*

For an instant he wavered. But such a message, especially from a man as steady as Tom Lawry, could not be ignored. Lifting off his saddle-bags he handed them to Cora. 'I hope not to be long.'

She nodded. 'The water's hot for your bath, and I got cold beef, pickles and fresh bread ready on a plate.'

At the inn's yard he handed the reins to the stable boy.

'Loosen the girth and give him a drink, but don't unsaddle him.'

Tom met him in the passage. 'What—?' Charles got no further.

'I'll tell you what,' Tom hissed, his expression dark and fierce. 'Your wife and her mother is upstairs. Arrived not an hour since asking for you. In some state they was, especially the young missus, her being in the family way.'

'It's not as it appears.' *Why was he excusing himself to an innkeeper?* Because this village, these people, mattered.

'You tell Miss Trevanion that.' Anger roughened Tom's voice. 'She heard them asking for you and fainted clean away, dear of her.'

Charles felt the blood drain from his face. 'She was here?'

'She'd come with the week's beer money.'

'Where are they now?'

Tom pointed upward. 'First room on the left.'

Charles took the stairs two at a time. Anxiety for Jenefer was swept aside by icy rage directed at the two women who had wreaked such havoc in his life. He wished he might never have laid eyes on them again. But though their arrival was unexpected and unwelcome, it presented an opportunity to end the matter once and for all. Knocking briefly he opened the door.

'Charles!' Eve's sulky frown swiftly evolved into a smile. 'Is this not a lovely surprise?' She extended a hand. 'Come, help me up.'

Closing the door he remained beside it. 'You have no business here.'

Widening her eyes, Eve rested one hand on her swollen belly. 'I'm your wife, Charles. I have every right—'

'No,' he cut her short. 'You have no rights. Not with me.'

'You can't!' Eve shouted. 'Tell him, Mama. He cannot set me aside.'

'Calm yourself, Eve. Getting upset is not good for your health or the baby's.'

'Tell *him* that, Mama. He's my husband—'

'Did neither of you hear me?' Disgust roiled in his stomach. 'This travesty of marriage is over.'

'You are angry,' Madeleine interrupted, desperation turning her smile into a grimace. 'I understand that. But before you make a decision you might regret—'

'Regret?' Charles roared as anger, so long contained, burst free. 'I'll tell you what I regret: my gullibility. You and Samson are - *were* - family. I trusted you. Yet you allowed - no, you *conspired* to have Eve marry me, knowing she was carrying another man's child'

Madeleine flung up her hands, her face crumpling. 'What else was I supposed to do?' she cried. 'We could not afford a scandal. Charles, please, I beg you. You know my husband is not well. You are like a son to him. Indeed, his plan is to hand you the business. Surely we could put this behind us? I know Eve bitterly regrets her behaviour. Don't you, dear?' Madeleine turned, extending her hand to her daughter.

Levering herself off the bed, Eve came forward, her blue eyes swimming with tears. 'I'm sorry, Charles. Truly I am. But you were away for so long and I was lonely.'

A rasping laugh tore his throat. 'You betray and trick me and it's *my* fault?'

'Well, it was.' Eve pouted. 'You should have—'

'Enough.' He shook his head, drained and sickened. He opened the door.

'Stop!' Eve shrieked. 'You can't leave me. What will people say? What will I do?'

Charles paused on the threshold. 'Whatever you wish. It's of no interest to me.' He eyed Madeleine briefly. 'Take your daughter home, madam. There is nothing for you here.'

'Nooooo!' As Eve sobbed hysterically, stamping her feet, Madeleine shouted after him.

'You'll be sorry, Charles. I'll make sure of that. If you think—'

He shut the door firmly, cutting off the rest of her threat, and looked down into the shocked faces of Tom and Esther who stood frozen at the bottom of the stairs.

*

After a while the storm of weeping passed, and Jenefer sat up, wiping her eyes and nose on a clean tea towel Lizzie took from the dresser drawer. She gulped and shuddered, sobs catching in her throat.

'Your shoulder's all wet,' she rasped, her voice thick and croaky.

'I've had a lot worse on it than your tears.' Lizzie patted Jenefer's knee. 'Remember the pilchard cellar?'

Jenefer managed a wan smile. 'Could I ever forget?'

Pushing herself up Lizzie crossed to the range and pulled the kettle over the fire. 'You wash your face while I make you a nice cup of tea, and some bread and jam. Then you get up over stairs. You had more 'n enough for one day. What you need now is sleep.'

Jenefer bit her lip hard to stop it quivering. She wiped her eyes again. They were swollen almost shut and felt hot and gritty. 'I can't believe— He seemed so—' She bent her head, fighting another upsurge of grief.

Lizzie made tea, refilled the kettle and set it to boil once more, then fetched milk, bread, butter and jam from the larder. 'Leave it, bird. You'll make yourself sick else.' She made a sandwich, cut it into triangles and put them on a plate. Then, wiping her hands on a cloth, she shook up the soft cushion in the armchair and beckoned. 'Come on over here by the fire.'

Exhausted from weeping, her limbs heavy, her head feeling as if it was stuffed with cotton, Jenefer pulled herself off the stairs. She ached all over and the occasional sob still caught in her chest.

'I'll tell you what you'll do.' Lizzie poured tea into a cup, adding milk and a spoonful of sugar, and moved it closer to Jenefer. 'First thing is, drink that.' She pointed then waited with one hand on her hip. 'After all they tears you'll have some terrible headache.'

As Jenefer picked it up, tea slopped into the saucer and she had to use both hands to raise the cup to her mouth. She sipped and pulled a face. 'I don't take sugar.'

'You do tonight. After the shock you've had, 'twill settle you down. And tomorrow you'll hold your head up and look the village in the eye just like you've always done.'

As her eyes filled and her mouth trembled, Jenefer gulped more tea and fought for control. She clattered the cup onto its saucer. 'I can't.'

'Yes, you can, but it don't have to be tomorrow. I'll tell Hannah you're sick with a bad cold. Now come on, eat up that sandwich. You need sleep, bird, and you'll rest better with something in your stomach.'

Lizzie stayed; washing the dishes while Jenefer took water upstairs, bathed her swollen face and changed into her nightgown. Unpinning her hair, she brushed it, avoiding her reflection in the glass as she braided it into a loose plait over one shoulder.

'Right, bird,' Lizzie called up. 'Everything's put away and I've made up the fire.'

Jenefer went down. 'Thank you, Lizzie.'

'Soon as I've gone, you put the bolt across then get up to bed.'

Pulling the covers up, Jenefer lay on her side and felt hot tears spill over her nose and soak into the pillow. *Charles.* She closed her eyes, felt herself falling, and welcomed oblivion.

She didn't want to wake, didn't want to move. But her mind kept reliving the previous day, then flinging up memories of the hours she and Charles had spent together: work shared, meals here and at Kegwyn, his teasing, his touch, his kisses. Conflict raged between her head and heart, tearing like sharp claws. Unable to bear it, desperate to escape, she stumbled downstairs. Three years ago she had lost everything that defined who she was. Seeking salvation in work she had rebuilt her life. If she had done it once, she could do it again.

No, she couldn't. She sank onto the armchair, hugging herself, rocking back and forward in anguish. It was different this time. The lies, the deceit and the loss were so much more devastating. *She could not bear it.* She had no choice. There was no going back, so she had to go on.

She wiped her face on the hem of her nightgown, and forced herself to move. She followed her morning routine, focusing on each task, not allowing herself to think beyond that. Her stomach too tender and tense for food, she drank hot chocolate. Lizzie arrived.

'Look at you, washed and dressed, your hair all neat, working like always. You're some brave maid.'

A lump swelled in Jenefer's throat and she shook her head. 'No, I'm hanging on by my fingernails.'

Reaching out, Lizzie patted Jenefer's cheek with work-roughened fingers that were infinitely gentle. 'That's what I mean. Right, I'm going down the shop to tell Hannah you been took bad with a cold.'

'No.' Jenefer's voice thickened and she swallowed hard. 'Don't say I'm ill. There have been enough lies.'

'You sure, bird? I just thought— '

'I know. And I appreciate it. But M— Mrs Polgray's arrival will be all round the village by now, so no one would believe you. If you are asked directly, tell the truth. I am, as usual, very busy.'

After Lizzie had gone, she closed the top door to keep in the warmth, pulled the table a little closer to the window to make the most of the light, and started work.

She was halfway through adding a column of figures when a brisk knocking made her start violently. Shock zinged along her nerves as hope flared, and just as quickly died. She knew Charles's knock, and that wasn't it. Why would he come here when his wife and her mother were at The Standard? *Trust me.* Plunging towards despair, she closed her eyes and clenched her fists. As the knock was repeated, she rose from her chair and went to open the door.

'William!' Seeing his expression of deep solemnity, her hand rose to her throat as fear blossomed inside her. *Betsy? Tamara? The baby?*

'May I come in? The news I have to impart is best told in private.'

'M–my sister?'

'No, no. As far as I am aware she and her family are all in excellent health. Jenefer, I want you to know that what I have to tell you gives me no pleasure—'

She knew then why he had come. 'I am glad to hear it. But if you are here to tell me that Mr Polgray's wife and mother have arrived in the village you could have spared yourself the trouble. I already know.'

'I fear the news must have come as a great shock to you.'

She gripped the door latch tightly. Pain lanced through her knuckles and she felt as if she was bleeding inside, but pride would not let her crumble.

'Why should you think so? Mr Polgray's domestic arrangements are a private matter between him and his wife. They are certainly of no concern to anyone else. Nor are they relevant to his plans for the harbour. So if that is all you came to say. . . .'

'I tried to warn you!' he blurted. 'I saw you responding to his attentions.'

'What you saw was my pleasure in being regarded as an equal and having my business ability respected and valued.'

'Charles Polgray is not—'

'That's enough, William. You came here relishing the opportunity to decry a man whose purpose in this village is to create work so people might comfortably feed and clothe their families. You came to crow. Shame on you!'

Flushing scarlet, he met her gaze. 'I admit the sin of jealousy. Despite my calling and all my efforts, it took me months to win the hearts and minds of the villagers. I am still trying to win yours.'

Suddenly weary, Jenefer sighed. 'You think this will help? Go home, William.' She started to close the door. He held it open.

'Wait, please. You must know my feelings for you. I— This is neither the time nor the circumstances I would have chosen but – I have received a legacy from an elderly relation. I am in a position to offer you a comfortable life. You know I respect your opinions, and I would greatly appreciate your help in expanding the school. We worked well together before. Do not answer now,' he said quickly as she opened her mouth. 'I admire and respect you above all women.

216

I feel sure that the friendship and fondness we share would, given opportunity, grow into love. For myself, there is no one I would rather have at my side for the rest of our lives.'

Jenefer's head was pounding. She had not expected – did not want – yet could not help but be touched. 'William, you do me great honour. But I don't deserve such praise.'

'We will not argue. I know you to be thoughtful and considerate. All I ask is that you think about my offer. Good day.' As he turned away she closed the door.

Returning to her chair, she rested her elbows on the table and buried her face in her hands. William was a good man who would care for her. But how could she accept one man when she loved another? Scalding tears seeped through her fingers. *You are everything to me.* How could he have said that? Why had he not told her he was married? Why had he allowed her to think – to hope? He had to have recognized her deepening feelings for him.

But the bitter truth was that while the village had begun to suspect – even hope – there was more than friendship between the two of them, he had never actually said as much.

He had kissed her with tenderness that made her heart tremble, and passion that left her weak and breathless and yearning. But he had never told her he loved her. He had taken cruel advantage. Yet he could have taken far more. That he had not done so indicated a glimmer of conscience. Unless – unless he had not found her desirable.

But he had. As she relived his arms around her, her body moulded to his, his mouth hot on hers, her blood raced and her skin burned. He had wanted her and she had ached for him. She pushed up from her chair, pacing as if she might somehow escape the agony, gasping as sobs racked her.

Eventually the wave of grief ebbed, leaving her with a grinding headache. She left the door unbolted so Lizzie would not worry, dragged herself upstairs, and lay on the bed.

She jerked upright, briefly disoriented. She hadn't expected to sleep. Her headache had gone, but her face felt tight and her eyes were hot. What had woken her? *That was Charles's knock. He was back.* Then she heard Lizzie's voice.

'Miss Trevanion isn't home to visitors today.'

Her heart thudding against her ribs she crawled to the window. Not daring to look out in case he saw her, she held her breath and listened. 'I understand.' His voice was hoarse with strain and exhaustion. 'Will you give her this letter?'

'You aren't going to give her no more grief.' Lizzie's tone hovered between question and statement.

'Please, give her my letter.'

Tempted to go down, to hear what he had to say, wanting to hit him and hold him, Jenefer scrambled away from the window. As she got to her feet she heard his footsteps receding and caught sight of herself in the glass. Her face was the colour of ashes except for plum and purple shadows beneath her swollen eyes, and her hair had come loose and hung in untidy hanks.

She heard the door open and hesitated at the top of the stairs as Lizzie glanced up and raised the letter.

'Mister just brought this.'

'I heard him.'

Lizzie laid the letter on the table. 'I'm going in and fetch you a nice bowl of beef stew.' She paused, her hand on the latch. 'He look like he haven't slept in days. Not that he deserve to. But don't go thinking he got off light. Hannah says half the village isn't speaking to him, and the other half is ready to scat him in the harbour. 'T isn't out of sympathy for his wife neither. Hannah heard from Esther that there was some terrible row between the three of them—'

Jenefer came slowly downstairs. 'Row? But he was away in Truro.'

'He come back no more'n an hour after they arrived. Tom had already sent the boy up to Kegwyn with a note for 'n to come d'rectly he got home. When mister got to The Standard there was some carry-on. The girl was screaming, her mother was begging one minute and shouting at him the next. From what Esther can make out, the girl was already expecting by another man when mister was trapped into wedding her, and her mother was in on it.'

Jenefer gasped, her hand flying to her mouth.

'I'll fetch your dinner,' Lizzie said. As the door closed behind her, Jenefer picked up the letter, her thoughts fizzing like sparks from a firework. As her heartbeat quickened, drumming in her ears, she broke the seal and unfolded the sheet.

Please, name a day and time to suit you, so I may tell you everything I should have told you when we first met. Nothing is as it appears.

Ever yours, Charles.

Though her head was bursting with questions, and her heart seethed with hurt, fear and anger, she pined for him, ached for him.

When Lizzie returned, Jenefer regarded the loaded tray with unease. 'I don't think— '

'Yes, you can, bird.'

'He wants to talk to me.'

'All the more reason for you to eat a proper dinner. You don't want to meet him looking like something the cat dragged in. Come on, now. Eat it while it's hot. I'll fetch the tray later.'

At the first mouthful Jenefer tensed, fearing her stomach would rebel. But the second was easier, and the third made her realize that the queasy feeling was actually hunger.

While she ate she pondered. The following evening would be best. At eight o'clock it would be dark. Anyone not at home would be in one of the public houses, which meant fewer people around to perhaps see and speculate.

When she had finished her meal she penned an equally brief note and gave it to Lizzie who promised Billo would deliver it as soon as he'd finished his dinner.

Jenefer spent the rest of the afternoon and evening finishing paper-work. The following morning she cleaned the cottage. In the afternoon she bathed and washed her hair, anxious to repair the ravages of the past few days. Lying awake had given her time to think.

Regardless of the circumstances he was married, and she could no longer afford to indulge her hopes. Thank God for her work. With so many people depending on the harbour project, she had no choice but to set aside her personal concerns.

By 7.45 she was dressed and ready. She had chosen a long-sleeved rose-pink gown that reflected a little colour into her pale cheeks. Her honey-gold hair was piled high and fine curls framed her face. Pink kid slippers whispered on the wooden stairs as she descended. After a critical glance round the spotless and tidy kitchen, she tipped a little more coal onto the fire then sat in her chair and folded her hands.

But she couldn't keep still. She polished two glasses and placed them on the table with a crystal decanter of brandy, then adjusted the bowl of cream roses and fragrant honeysuckle, breathing in their delicious scent. She sat down again and took deep breaths, trying to slow her racing heart and calm her nervousness. *He was married. There was no future.*

His knock, instantly recognizable, was quiet. Taking one last deep breath she went to the door and opened it. He removed his beaver hat and as the lamplight illuminated his face she knew Lizzie had not exaggerated. Strain had carved new lines and given his features a hard edge. His expression was aloof, unreadable. But his eyes betrayed him. Haunted and full of shadows, his gaze met hers.

He bowed. 'Thank you for agreeing to see me.'

She stood back and gestured for him to enter. 'How could I not,' she said softly, 'if I am to understand?' She sat down and, setting his hat on the table, he took the other chair, his knee only inches from hers.

He cleared his throat. 'I have so much to tell you. But first, let me say how deeply and sincerely sorry I am for not telling you my situation before. When I first came to Porthinnis I did not consider it anyone else's business. Nor was it relevant to the project. But then I met you. I never expected – wasn't prepared—' He shook his head, took a deep breath and continued. 'The arrival in the village of Mrs Kerrow and her elder daughter will have led you to believe that I am married. I was, but that is no longer the case.'

Jenefer felt her eyes widen and she flinched as her heart gave a sudden painful kick. A tiny green shoot of hope broke through the dark despair that had filled her soul, and she realized that her brave determination to put this – him – behind her and move forward with her life, had been a desperate pretence with no more substance than mist. 'Not married? But, I don't understand.' She watched him reach inside dark-green frock coat and withdraw a folded document.

'This is a decree of nullity. I applied for it back in June, as soon as I discovered the deception that Mrs Kerrow and her daughter had perpetrated. I have been waiting for it ever since.' His gaze met hers. 'With increasing impatience and anxiety. When I left here after learning of

Barton's failure, I did indeed go to Truro. But after conducting my business there, I rode on to Bodmin to appear before the Archdeaconry Court. Unfortunately I was not told the outcome of the hearing. Every day I looked for the post. Then we had the gale and I had to return to Truro to see Ralph Daniell. When I reached home I found the decree had arrived. But also waiting for me was a scrawled note from Tom Lawry bidding me to The Standard immediately. The rest you know.'

'So your marriage is dissolved?'

He offered her the document and, when she shook her head, tossed it onto the table. 'In the eyes of the church I have never been married.'

'Why didn't you tell me?'

He recounted his promise to Samson, his shame at having been duped, and his fear that once she knew he was married she might want nothing more to do with him. 'You see, until I received the decree I had no proof of a story that to many would sound unbelievable. Yet I knew I could no longer keep silent. I could not bear to see you suffer in the belief that I did not care for you.' As he spoke he reached for her hand. Her fingers twined with his and his touch infused her with strength and deep joy.

'I have never loved,' he said simply. 'Then I met you. You changed my life. I hate having caused you pain. But the prospect of losing you was too terrifying to contemplate. Even so, I knew I had to tell you the truth. Then on each occasion I tried, we were interrupted.' He stood, and she rose with him.

'Oh' She realized, and smiled up at him. 'Yes, I remember. It was never the right time.'

'It is now.' He slid his hands down her arms then rested them on her hips. Hers lifted as naturally as breathing to his shoulders. 'I never imagined feeling what I feel for you. You fill my heart. I love you, now and always.'

His image blurred as tears of joy welled up and spilled down her cheeks. Blinking them away, Jenefer laughed. 'Oh, Charles. You have taken the words from my mouth. I love you so very much.'

He lowered his head and touched his lips to hers in a tender kiss of homage and commitment. Her eyelids fluttered down and her heart opened like a flower. She welcomed him in and knew he would never leave. She slipped her arms around his neck and her fingers curled in his thick hair. 'More,' she whispered against his mouth.

His arms tightened around her moulding her body to his, and passion leapt between them, a glorious white-hot flame that fused soul with soul. What his mouth demanded she gave, glorying in his strength. All she offered he took, and when eventually they parted, both breathless, her legs were trembling and his heart pounded against her breast. It moved her that he should be as deeply affected as she was.

'Jenefer?' he murmured hoarsely. 'Will you do me the very great honour of becoming my wife?'

Radiantly happy, she looked up into his beloved face. Relief had softened the lines of strain, and in his tired eyes she saw a hunger that elicited an answering tug deep within her. 'I will, for I should like that above all things. When?'

'If I get a special licence, within the week.'

'I must wait that long?'

The laugh that erupted from his throat warmed her. Drawing her close he kissed her again. But as desire leapt between them he placed his hands on her shoulders and eased her away, his gaze burning into hers. 'I want – but I will not. It must be right for us.' He raked his hair with an unsteady hand. 'God grant me patience.'

She touched his mouth then her own with her fingertips. 'I love you.' She could still feel him, taste him. *He loved her.* 'Perhaps you will pour us both a little brandy, and tell me what Mr Daniell said?'

'It was as I feared.' Charles gently swirled the cognac in his glass. He had pulled his chair closer so their knees touched. 'He will not increase the loan or the repayment period. However, Mr Casvellan called on me to reiterate his interest in becoming a shareholder.'

Jenefer sipped and the spirit added its own warmth to the glow inside her. 'That is excellent news. You haven't forgotten I promised you a loan?'

He raised his glass in salute, and her heart turned over at his smile. 'I haven't forgotten.'

'What do you think about me approaching Mr Lukis, the Guernsey merchant? He might well be interested. You could invite the villagers to become shareholders. Now they have regular wages coming in, they might like the idea of investing. It would give them a sense of owner-ship. They would be working for themselves as well as the company.

We could arrange with Tom Lawry to have a meeting in the long room at The Standard. I'll tell Hannah, and you announce it to the men before they begin work— What?'

He regarded her without speaking; his head tilted slightly, a smile lifting the corners of his mouth. 'One, how did I manage without you? Two, I am beginning to realize what a formidable asset you will be to my business. And three, when should we hold this meeting?'

A flush of pleasure tightened her skin. 'The sooner the better. Say the day after tomorrow?' Her fingers tightened on her glass. 'Charles, you have always done a great deal of travelling.'

He nodded. 'True. But much has changed these past months. My priority is to complete the harbour expansion and increase the through flow of cargo. I have not yet decided if my future includes any connection with K&P. That is something for you and I to discuss. Meanwhile, know this: my heart and my home are here in Porthinnis.' He drained his glass and stood up. 'I hate to leave you.'

'I hate that you must, but it won't be for long.'

He picked up his hat and paused at the door. 'When we are married, will you be happy to live with me at Kegwyn? We could look for somewhere else if you prefer.'

Reaching up, Jenefer kissed his cheek. 'I would live with you in a cave. But I shall be very happy at Kegwyn.'

'You won't mind leaving here?'

She looked round. 'I have been happy here, and blessed with the kindest of neighbours. But my life and my future lie with you.'

'Sleep well, my love.' Leaning down he kissed her, a sweet, cherishing kiss. 'Until tomorrow morning.'

'Goodnight, Charles.' She listened to his receding footsteps, then closed the door and gently pushed the bolt across. Tomorrow: the first day of the rest of their lives.